the dead and buried

ALSO BY KIM HARRINGTON:

Clarity
Perception: A Clarity Novel

the dead and buried

KIM HARRINGTON

Point

Library of Congress Cataloging-in-Publication Data

Harrington, Kim, 1974–
The dead and buried / Kim Harrington. — 1st ed.
p. cm.
Summary: New student Jade uncovers a murder mystery when she moves into a house haunted by the ghost of a beautiful, mean girl who ruled Jade's high school.
ISBN 978-0-545-33302-3
[1. Haunted houses — Fiction. 2. Ghosts — Fiction. 3. High schools — Fiction. 4. Schools — Fiction. 5. Murder — Fiction. 6. Mystery and detective stories.] I. Title.
PZ7.H23817Mu 2013
[Fic] — dc23
2011043877

10 9 8 7 6 5 4 3 2 1   12 13 14 15 16/0

Printed in the U.S.A.   23
First edition, January 2013
Book design by Elizabeth Parisi

To Ryan

W.W.A.B.M.L.B.

"One need not be a chamber to be haunted.

One need not be a house.

The brain has corridors surpassing material place."

~ EMILY DICKINSON

From the Diary of Kayla Sloane

I'm not stupid. I know half of them only worship me because they fear me.

With popularity comes power and I could crush any of them with a simple text blast. Any day, at any moment, at my whim, I can change lives for the worse.

I see it, sometimes. In their too-eager compliments. Forced laughs. A smile that ends a moment too soon to be genuine. It's not love, it's fear.

I'd worry about retribution for the things I've done, but really, let's be honest. I'm at the top of the food chain, baby. I'm untouchable.

What could any of them do to me?

chapter 1

Colby had a secret.

I knew this from the way he was holding his lips tight, trying desperately not to smile. He was five years old, so it was probably a mildly mischievous prank, like he'd hidden Marie's keys again. But an unusual look in his eyes made me wonder if, this time, it was something more.

Whatever it was, he definitely didn't want Dad or Marie to know. He didn't speak as Marie hovered around us in the kitchen, triple-checking that she'd put everything Colby could possibly need in his backpack.

Dad swooped in and gave us both kisses on the tops of our heads.

"Have fun in kindergarten," he said, ruffling Colby's hair a bit, but not too much since Marie had already slathered gel on it. Gel. On a five-year-old.

"Enjoy your first day of senior year, Jade," he said to me, and winked. He kissed Marie on the cheek, grabbed his laptop case and garment bag, and left. I could tell Marie was miffed that Dad was missing drop-off for Colby's first day of school. But he had a plane to catch. A plane that brought him to meetings that paid for things that Marie liked. So she kept her mouth stiff, but closed.

Colby stopped staring into space with that mysterious expression and turned his attention to his bowl of Cocoa Puffs, which he stirred vigorously. He refused to take a bite until the milk had magically turned into chocolate milk. He did this every morning. On an adult, it would be an annoying quirk. On Colby, it was cute.

My mother died when I was nine. Dad remarried two years later. And then, after twelve years of being an only child, I became a sister. During Marie's pregnancy, I was *not* looking forward to the addition to my new family. My life had been through enough turmoil. I sulked anytime they talked about the baby. I spent the baby shower locked in my room. Even though they knew the baby was a boy, I constantly referred to the bump in her stomach as "it."

Then Colby was born. In the hospital, they sat me in a chair and carefully placed him in my arms. It was the first time I'd held a baby. I think my dolls weighed more than he did. He was wrapped up tight in this white hospital blanket, a blue hat on his little, bald head. His eyes were wet, glassy, and unfocused. But he stared right at me. Almost through me, in a way. And all the hatred, the anger, and my selfish, petulant feelings evaporated. They rushed out of me like air from an untied balloon. And I filled back up with love.

I was seventeen now. Next year, I'd be going off to college somewhere and Colby would have his turn to be an only child. He'd miss me, though. And I'd miss him. He was a cool little dude. His favorite color was purple, because most boys pick blue and he liked being different. He loved to make up his own dance moves when I blasted my music. And SpongeBob made him laugh so hard he sometimes couldn't catch his breath.

Though Marie looked like she needed a horse tranquilizer, I wasn't worried about Colby in kindergarten. He'd have no trouble making friends. He'd beam that giant baby-toothed smile and they'd all share their LEGOs.

Me on the other hand . . .

"You excited for school?" I asked, my spoon clinking against the cereal bowl.

Colby's face lit up. "Yeah! When I went to the open home —"

"House," Marie corrected as she loaded the dishwasher. "Open *house*."

"They had a ton of toys in the classroom," Colby continued. "Way more than my preschool back home."

"This *is* home," Marie said.

My fingers tightened around the spoon. "He meant our *old* home." I held back from adding, "obviously." I hated how Marie constantly corrected him.

The town I'd grown up in was in Western Massachusetts, almost at the Vermont border. My house was old, drafty, and small. Our closest neighbor was a half mile away. My high school was regional, made up of three bordering rural towns, but still my grade only had thirty kids total. I'd always dreamed of living in one of those upscale suburbs close to Boston with great schools, big malls, and actual fun stuff to do. I'd begged my dad year after year, but he'd always said moving wasn't an option. We could sell our house but it wouldn't be enough money to buy a house in one of *those* towns.

So color me surprised when Dad and Marie called a family meeting over the summer to tell us my dream was coming true. Now. When I only had a year of school left. The timing made their motivation obvious. Colby was about to start kindergarten. And our town's school system wasn't good enough for him, even though they'd made it plain over the years that it was good enough for me. I wasn't bitter over the reason, though, just happy it was finally happening.

Marie got a job as a night-shift nurse at a Boston hospital, which paid much better than her old one. And Dad could work from wherever since he traveled most of the time rather than going to an office. He sold data systems. Whatever they were. But still, I wondered how all of a sudden we could afford it.

Our new house was big and beautiful, pale yellow with black shutters. White trellises climbed up either side, ivy snaking through the latticework. Our old house always had something broken, something crumbling, something needing a fix. The new house was perfect. The only change Marie and Dad made was to add a carpet runner on the main staircase. Marie thought the hardwood stairs were unsafe for Colby.

I used to watch teen movies where everyone lived in big, nice houses and threw amazing parties and prom was this *Event* held somewhere fancy like a hotel. Call me superficial but when I watched those movies . . . I wanted that. Instead of my little old house, the one party I'd been to (in a barn), and a junior prom in the school gym, which smelled like sweaty socks.

Now here I was. In Woodbridge. Living the dream. I didn't know how Dad and Marie were swinging it, but I wasn't going to question. Just appreciate.

I rose and rinsed my cereal bowl. Then I headed back upstairs, brushed my teeth, and took one last glance in the mirror. My long brown hair was almost to my waist. It probably needed a cut. But the blond highlights that appear every summer still glowed, so it didn't look half bad. I wore a yellow tee that brought out the flecks of gold in my hazel eyes, and a brand-new pair of jeans.

Last night, when Dad and I were alone downstairs, he told me I looked more and more like Mom every year. I loved that. My mother had been beautiful — in that natural, graceful way that made strangers on the street stop and stare. But my delight in our resemblance had nothing to do with beauty. I just felt like, if I was walking around with her blood, her DNA, looking like her . . . maybe she wasn't completely gone. My existence kept her a little bit alive.

A silly thought, I know.

She died quickly. People tell me that was a gift, considering it was cancer. She had headaches, but she'd always suffered from migraines so no one thought anything of it. Until the day she started mixing up words. She said we were going to order a toaster for dinner, when she meant pizza. I'll never forget the look of horror on her face when she looked at me and said, "I can't remember your name. I know it, but I can't say it."

One MRI later, we saw a picture of the tumor that had been silently killing her. She didn't survive the surgery.

Marie had been a nurse in the hospital. She'd even met my parents. A year later, she'd run into my father again and they'd started dating. It was just one massive life change after another from that point on, leading up to today, my first day at a brand-new school.

I checked my phone and wasn't surprised to find no new texts. My only friends back home were Nicole and Elizabeth, but I'd always felt like the third wheel on their BFF bike. School had already started for them and they were so busy, it was taking them days to respond. I'm a realistic person. I knew we'd do that "slowly drift apart" thing friends do when they move. I'd just expected it to take longer than two weeks.

"Jade?"

I turned away from the sink. Colby was standing in the bathroom doorway. "What's up, little dude?"

"I want to tell you something."

Ah, the secret. "Okay." I bent down and whispered conspiratorially in his ear, "Follow me."

He tagged along down the hall to my room, his little legs almost running to keep up with my strides. I closed the door behind us. "What's going on?"

"I'm worried," he said, sinking into his favorite beanbag chair.

"About school?"

He nodded slowly. "What if the kids don't like me?"

"Of course they'll like you! Everyone in preschool liked you."

"What if the kids are different in this town?"

I swallowed hard. Twelve years between us and we were basically worrying about the same thing.

"I was wondering . . ." Colby trailed off, like he was scared to ask.

"What, buddy?"

His eyes went to the box I kept on top of my dresser.

"Something about my collection?" I asked.

A little pink colored his cheeks. "I was wondering if any of your pretties could help me."

I collect gemstones. Some as jewelry pieces, some loose, some inherited from my mother, some collected on my own. I'd passed a lot of time with Colby showing him the gems, talking about their colors, their names, what meanings they each had. I first showed them to him when he was two. He called them my "pretties." Even though he knew the word "gemstones" now, "pretties" had stuck.

"I don't know if a gem exists that can make people like you," I said.

"How about one that will make me stop worrying?"

The truth was that the gem he probably needed was the one my mother named me after. Jade: protector of children. But the only jade I had was a pendant. Sending him to school wearing a girl's necklace probably wasn't going to help.

He read the answer on my face and his lower lip turned down in disappointment. I hated seeing him all nervous. I went to the box, sifting through the gems, avoiding the one at the bottom that no one was allowed to touch, and pulled out the jade pendant.

"This is very special to me," I said. "You promise you won't take it off or show it to anybody?"

His eyes widened with wonder at the dangling, smoky green jewel. "I double-promise."

Normally, I'd trust a five-year-old boy with a delicate piece of jewelry as much as I'd trust a thief with an ATM password, but Colby was different. I knew he'd take good care of it.

"Okay, then." I slipped it over his head and hid it under his shirt. "This jade will hang over your heart all day and protect you."

He wrapped his skinny little arms around my neck. "Thank you, Jade."

"You're welcome, buddy."

He began to skip out of the room, but stopped as if he'd forgotten something. He turned back to me with a smile. "I'll tell you now . . ."

I blinked quickly. I'd thought being nervous about school *was* what he had to tell me. "Okay." I crossed my arms and grinned. "What?"

He went to the doorway and looked both ways down the hall, then came back to me. He lifted himself up on his tiptoes and whispered into my ear, "There's a girl in my room."

"Right now?" I whispered back with a smile.

"No, just sometimes."

"A pretend girl?" I asked, my eyebrows raised.

"No, she's real. But I can see through her."

An icy sensation tickled the back of my neck and worked its way down my spine. "You can see through her," I repeated.

"Yeah." He nodded enthusiastically. "And she . . ." He paused as he shuffled through his five-year-old vocabulary to find the best description. His eyes lit up as he hit on the word he needed. "Glimmers. Yeah, she glimmers."

chapter 2

I sat in the office of Woodbridge High School, clutching the paper with my schedule and locker combo on it. Colby's admission had freaked me out a little. *He* wasn't scared, but that didn't stop *me* from looking over my shoulder a couple of times before I'd left the house for school.

When I was little, I'd loved ghost stories. And I'd been completely convinced that ghosts were real. But then I grew up and figured they were just part of legend — like vampires and werewolves. Haunted houses were just old, run-down places whose "ghosts" could be explained by drafty windows, loud pipes, or lying tenants looking for attention.

But our new house was only twenty years old and in perfect shape.

And Colby didn't lie.

I shook it off and focused on the schedule in my hand. There were no surprises, since we'd been in contact with the school over the summer and sent them my transcript. When I'd arrived at the office, the school secretary had told me to wait there for my "Newcomers Club Buddy" to assist me through my first day.

We didn't have anything like that at my old school. But then again, we never had new kids, either. My whole grade fit into one dingy old classroom. Woodbridge High School, though, was a two-story brick building with a clock tower at the entrance and was surrounded by fields so perfectly manicured they could have been on ESPN.

I looked through the office's glass window into the hallway and felt a surge of anxiety. Throngs of kids meandered through the hall, stopping at lockers and calling out to each other over heads and backpacks. Kids who'd known each other for years. And I was stepping in, having no history, knowing no one. My stomach clenched like a fist.

A boy entered the office. He was tall, but you wouldn't immediately know it from the way he stood slightly hunched forward. He wore a black T-shirt and dark jeans, with his hands stuffed in the pockets. An aura of sadness clung to him like bad cologne. He kicked at the ground as he mumbled to the secretary, "Um . . . the Newcomers Club."

She pointed at me and he turned my way, not looking anywhere but at the ground as he trudged over. Still, I felt a bit of relief. I wasn't alone anymore.

"I'm your guide for the day," he said, apparently to my shoes.

"Hi. I'm Jade Kelley?" I knew that was my name, but somehow it came out sounding like a question. I stood, hoping he'd finally look up. When he did, my heart sped up a bit.

I didn't have a ton of experience with boys. There were only fourteen of them in my grade back home and we'd all gone to school together since kindergarten. It was kind of hard to be attracted to a boy if you could remember him picking his nose in first grade. Though I did go on a date once, my freshman year. And by "date" I mean we went to a dance together, kissed once, he tried to do more and I stopped him, and then he told everyone at school my breath smelled like a toilet. So . . . my track record . . . not so good.

But this guy standing in front of me seemed a little different. His dark hair was messy and too long. It hung down over the palest blue eyes I'd ever seen. Eyes that no one should hide. But they were also ringed with dark circles. He'd be pretty hot if he got a little more sleep and put a modicum of effort into his looks. But he seemed more than tired. He looked . . . haunted.

"Thanks for taking the time," I said with a gratefulness that I meant. "I'd be lost without help today. This school's much bigger than my old one. And coming in as a senior, when everyone else already knows each other, it's so much pressure."

Oh no. I'd started babbling. And my voice had this hysterical-girl edge to it that I hated. I'd become Nervous Babbling Girl. My right hand went up to my ear. I was wearing my blue topaz stud earrings. Blue topaz was supposedly useful for verbalizing feelings. So either they weren't working or were overworking. Regardless, a stream of verbal vomit continued to spew from my mouth.

He pulled a lock of hair behind his ear, his eyes at full force now, and gave me this entertained, lopsided grin. I modified my original judgment. This boy was *already* hot. He just hid it well.

I took a breath, and he was able to sneak in a question. "So where did you move from?" He didn't mumble it, like before. He seemed interested. Like he'd finally woken up from the half coma he was in.

"A small town in the western part of the state. I'm sure you've never heard of it." I added a little giggle. Now I was Giggle Girl. Just . . . kill me.

"That's cool," he said. "Where did you move to in Woodbridge?"

"Um, Silver Road?" I said, again making it a question.

His whole face suddenly changed, and he took a huge step back, as if he'd just realized I had a debilitating contagious disease. He turned away from me and returned to the counter. "I, uh, can't do this," he said to the secretary, who didn't look too surprised by his behavior.

With that, he was out the door. No explanation, nothing. I stood with my mouth open. I should have been appalled. I should have considered him the rudest boy on earth. But the moment when his face changed for some reason reminded me of this morning when Colby told me about the girl in his room. So instead of anger, the icy feeling returned. I rubbed the back of my neck.

Just as I was about to contemplate finding my locker on my own, another girl, who'd been standing in the office, walked over.

"Hey. I'm Alexa Palmer." She didn't say it in a friendly way. More matter-of-factly. Her hair was black, straight, and shiny, with bluntly cut bangs. "I'm also in the Newcomers Club," she continued. "I'll be your Newcomers Club Buddy today. Even though you were Donovan's assignment."

Donovan. So that was his name.

"So what was his problem?" I asked, aiming my thumb in the direction Cute Boy had fled.

"Donovan? Don't mind him. Let's see where your first class is." She took the schedule out of my hand. "Only AP in Math, huh?" she said, not looking at me. Come to think of it, she hadn't looked me in the eye once yet. "I'll be in that class with you." Then she handed the schedule back to me and clapped her hands together once. "Okay, let's get you to your locker and to History. I will meet you at the end of each of your classes and shepherd you to your next. I'll sit with you at lunch. And then tomorrow you can be on your own."

I felt like I'd just been dismissed from a business meeting. "Um, okay. Do you want to jot down the room numbers so you'll know where to go?"

Alexa raised one eyebrow, but still didn't look at me. "Of course not. I memorized them."

She turned around and walked right out the door without looking back. I hurried to follow her. There was no small talk on the way to my locker or my first class. And no platitudes when she dropped me off. I wished I were confident enough to tell Alexa I could face the rest of the day on my own. The girl was clearly strange. But the idea of having someone walk me around all day and sit with me at lunch did help keep me from hyperventilating.

My morning classes went by quickly, with Alexa dutifully meeting me after each one and walking me to the next. All the classes seemed a little harder, a little more intense than the schoolwork back in my old town. I'd have to work hard to keep up. That Donovan boy was in three of my classes. I caught him looking at me once, and he immediately dropped his eyes back down.

My old school offered no advanced placement classes. This school seemed to have an AP for everything, but I was only scheduled for Math. My grades must have been good enough for me to get in, but I had a feeling AP Calculus here was an entirely different beast from Math at home.

I sighed. I had to stop doing that. Marie was right with that particular nag. My old town wasn't home. This was.

I survived all my pre-lunch classes. When it was lunchtime, Alexa went to use the girls' room so I waited for her, leaning against a row of lockers. Just then, a girl approached me. Her bold makeup and overhighlighted hair added up to pretty, but in a "trying too hard" kind of way. And she smelled like a Bath & Body Works had exploded all over her.

"Are you the new girl?" she asked.

"Yeah. I'm Jade Kelley." I thought about holding my hand out, but something told me this wasn't a "let's be pals" introduction. It had some sort of purpose.

"Where do you live?"

She didn't reply back with her own name, which was strange. "Here," I answered tentatively. "I just moved to town."

The girl heaved her shoulders with impatience. I noticed a

gaggle of three other girls watching us from a distance. "No, like, *where* in town?"

"Silver Road."

Her eyes widened. "Which house?"

"Number six," I said, not liking this conversation and its one-sided feel. "The yellow one."

My interrogator's mouth opened, then shut wordlessly. She scurried back to her group and they all huddled in as she whispered. I only heard a few words . . . *"new girl"* . . . *"house"* . . . *"Kayla Sloane."* Who was Kayla Sloane? And what was the big deal about my house? It certainly wasn't the biggest in town. Did they give this third degree to every new student?

I felt a swoosh of wind and Alexa called over her shoulder, "Let's go," as she breezed by me. I jogged a few steps to catch up to her.

"Would you stop doing that?" I said with more annoyance in my voice than I'd normally use. But between Fruity-Smelling Girl's questions and Alexa's oddness, I'd just about had it.

Alexa looked at something above my head. "Stop what?"

"Walking so fast that I have to run to keep up with you."

"Well, I'm taller than you," she said flatly. "Longer legs."

"Yeah, but it's rude."

She stopped then, her forehead creased. "Why?"

I had to explain this? Really? "Because when you're going somewhere with someone you should walk together side by side at a comfortable pace. Not breeze by them, yelling over your shoulder, and forcing them to go faster. Especially when it's someone's first day and that someone is kind of nervous." I let out a big breath.

Alexa's face sagged. She looked like she actually felt bad. Like it just dawned on her now that what she was doing wasn't cool. "I'm sorry," she said. "I didn't know."

We walked the rest of the way a little slower and I saw her take a few peeks at my feet, like she was mentally calculating speed or something.

The cafeteria had long tables in the center, and several round tables lined the perimeter. After we got our food, we grabbed two end seats at one of the long tables. I expected other people to join us, but after a few minutes it was clear that wasn't happening. I momentarily wondered . . . if I wasn't sitting with Alexa today, would she be alone at lunch? I didn't want to ask, though, and make her feel self-conscious.

I took a tentative first bite of my lunch, Chinese chicken stir-fry with lo mein noodles, and nearly moaned. It was so good. So *not* the school lunch I was used to. I didn't even mind that Alexa obviously wasn't one for small talk. All the more time for me to shovel this awesomeness into my mouth.

But then I was full and a glance at the clock told me ten minutes remained. I felt the need to fill in the silence. "So," I struggled to think of something to ask. "Can you tell me about the other students here?"

"Sure," Alexa said, wiping her mouth with her napkin. She nodded toward a girl standing nearby who had long dark hair. "That's Meghana Patel." She looked away. "And that's Kane

Woodward, and that's Johnny Xu, and that's Laura Preston."
She rambled on, pointing out people here and there. But they
seemed to be at random. They weren't even people who sat
together.

"Are they your friends?"

"No. They're the top ten."

"In what?"

Alexa simply said, "Class rank."

Ahh. She was one of those overachievers. "Okay. Can you
tell me anything about someone who *isn't* your competition?"

Her eyes flicked around for a moment, then she just
shrugged. Ooookay. I glanced around the cafeteria and spotted Donovan, who was sitting at one of the round tables with
a group of boys. They all wore black T-shirts with band names
or gamer-related logos. Donovan kept his head down and
didn't seem to be involving himself in conversation.

"What about him?" I asked, nonchalantly pointing him out.

Alexa peered over her shoulder, then returned her eyes to her
plate. "Donovan O'Mara. Above average. Rank thirty-three."

"No, what does he do? Besides school."

Confused at first, Alexa thought for a moment, then said,
"I've seen him in the art room after hours. He talks with other
boys about video games. If he spent less time gaming, he could
have come in at twenty-six through twenty-eight. No higher
than that, though."

I sighed. "But what's he *like*? You know, his personality." I
watched as he picked apart a sandwich.

"He used to smile a lot. It looked nice." Alexa added softly, "But he doesn't smile anymore."

It took all my effort to tear my eyes from him. He just made me feel so curious. I wanted to know why he was so sad.

I wanted to fix him.

chapter 3

The next morning, the sun in my eyes woke me up well before my alarm. I must have forgotten to pull down the shade, though I thought I'd remembered doing it.

I sat up and stretched, looking around. I still had a few boxes left to unpack, but my new room was so huge they didn't even get in the way. I had the same furniture, the same blue bedding, the same Interpol poster on similarly colored cream walls, but everything had changed. Now I could keep a desk and my computer in here, rather than the living room, giving me more than a place just to sleep. It was a place to *be*. A place that was all mine and private.

I laid an outfit — jeans and a purple V-neck — on the bed, then dug through my jewelry box for something to spice it up with. Despite knowing the history and meaning behind every identifiable gemstone, I still couldn't color coordinate. I liked the garnet pendant, but did red go with purple? I closed the lid, shrugged, and headed into the bathroom to shower. In our old house, if someone had showered right before me, I'd have nothing but cold water left. Not here, though. The water was so hot and relaxing, I almost hated to get out, and my fingers were pruned by the time I did.

I opened the door and steam trailed along as I slipped into my room, a towel wrapped around me. I returned to the clothes I'd laid on my bed when my eyes registered something. Something wrong. Out of place.

My long gold necklace with the black onyx pendant lay placed over the shirt. I hadn't put it there. And I'd closed my jewelry box, though it now stood open atop my dresser.

I padded down the hall to Colby's room where he was playing with his train table. I held the necklace up. "Did you take this out of my jewelry box and put it on the outfit I had on my bed?"

"Nope," he said, smashing two trains together.

"Did Mar — Mom do it?"

He shook his head. "Nuh-uh. She's downstairs."

I furrowed my brow in confusion, staring at the onyx dangling from my hand. It was a good choice, actually. The color matched my purple shirt. And onyx protects against negativity. That would be helpful if I ran into that fruity-smelling girl again today.

"It must have been her," Colby said.

"Who?"

His eyes panned the room like he was looking to see who else was there. "You know," he whispered. "The glimmering girl."

Goose bumps rose on my skin and I held the towel tighter. Despite the steam still flowing out of the bathroom . . . I wasn't hot anymore.

"What does she look like?" I asked, thinking maybe if I prodded him for details he'd admit the girl was an imaginary friend.

He turned the toy train over and over in his hand. "She's a big kid."

"A teenager like me?" I clarified. "Big kid" to Colby could mean anyone older than him.

"Yeah, but she doesn't have your hair. Hers is black."

"What's her name?"

He shrugged. "Dunno. She moves her mouth, but she can't talk."

I drove my ten-year-old clunker to school and parked it between two shiny new luxury cars. As I walked toward the open doors of the school, I wondered why Colby was doing this. He'd never lied to me before. Maybe moving and starting school was taking a toll on him. He *had* to have been the one to put the onyx on my bed. He had to be making up the stories about the glimmering girl. Because otherwise . . .

I *wanted* to concentrate in my classes. It was only the second day, but already the teachers had kicked it up a notch and my hand was aching from all the note taking. But I had trouble focusing. I couldn't shake the feeling that a secret was being passed around. And it involved me.

When all eyes were on me as I walked down the hallway, I chalked it up to being the new girl. When I caught a boy staring in Science, I figured it was curiosity. When two girls whispered behind their hands in English, then looked at me in unison, I hoped for a coincidence. But when I walked into the cafeteria for lunch and heard one gasp, followed by a quick, "There she is," I knew for sure something was up.

I got into line, quickly chose a prepackaged salad, and wandered into the seating area. I glanced around, looking for a friendly face. But everyone regarded me with a kind of hungry suspicion. A bead of sweat slipped down my back.

An outburst of laughter came from my right and I turned to see what was going on. Alexa was seated by herself, in the same spot as yesterday, a textbook open beside her tray. A tall, skinny boy stood behind her, doing some sort of robot dance with his arms. A group of girls giggled and the words "Robot Girl" floated through the air. Clearly a mean-spirited nickname for Alexa. She didn't turn around, didn't react in any way. But she had to know what was going on behind her. Had to hear it.

My face flushed hot with anger. I marched over to her table, glaring daggers at the boy the whole way. He stopped his dance and moved on, his fun over.

I slid into a seat across from Alexa and opened my salad. She looked up from her book. "You're sitting with me again?" she asked. She didn't seem disappointed, just surprised. And maybe happy. I couldn't quite tell with her.

"Yeah, sure," I said. Sitting with Alexa seemed like my best bet. She was apparently the only one *not* whispering behind my back.

I moved the salad around the container with my fork, too worked up to feel hungry. When I glanced up, I saw Fruity-Smelling Girl at a nearby table. She sat next to a guy who looked like he'd been clipped out of a hotness catalog. Tall and broad shouldered? Check. Perfectly ruffled blond hair?

27

Check. A smile that was obviously making every girl at the table swoon? Check.

Fruity leaned in close to him and whispered something in his ear. Something that made him stop smiling. And then he looked over at me.

My eyes darted down to my plate. "What's going on?" I asked, not even bothering to keep my voice level.

"Chemistry," Alexa replied, looking up from her book.

"People are talking about me," I explained. "But I don't know why. Do you?"

Alexa eyed Fruity-Smelling Girl and Perfect Boy, who was looking at me with a mixture of sadness and interest.

"I'm not in that crowd," she replied. "Or any crowd. I don't get the gossip. Sorry."

I let out a long breath. Alexa wasn't going to be much help in finding answers, but at least I could talk to her and try to get my mind off being the sudden center of attention.

"So is that AP Chemistry?" I asked, motioning to her book with my fork.

"Yeah."

"You're taking two AP courses, huh?"

"I take as many as the school offers. And I'm forty points from a perfect score on the SAT."

"Oh." Holy canola oil. She was a genius.

"So . . . you still want to sit with me?" she said softly.

"What do you mean?" I asked, honestly confused.

"Now that you know what a nerd I am."

Her voice was bitter, and that one line told stories. She'd probably put herself out there before, only to get hurt. Maybe she helped other Newcomers Club Buddies only to get shunned as soon as they latched on to more popular people.

"I don't care about that." I shrugged. "I think it's cool you're so smart."

"Really?" Her brow furrowed.

"Yeah," I said, and I meant it. Alexa was a little bit different, but I liked that. She seemed honest, anyway, and what more could you want in a friend than that?

Alexa looked at me sideways. "You're not . . . playing a joke on the weird girl?"

"No." I tried to think of how I could prove it to her. "Hey, we both have seventh period free, right? Come with me to my house and I'll show you how *I'm* weird."

"I can't," she said. "I have too much work. I'm going to be in the school library all period."

I nodded. "Okay, then. I'll bring the weird to you."

I clutched the box tightly in my hands and scanned the tables in the school library, looking for Alexa's face. Then I felt a light tap on my shoulder, and a boy's voice asked, "Are you Jade Kelley?"

I turned and was surprised to see Perfect Boy standing there with a cute, petite blond girl beside him. Not Fruity-Smelling Girl, thank goodness. Someone else. She gave me a small, almost-welcoming smile.

Perfect Boy towered over me, giving me the opportunity to let my eyes graze as they traveled up to meet his. He wore scuffed sneakers, faded jeans, and a Woodbridge Lacrosse windbreaker. It wasn't really cold enough for a jacket yet, but it was probably a matter of pride to him.

I finally found my voice. "I am."

"I'm Kane Woodward," he said. "And this is my sister, Ellie."

"I'm only a sophomore," she said softly, like she wasn't worthy of speaking to me because I was a senior.

"Very nice to meet you." I extended a hand and smiled to put her at ease.

"Do you play any sports?" Ellie asked.

"No." I squinted at Kane's jacket, pretending I hadn't already noticed it before. "So you play . . . lacrosse?"

"Yeah," he beamed. "You a fan?"

"I honestly don't know much about it. My old high school didn't have a lacrosse team."

He held a hand over his heart in mock distress. "How tragic!" Ellie laughed, but not in a mean way. Not at me. She nudged her brother with her elbow, then said she was off to meet some friends.

As she walked off, I gave a shrug and looked back up at Kane. "It was a small school."

"Well, welcome to Woodbridge, Jade. If there's anything I can help you with . . ." Kane paused a little too long and was staring a little too much. What for, I didn't know, but I felt a familiar prickly sensation on my neck.

Most people have the ability to hide it when they are embarrassed or feeling a particularly strong emotion. At worst, a little pink may rise into their cheeks. I, on the other hand, have been struck with this problem where my neck turns bright red and splotchy. There's no hiding it. Unless I wear a turtleneck every day. And I could feel it happening right now. My hand involuntarily rose to the pendant on my neck and fiddled with it in an attempt to cover up my red Neck of Shame.

"Um, I need to find Alexa Palmer," I said.

"Yeah, I know her. She's in a few of my classes."

"AP classes?" I must have creased my forehead or made some sort of surprised look because he raised one eyebrow and tsked at me with his finger.

"You assumed I was a dumb jock."

"No, I didn't!" The splotches started tickling my neck again.

"Yeah, you did," he said, smiling. "Just admit it."

"Well, not dumb," I bumbled. "But I didn't expect you to be . . ." I stopped and couldn't find any way to put this into words that didn't make me out to be a big jerk.

"It's okay," he said, smiling. "I'm only messing with you. I don't mind. I make assumptions about people all the time. It's human nature."

I really wanted to know what assumptions he'd made about me, but he pointed over my left shoulder. "There she is, in the corner."

I looked and saw Alexa hunched and scowling over a laptop.

"Thanks," I said to Kane. "See you around."

I made my way past a cluster of tables. Had Perfect Boy . . . ahem . . . Kane been flirting with me? Or was he just being nice and welcoming? I was like a traveler without a map in this place.

I passed by Fruity-Smelling Girl and a friend of hers sitting at a table. They seemed to be arguing about something. Fruity-Smelling Girl made a point to stop, midconversation, and give me the hairy eyeball as I passed. She hadn't exactly been scrambling to be my friend before, but there hadn't been hate in her eyes until now. Something had changed.

But before I could ponder that, I reached Alexa's table. I sat down and placed the box in front of me.

"I'm glad you're here," she said. "I'm tearing my hair out on this and need a two-minute break."

"Wow, two whole minutes?" I said, laughing. "What's got you so frazzled?"

She groaned. "My application essay to MIT."

"Wow, MIT, huh? Impressive." Schools like that weren't even on my radar. In fact, I hadn't even started my college applications. That was number five on my top ten list of Stuff That Was Giving Me Anxiety this week.

"Both my parents went there," Alexa said. "So it's sort of expected for me to go. No pressure," she snorted.

"Well, you're a double legacy, then. Plus, you have perfect scores and perfect grades. You have nothing to worry about."

"They don't take legacy into consideration." Alexa wrung her hands as she talked. "And even with my numbers, it's no guarantee. I think I came across as cold in my interview. And I don't play sports or have much for extracurriculars. And this essay is super important."

"What do you have so far?" I turned her screen toward me. It was blank.

"Nothing," she said, throwing her hands into the air. "A big fat nothing. This essay is going to be the death of me. It's all I think about lately. And I'm just blocked. It counts for so much and I can't even write one word."

"Just relax," I said, though those words to Alexa were about as useful as spit on a forest fire. "There's no right or wrong answer in an essay."

"That's why I hate it!" she yelled, drawing two dirty looks and one shush from the other tables. "I like things to be black-and-white. Right and wrong. That's why I love math and science. There are concrete answers. Things that can be tested and proven."

"Okay," I told her. "Sounds like you do need a break." I opened the top of the box I brought and grinned at her. "Want to see my collection?"

She dragged her hands through her hair. "Please tell me it's not rodent skulls or something because I don't want it to be *that* weird."

I looked through until I found one of my favorites. I held up the sliced crystal. It was one of my loose gems, not set into a jewelry piece.

"This is watermelon tourmaline." I turned it around in the palm of my hand so she could see the contrast of pink enfolded in green. "It's supposed to help you see the silver lining in every situation." I replaced that one and pulled out my red ruby earrings. "Rubies are useful against psychic attack. They're supposed to darken when danger lurks." I gave a little smile at her raised eyebrows.

I pulled out a pendant and let it dangle from my fingers. "This is bloodstone." It wasn't hard to figure out how they came up with that name. The stone was dark green with a spattering of red spots. "It also goes by the much less cool name heliotrope. This was used to banish evil and control the weather."

I went through and held up a few more of my favorites, explaining the meaning of each. Yellow sapphire attracts wealth. Aquamarine protects against drowning. Amethyst keeps you sober.

I avoided the one I never touch.

"Do you really believe in all this?" Alexa asked warily.

"Not really, no." I gave a tiny shrug. "It's just a hobby." I didn't want to go into the real reason behind my obsession with the stones. Not now, anyway.

"That's kind of cool," Alexa said, and I knew she meant it.

"So . . . you still want to sit with me?" I asked, my voice laced with teasing sarcasm. "Now that you know how weird I am?"

"Yeah, yeah, I get the point," Alexa said, the side of her mouth lifting. She reached in and pulled out a ring. "What does this one do?"

"That's marcasite. It helps with memory and clear thinking."

"Maybe that will help me write my essay!"

We laughed until we were shushed back to whispers. But I was glad the air was cleared. Yeah, she's weird. I'm weird. Who cares? If people showed the honest versions of themselves instead of the scrubbed, toned-down versions, we'd all be a little more interesting.

Fruity-Smelling Girl and her friend stood and began packing their things one table over. "Who is she?" I whispered and aimed my eyes toward them.

"Ugh, that's Faye Bettencourt. She's much less wonderful than she thinks she is."

I smiled. That little description seemed spot-on.

"I'll let you get back to work," I said, scooping the box into my arms. As I passed Faye, she held her hand out, stopping me. "You know, my mom's a realtor and she told me that it should be on the disclosure statement."

I blinked in confusion. "What are you talking about?"

Faye's friend giggled from behind her, but Faye just looked me in the eye. "Look at the paperwork from the sale of your new house. Then you'll know why everyone's talking."

The empty driveway told me Marie and Colby were out. I wasn't sure which Mommy and Me class they were at today, but it didn't matter. All that mattered was that I'd have the house to myself.

I had some snooping to do.

As I headed up the front walk, I saw a dark form in the window of the brown house next door. I knew an older man lived there. I'd seen him puttering around his yard a couple times. But he'd never come over to say "hi" or "welcome to the neighborhood" or anything like that. Seeing him standing there in the window, unmoving, obviously staring at me as I hiked my backpack up higher on my shoulder, gave me the creeps.

I let myself in the house, and the sound of the door slamming echoed in the quiet.

"Hello?" I called out, just to be safe.

No one answered, so I dropped my bag on the floor and bounded up the stairs. My dad used the fourth bedroom as his office. I hadn't spent any real time in there yet. He had a stack of boxes piled up in the corner, stuff from his old office he'd probably never need. The house papers wouldn't be in there, though. They were recent, only a couple weeks old, so they'd be somewhere handy.

I started with the top of his desk. There were bank statements, a few change-of-address papers, but nothing related to the new house. My eyes were drawn to the desk drawer.

It would be in there, I thought.

And a shudder ran through my body. I stiffened and listened hard, holding my breath. I was suddenly sure that someone else was home.

And they were watching me.

I ran over to the doorway and looked both ways down the hall. Nothing. Other than the muted ticking of the grandfather clock drifting up from downstairs, there was silence. But still . . . I felt someone there.

I stepped back into the room and took a deep breath. It was probably only my guilty conscience. Here I was in my father's office, searching through his belongings. It was just wrong. And that was why I felt this palpable anticipation in the air. It was guilt, that was all.

I slid open the drawer and found a manila file folder labeled 6 *SILVER ROAD — CLOSING*. That was it.

An icy breeze traveled past me, slightly lifting my hair. I glanced at the window. It was closed. But there was definitely a draft coming in from somewhere. Goose bumps rose on my skin, but I couldn't stop now. I felt something urging me on.

My shaky fingers opened the folder. The feeling in the room changed slightly, from anticipation to satisfaction, as I saw the paper on top. The title, *DISCLOSURE STATEMENT*, glared up at me in all caps. Exactly what that girl Faye had told me to look for.

And there, at the bottom, was what she had wanted me to find.

I closed my eyes tightly, the paper trembling in my hand. I didn't want it to be this. Anything but this.

I reopened my eyes, but the words remained the same.

Death by unnatural causes.

I was living in a murder house.

From the Diary of Kayla Sloane

It's time for a new school year. I feel like I should have something exciting to say, but there's really nothing. I am <u>so</u> ready for college. Parties with the WHS crew are boring me to death. Sigh. Only two more years.

Junior year starts tomorrow. We'll see what that brings.

My phone's been buzzing nonstop. All the girls want to know what I'm wearing for first day. Damn, 14 sent me over a dozen texts herself. 14 has her nose so far up my butt, it's hilarious.

I'll have my pick of the boys this year. Who should I snap up? 18? 13? The obvious 7?

Or maybe it's time for a new acquisition . . .

chapter 4

eath. Death. Death.

D   In my house.

Dad and Marie knew. And they hadn't told me. They deliberately made the choice to keep it a secret. This was how we could afford the house. It'd probably been heavily discounted because no one wanted to live where someone had been killed.

I stayed upstairs in my room all afternoon, pacing. Getting through dinner was torture. I wanted to confront Marie and Dad, but wouldn't do it in front of Colby. He was having enough trouble transitioning as it was. So I plastered on a smile and pretended to be interested in my dad's stories about the awful lady he had to sit next to on the plane. All the while, inside, I was screaming.

After Colby went to bed, I entered the living room, fists clenched at my sides. Dad and Marie were cuddling on the couch, getting ready to settle in and watch a show.

"We need to talk." My voice was authoritative and serious. It barely sounded like me.

Concern fell over Dad's previously tranquil face. My father had the body of a basketball player, almost comically tall and skinny, like he'd been made of clay and stretched too far. His job had him gone more than home, but he always had a smile for me. No matter how bad his own day might have been, he compartmentalized and never brought work frustrations into the house.

I hated being mad at him. Marie could be manipulative when she had to be, to get something she wanted for herself or Colby. I guessed the secrecy had been her idea. But Dad had obviously agreed to go along with it, so I couldn't lay my anger all on Marie. They'd both earned it.

I crossed my arms. "Were you ever going to tell me that we're living in a murder house?"

Dad's mouth opened, but no sound came out.

Marie straightened and spoke up quickly, "What on earth are you talking about?"

"Don't even lie to me." I held my hand up, palm out. Tears threatened to spring to my eyes and I closed them for a moment to regain control. This was why I hated confrontation. I couldn't stay unemotional.

I took a deep breath and reopened my eyes. "I know the truth."

"It's not a murder house," Marie said, slowly enunciating each word.

"Well, they don't know for sure if —" my dad began but was interrupted when Marie snapped his name. "Lawrence! We don't need to go into the details."

I gave an exaggerated shrug. "I can get the truth from you or I can get it from kids at school. Which would you rather?"

They looked at each other on the couch, weighing my ulti-matum. I stayed standing, liking the feeling of being higher while they sifted through their uncomfortable feelings. It was gratifying after the last few hours of holding all my anger inside.

"Fine." Marie remained calm and clasped her hands on her lap. "A teenage girl died in the house before the end of the school year."

I gasped. "Just a few months ago?"

Marie nodded. "Her name was Kayla Sloane. She fell down the stairs, hit her head, and . . ." she trailed off but I knew how that sentence ended.

Kayla Sloane. The name I'd heard among the whispers at school.

Marie's eyes traveled over my shoulder to the staircase behind me. The stairs I'd climbed up and down countless times in the past two weeks without knowing their true history. But Dad and Marie had known all along. That's why they added the carpet runner to the stairs. The only change they made to the house.

"To be completely truthful," my father began, despite an icy look from Marie, "the realtor told us that the police had never been able to determine if it was an accident or not."

A big dry lump formed in my throat. "So she might have been pushed," I croaked.

"There were rumors, but . . ."

"They're only that," Marie said. "Rumors. No proof."

"How did you find out, Jade?" my father asked softly. I could tell he felt bad about keeping the truth from me.

I didn't want to tell him I'd snooped in his office. No matter how angry I was, I still never wanted him to be disappointed in me. Instead, I told a half-truth. "From someone at school. Everyone at school knows. I'm apparently the only one who didn't know. So thanks for making a fool out of me."

"That wasn't our intention," Dad said.

"We just wanted to protect you both," Marie added.

"I understand not telling Colby," I agreed. "But I'm seventeen. Not five. And did you really think I wouldn't find out?"

"We planned on telling you eventually . . ."

"But just *after* we bought the house, right?" I said sarcastically. My anger was rising again, bubbling up like boiling water, threatening to spill over. "*After* we moved in. So if I was uncomfortable with the idea, it would be too late for my opinion to matter."

"You're leaving for college next fall —" Marie started.

"That's a whole year. I'm not staying here. In some . . . house of the dead. It's creepy. How am I supposed to sleep at night?"

"If we'd bought an old house, chances are someone would have died there," Marie pointed out. "Heart attacks, accidents."

"But this is different," I insisted.

"You're the one who always wanted this, Jade." Marie stood now, clearly losing her patience. "You're the one who wanted the big house in the nicer town with more kids and more stuff to do."

"Not like this. I would never have wanted this." I turned to my dad. "And you know it."

I looked into his eyes, pleading for understanding. He knew how I always went out of my way to avoid a fight. So for me to stand my ground like this, I had to be really upset. He knew that. He'd side with me.

He pushed himself off the couch and slowly straightened to his full height. "I think Marie's right."

"*What?*" My voice cracked on the word.

"I know it's hard to learn about it, honey. But we thought this through carefully and decided it was an opportunity we couldn't pass up. We never would've been able to move here otherwise, and it's the perfect town for our family."

He reached out for me but I pulled my arm away. I found myself holding back tears. I was sad for the girl who'd died. I was upset that my dream house had this giant cloud over it now. And I was angry that Dad and Marie had kept the truth from me. It stung like a betrayal. Two against one. They were a team. Against me.

I ran upstairs, slammed the door to my bedroom, and threw myself across the bed. I cried it out for a while, but knew I wouldn't be able to sleep. The feeling in the air had changed. I felt like an intruder, a thief, an uninvited guest sleeping in someone else's home.

I pushed the tears off my cheeks with the palms of my hands and sat up. Morbid curiosity niggled at me. I had to know more. I had to read it for myself.

I sat in front of my computer and typed "Kayla Sloane,

Woodbridge" into the search engine. I clicked on the first link — a news article.

> **Woodbridge, MA — *A Woodbridge High School junior was fatally injured when she fell down the stairs in her home. Kayla Sloane, 16, died from trauma to the head and neck. Her mother, Katherine Sloane, found her daughter's body at the bottom of the stairs when she returned to the home. The teenager was unresponsive and pronounced dead by paramedics.***
>
> ***Police aren't commenting on the nature of the death, only saying the injuries sustained are consistent with that of an accidental fall down the stairs. However, a source close to the tragedy says the police are also following up a lead that Kayla may not have been alone at the time of the fall, spurring rumors that her death was, in fact, a homicide.***

I gripped my abdomen as nausea roiled in my stomach. I shouldn't have looked it up. The details only made me feel worse. My eyes drifted down to the picture of Kayla they'd included with the story. It looked like a yearbook photo. I was immediately struck by how beautiful she was. Flawless skin. A Hollywood smile. Electric green eyes that gave her an exotic look. And long black hair, parted down the middle, that fell in waves over her shoulders.

Long black hair.

I stifled a gasp.

Colby had said his glimmering girl had black hair.

No, I told myself. *Just no.*

Finding out the history of my house was traumatic enough. I didn't need to go there. Colby was making up stories. That's what five-year-olds did. His girl was imaginary.

Not real.

chapter 5

I went to school early so I could avoid Dad and Marie. I walked down the main hall, searching for somewhere to be alone. Fluorescent lighting leaked out of a large room on the left, the door wide open, so I went through and, finding it empty, sighed in relief. One half was full of easels, the other, desks. I sat down at the closest desk, unzipped my bag, and took out the Calculus assignment that I should have done the day before. Now that I was out of the house, it was easier to clear my mind, and I ticked off the problems quickly. I was on the last one when I heard a sharp intake of air.

I looked up and found Donovan staring at me from the doorway. He had a bowl in his hand, with a few paintbrushes sticking out of it. I remembered Alexa mentioning he was in the art room often.

"Sorry," I said, breaking the silence. "Were you working in here?"

"Yeah." He set the bowl down and pushed the hair out of his eyes.

Those eyes again. My body tensed. I gripped the pencil harder in my fingers and forced myself to look down at the paper.

"But you don't have to leave or anything," he added.

"I just had some homework to finish," I explained.

He motioned with a brush. "Keep on keeping on, then. I won't bother you." He flashed a tiny smile, releasing a flood of warmth through my body in response. Particularly my neck, which was probably neon red. Then he turned his attention to whatever he was working on at the easel.

My attention was gone, though. I tried to focus on my last problem, but I kept wondering if Donovan was looking at me. So I'd sneak a glance, see him working away, then end up disappointed.

Why did I even *want* him to be looking at me?

He'd acted so strangely back in the office. But then I remembered what had brought on his attitude change — my address. And now I knew why. Still, he could have just told me I was living in a famous death house rather than run away and leave me hanging.

"So which one are you wearing today?"

Donovan's voice snapped me out of my rambling thoughts. I looked up at him. He looked less like the emotionally frozen guy who'd sat silently in the cafeteria and more like he had that day in the office. After he'd met me, but before he'd found out my address. A bit of life had entered him again. He stood straighter, had an inquisitive smile.

And I totally forgot his question.

"Huh?" I said.

He pointed at my chest. I looked down and realized I'd been absentmindedly fiddling with my pendant.

"Every day, you wear a different one," he said.

He'd noticed that. I licked my lips, suddenly nervous. "This is, um, a clear quartz."

He stepped closer and squinted at it. "The black one you wore on your second day . . . was that onyx?"

My eyebrows rose in surprise. Not only did he notice *me*, but he noticed I wore pendants and not the same one each day. And now he even knew the name of one. I was impressed. "Yeah," I said. "How'd you know? Staying up too late watching the home shopping channels?"

I smirked at my little joke, but he didn't laugh. The light in his eyes went out and that closed-off look fell over him again. He crossed the room and faced the window, staring out at the kids pouring out of a bus. "I bought a ring for someone once, with that stone in it."

He added, almost too softly for me to hear, "She loved it."

The bell for homeroom rang, but he didn't move from the window. I wordlessly picked up my books and left the room. What had started out awkward had turned promising and then just plain strange.

All morning I wanted to talk to Alexa about the house, but didn't get the chance until we sat down at lunch. My appetite had returned somewhat, and I stabbed my penne with a fork as I told her the news.

"So you live in Kayla Sloane's house," Alexa said, shaking her head. "Creepy. No wonder everyone was talking."

I held my hands out wide. "Why didn't you tell me?"

She blew her bangs out of her eyes. "I didn't know where you live, and I'd certainly never been to Kayla's house before. And I'm not on Faye Bettencourt's gossip grapevine."

"Yeah, I know," I said. "I just hate that everyone knew something I didn't."

"I can't believe your parents didn't tell you."

"No kidding," I agreed. I paused as I chewed through a mouthful of ziti. "So would Kayla have been a senior this year?"

"Yep."

Part of me wanted to forget Kayla ever existed, but another, more-insistent part of me wanted to know everything I could about her. "What kind of girl was she?" I asked with forced nonchalance.

Alexa snorted. "She was the girl who had everything."

"What do you mean?"

"She was smart *and* athletic. She got the grades and made all-state in soccer."

I sensed a jealous tone in Alexa's voice. I remembered her freak-out over college applications, how she had the best grades but no extracurriculars. Kayla, it seemed, had both. Plus, I'd seen Kayla's photo, so I knew she was beautiful. But Alexa didn't mention that. Looks apparently weren't something Alexa envied.

"Was she popular?" I asked.

Alexa rolled her eyes. "That's an understatement. More like worshipped."

Wow. "Everyone must have been so sad when she died."

Alexa had a faraway look in her eyes as she spoke. "You would think so."

"There were rumors that she was . . ."

"Pushed?"

I nodded.

"I don't believe it for a second. Donovan's one of the only kids in this school who's nice to freaks like me. He's not capable of murder."

My fork clanged loudly as it hit my plate. "Wait, Donovan O'Mara?"

"Yeah, what other Donovan would there be?"

Something in my heart twisted. *Donovan* was the suspect mentioned in the article? "Why did they think he killed her?"

"He was her boyfriend."

A tiny spark of jealousy twinged inside me.

Alexa continued, "And he was the last one to see her alive. A witness saw him go into the house with her and come out alone. Then her mother came home and found her body in a heap at the bottom of the stairs." Alexa paused. "Donovan swore she was alive when he left. The police couldn't prove it one way or the other. All of Kayla's friends turned on him, but the rest of the school knows he would never do something like that."

I glanced at his usual table, but he wasn't there. This explained everything about Donovan. The girl he loved had died and then he was shunned at school. Suspected. Labeled a social pariah.

I felt guilty for my snap judgment earlier about his behavior in the office. He wasn't a jerk. He was just . . . broken.

Alexa and I finished our lunch in silence but my mind was in overdrive. I thought about my quick conversation with Donovan in the art room. He had mentioned buying onyx jewelry for someone. Obviously, that someone had been Kayla. And the day I'd had trouble choosing a pendant, *the onyx had been laid out on the bed for me.* A chill went through me.

Coincidence, I told myself. I was a rational person. I was not going to jump to insane conclusions. The easiest answer was the most likely one. Colby had taken the necklace and put it on my bed, not a ghost. And it was only by chance that it was onyx, the same stone Donovan had given Kayla.

Because if it wasn't a coincidence, the other option was that my house was haunted and a ghost chose the onyx to send a message to her ex-boyfriend.

And that was 100 percent pure, unfiltered crazy.

But, while I tried to convince myself of that, my mind also thought about what the message might be. What I'd want to tell my boyfriend, if it was me drifting out there, all alone, still haunting the house I'd lived and died in. If it was me, I'd want him to know —

I'm still here.

That night, I lay in bed but sleep wouldn't come. I couldn't shut my mind off, couldn't stop thinking about Kayla. She'd lived in this house and done the same things I did. Ate in the kitchen. Showered. Did her homework. Slept. And now here I was. Living in her house. Going to her school. Meeting her friends. Finding myself drawn to her boyfriend.

I tossed and turned, then got up, thinking that a breeze from the window might help. I slid up the sash and crawled back into bed, but the night sounds of crickets were distracting, not lulling. The September air was a bit too chilly. And the breeze kept making my sheer white curtains dance. Even with my eyes closed, I sensed their movement.

I groaned and got up again, shut the window, and returned to bed. If I didn't get to sleep soon, I'd be in a coma all day in school. But the more I thought about that, the more anxious I became, and my now racing heart made me even more awake.

I sighed and pulled the comforter tightly up under my chin. The ticking of the grandfather clock downstairs, distant yet distinct, eventually calmed me. I imagined my heart slowing and beating to the rhythm of the clock. And soon my eyes got heavy and closed.

But then reopened.

A voice drifted down the hallway. Unfamiliar and muffled. Was it calling my name? My body tense, I held my breath and listened.

"Jade . . ."

The voice came again. Sure now, I threw off the covers and padded into the hallway, wincing at the noisy floorboards. I peeked my head into Colby's room. He was sleeping — fitfully. He groaned and rolled over, then back again. I tiptoed down to my parents' room. Marie was sleeping on her side, one hand hanging off the bed. Dad was lightly snoring.

So who'd called me?

I turned slowly, now at the top of the staircase, and peered into the darkness below. This was where it had happened. Where Kayla fell . . . or was pushed.

I placed my hand on the banister, closed my eyes, and imagined Kayla placing her hand in the very same spot, trailing her fingers over the polished wood . . . then feeling her balance go out from underneath her. I imagined what she must have felt in the instant she realized she was falling through air. The terror that must have gripped her heart. The panic rushing through her veins as she rushed toward the bottom.

I saw the floor coming up to meet her, fast and furious, but then realized in horror that I wasn't imagining anymore. My hand no longer gripped the banister. I wasn't picturing Kayla falling. *I* was falling.

What happened? Did someone push me? Did I fall on my own?

I screamed but no sound came out. The air rushing at my face told me I was falling fast, but it seemed to be happening in slow motion. I tried to put my arms up, to soften the blow I knew was coming to my head, but I couldn't move my limbs. I was paralyzed.

And then I hit bottom.

My face crushed into the hardwood. Instant pain reverberated through me. I couldn't move, couldn't open my eyes. All I could do was wait for death to take me away.

Someone was calling my name again. But this time it was familiar. It was Colby, his voice panicked.

"Jade!"

I blinked as forms came into view, familiar but at wrong angles.

"Are you okay?" Colby asked, worry making his voice tremble.

I pushed myself up on my elbows. The confusion was burning away, though the ache in my cheekbone remained. I was on my bedroom floor. I quickly figured out what had happened. I'd fallen out of bed, woken Colby with my loud thump, and he'd come in and turned the lights on.

"It's okay, buddy," I said softly. "You can go back to bed."

He blinked his glassy, tired eyes, nodded, and slowly retreated to his room. My bones cracked as I pulled myself up and stood in front of the mirror. Sweat plastered my hair to my face. I pulled it back and saw the raging red mark under my left eye. I'd have a bruise there tomorrow. How would I explain that in school?

Oh yeah, I dreamt I was Kayla falling down the staircase, but really I'd fallen out of bed and hit my face on the floor. Even though I've never fallen out of bed before in my life. Yeah, that makes sense.

A tightness pulled across my neck and I realized I'd forgotten to take my pendant off before I went to sleep. The clear quartz. I unclasped the necklace and stared at the stone uneasily for a few moments. The gem hung from a silver mounting and was delicately tapered to a pointed end. I shuddered as I thought of the crystal's use: to promote out-of-body experiences, lucid dreaming, and communication with the dead.

From the Diary of Kayla Sloane

Hola, Diary. Long time, no write. Been super busy with soccer, classes, parties, hazing the freshmen. Good times.

14 keeps asking me every day who I'm going to go after this year. She wants to know if I'm taking dibs on 7, obvs. I don't think I will. Mainly because everyone expects me to. And 7 will always be in my back pocket, no matter what. I don't even have to claim dibs. 7 is mine, natch. No matter who else he's with at the time.

But, no, I have my eyes on someone new. Someone different. I've actually never even written about him in here before, so he's going to need a number. And the next available one is . . . 28.

So, 28 was at 15's party Saturday night. I wore my tightest jeans and that spaghetti-strapped red tank. Looked so hot I even caught 9 staring at me through the window. The creeper. Anyway 28 was all shy and adorkable, wearing some Halo T-shirt with paint stains on his fingertips. He's not emo or anything. Just one of those artistic guys.

And I'm thinking . . . time for a taste of something different?

chapter 6

"What the hell happened to you?"

"Thanks," I mumbled. Apparently concealer did not work wonders. The fluorescent lighting in the school bathroom wasn't helping any, either. "I fell."

"Into a fist?" Alexa finished drying her hands and stomped up to me, suspicion in her eyes.

"No. I fell out of bed."

"Face-first?"

"It's a hardwood floor," I explained. "And I'm embarrassed enough without the twenty questions."

A flush came from one of the stalls and I rolled my eyes. Great, one more person who'd know I was a klutz, even in my sleep. The door opened and Faye walked up to the row of sinks. She hitched her giant bag up on her shoulder and eyed my injury, which was obvious now that it'd been pointed out.

"What did you try to cover it up with?" Faye asked.

"Liquid concealer," I said.

"Did you powder over the concealer after?"

"No . . ." I said cautiously.

Faye hefted her bag up onto the counter and sifted through

its contents for a minute, eventually pulling out a concealer pen and a powder compact. "Face me," she said.

I snuck a wary look at Alexa, who was having a staring contest with the tile floor.

"Okay," I agreed. *What's the worst she could do?*

Faye worked on me for a minute, then backed up a few steps and nodded with satisfaction. "That'll work."

I turned toward the mirror, expecting to see the Joker's face in the reflection, but it was only me. Unbruised. Maybe I'd been imagining the stench of evil coming off Faye the past few days. Maybe she wasn't so bad.

"Thanks," I said gratefully. "I can't even see it anymore."

Faye repacked her bag. "No problem."

On her way out, she stopped and turned. "Do you mind if I give you one more tip? Girl to girl?"

I shrugged. "Sure."

"Be careful of Kane Woodward. He's probably going to be all over you like a nerd on math, but it's because you're fresh meat. He's already torn through all the girls in this school, even the freshmen." Her mouth turned down in contempt. "If he decides you're next, he'll pursue you hard, get what he wants, then drop you." She stiffened her shoulders. "You hear me?"

I thought about the way he'd come up to me in the library and offered to help me with *anything*. "I hear you," I said. "Loud and clear."

After the door closed behind Faye, I looked up at Alexa, who shook her head and said, "Don't even ask me. The mating rituals of teens are as much a mystery to me as the additive number theory."

We joined the bustling hallway crowd and I clutched my books tightly to my chest. I was nervous about seeing Donovan, nervous about seeing Kane. When I spotted a giant banner reading SUNDAY OPEN HOUSE! I was glad for a distraction. "What's all that about?" I asked Alexa, pointing.

"All the clubs will have their booths in the gym that day," Alexa explained. "So if you're thinking of joining any extra-curriculars, it's a good idea to walk around and see what you're interested in."

"Are you going?" I asked. I wanted to go, but also wanted someone to go with.

"Nah. I'm on the math team. On top of all my accelerated courses, that's enough for me." She didn't say it in a bragging way. I didn't think Alexa even knew how to brag. She just stated facts.

"That's cool," I said as we rounded the corner to the back hall. "I didn't know there was a math team."

"Why would you?" Alexa's eyes flared and she abruptly stopped walking. "It's not a priority to the school. The football team wins one game on Thanksgiving and it's all, 'Woo! We rule! Banners everywhere! Let's celebrate! Congratulate all the players!' But when the math team finished in first place in the state competition, did we get congratulations? No! Did we get banners all over the school? No. Did Principal Bremer even mention it on the morning announcements? Not until three days later when we protested. Ugh!"

Alexa was flailing her arms in the air. I'd obviously hit on a hot-button issue for her. "I'm sorry," I said. "That really sucks."

"The priorities are all wrong," she continued. "And then there's the Bodiford Scholarship, don't even get me started on that."

"What is it?" I didn't want to egg her on, but was genuinely curious.

"It's a scholarship trust run by some rich old guy in town who owns four corporations. It can be given out to one graduating senior each year if someone meets the requirements. It provides free tuition to any college for four years."

That sounded amazing. "What are the requirements?"

"You have to have a class rank in the top ten and make all-state in a team sport. And, of course, the math team doesn't count. Athletics only."

I frowned. "That doesn't seem fair."

Alexa nodded firmly. "I considered petitioning the foundation, but my parents told me that since it's a private organization, they can put any conditions they want on their scholarship."

"Who's going to get it from our graduating class?"

"Actually, Kane Woodward, so I don't really mind. He kind of deserves it. Plus," she added, "the scholarship wouldn't matter for me, anyway."

I was about to ask why, but the bell rang and I realized we were the only two left in the hallway. Thankfully I was right outside my classroom door, so I bolted in and kept my eyes down as I slunk into my seat.

Mrs. Bourque started speaking in French. It was one of my favorite classes, but I wasn't into it today. All my feelings about Donovan, Kane, Kayla, the house, the awful dream, and my fall swirled around in me.

When the school day ended, I walked through the parking lot with Alexa. For someone who seemed to have problems reading people, she knew something was up with me. After a bit of prodding, I opened up.

"My parents want me to get over it, but I can't just get over it like that." I snapped my fingers. "How can I walk up and down that staircase, day after day, and not think about it?"

My voice had a high, almost-hysterical tone to it all of a sudden, from my bottled-up feelings finally breaking free. Alexa shuffled her feet and looked off to the side, obviously uncomfortable with my show of emotion, but she listened, and that was really all I needed.

So I continued. "My stepmother said, 'It's too late now. You were the one who begged for a house like this.' Yeah, I'd wanted a big house in a nice town. But one without a ghost, thanks."

Alexa shot a hand out to stop me. "Wait, what? A ghost?"

Oh. I hadn't meant to let that slip. "Not really. My little brother says he can see a girl sometimes in the house. A girl who glimmers. I know ghosts aren't real, but it's freaking me out a little."

Alexa whistled. "Man. That's crazy."

"Seriously." A film of wetness came over my eyes and I rubbed them with the palm of my hand.

Alexa took a giant step backward. "Are you going to . . . cry?"

"No, I'm not," I said, suddenly embarrassed.

"Good."

I figured she was about to say that she was uncomfortable with outward displays of emotion, but instead she said, "It's a waste of time."

I shouldn't cry because it was . . . inefficient? I shook my head. "You're a weird one."

"Or," she said, holding up a finger, "I'm normal and you're the weird one. It's all about perspective."

I laughed then and Alexa smiled. She gave me a light, quick pat on the shoulder and jingled her keys on the way to her car. She'd done her job. I was now laughing instead of crying.

And I knew exactly what I had to do when I got home.

I paused outside of Colby's room. I had to talk to my brother and get him to tell me the truth, once and for all. I heard his muffled voice coming from behind his closed door. He was probably playing with his Star Wars figurines, reenacting scenes from the movies. I inched up to the door and pressed my ear against it. Now it was silent.

A rush of cold suddenly pushed through the cracks in the door and traveled up the length of my body. The temperature was so shocking, I staggered back a bit.

And, just as quickly as the cold had formed, it was gone.

Icy fingers tiptoed up my spine.

I opened Colby's door and poked my head in. "You got a window open, bud?"

"No." He was sitting cross-legged on his bed, plucking at a lint ball on his comforter. There were no toys out. I shut the door behind me and glanced around the room. His window was closed, but I really didn't care about the draft anymore. He looked so sad, sitting there, his face slack. Like he was disappointed in something.

"Everything okay, Colby?"

He nodded.

I eased myself down on the bed and sat cross-legged, mirroring him. "Did you have a bad day at school?"

"I had a great day," he said. "We had two outdoor recesses."

"What did you do after school?"

"Music class with Mom."

"Did something happen there?"

"No, it was good. I like playing the keyboard. I can do three songs now."

Sounded like a whole lot of kindergartner good times, but his voice held no enthusiasm. His energy was sapped. This time of day, he was usually jumping on his bed, not pouting on it. I prodded, "Moving is tough, huh?"

He lifted one shoulder up in a half shrug. "S'okay."

Time to get direct. I cleared my throat. "Colby." I put on my super-serious, big-sister face. "I need to know. For real. Are you making up the ghost girl thing?"

He peered up into my eyes and said softly, "No, she's real."

"Pinky swear?"

He held up his tiny finger in the most solemn of our oaths and wrapped it around mine. "I pinky swear she's real," he said. "But I don't want to play with her anymore."

I let go of his little finger. "Why?"

He crossed his arms tightly. "She's not nice."

A shiver coursed through my body. "I thought you said she couldn't talk."

"She tries, but I can't hear her. I can just sort of . . . feel it. I think that makes her even angrier, when her mouth moves but I don't know what she's saying. She's gotten to be too mad all the time. I'm a little bit scared of her. So I told her to go away." He dropped his hands to the blanket again, rubbing his fingers back and forth over a seam.

"Has she?" I asked.

He shrugged his narrow shoulders, keeping his eyes down. "I don't know. It hasn't been long enough."

"When did you tell her to go away?"

He looked back up at me. "Right before you came into the room."

chapter 7

Last year, Dad and Marie took us to an amusement park.
There was this ride there called the Twister. It's a giant
cylinder and everyone stands with their backs to the wall. It
starts to spin in a circle, faster and faster. And then the floor
drops. There's this moment of panic. You're spinning a gazil-
lion miles an hour, you can barely see, and your feet aren't
touching ground. You think you're about to launch into the
air, you wonder why you haven't fallen to your death yet. And
then you realize . . . gravity has stuck your body to the wall.
But before you have a chance to really enjoy the fact that
you're not going to die, the floor comes back up, the ride slows
down, and then it's over.

In Colby's room, I felt like I'd just taken a ride on the
Twister. I realized with absolute, panicked fear, that my little
brother was telling the truth. The cold air I'd felt over my skin,
blasting out of his room . . . had been her. The glimmering
girl. Kayla.

I couldn't deny it anymore. My house was haunted.

The room started spinning, my eyesight wavered, and I
thought I felt the ground slipping from beneath me again. But
Colby's worried voice brought me back.

"Do you think she's gone now?" he asked.

"I don't know, buddy." I tried my best not to let terror leak into my voice. "I hope so."

"Can you *make* her go away?"

My chest tightened. "I can try."

I left his room on legs made of rubber and sank into my desk chair. I remembered that Dad had left for another trip this morning.

I'd have to talk to Marie alone.

Things weren't always so strained between Marie and me. They'd started out great, actually. After a year of having no female influence in my life, Dad slowly introduced Marie into our day-to-day routines. Eventually Marie and I started doing stuff on our own, like movies and shopping. She took me for my first manicure. I liked her, even though she seemed to be trying almost too hard to win me over.

But then Dad announced that they were going to get married. That's when uncertainty crept into my belly and grew larger, day after day. Marie took over the house, became the person in charge, gave me chores, told me what to do. Instead of trying to be my friend, she was trying to replace my mother. I was hurt, confused, bitter, and angry.

I let her know it.

Not directly, but in small passive-aggressive ways. Culminating in the day, a month after their wedding, when she sat me down and told me it was all right for me to call her Mom.

And I responded coldly, "I only have one Mom. She's dead." Our relationship changed then. In that one moment. We both built our walls up, almost instantaneously. And the distance had remained ever since.

I only called her Mom in front of Colby, mainly to keep things simple for him. He knew my mother had been someone else and had died, but it wasn't something we talked about. Though Dad mentioned her in private now and then, I honestly couldn't remember the last time my mother ever came up in conversation in front of Colby or Marie. She was always there, though, hovering, in the cracks of conversations, in the corners of my thoughts. Never too far away.

Especially now. Finally accepting the idea that Kayla Sloane was haunting the house made me wonder . . . why not Mom? Why hadn't I felt her presence in our *old* house? Smelled her jasmine perfume? Heard her voice in a whisper down the hall? Why Kayla and not her?

After dinner, I watched Marie as we collaborated on the dishes. When she'd first started dating Dad, she had long, black curly hair. I always wanted to touch it, to try to separate the curls with my fingers. Now it was shorter. She'd done the mom-cut thing after Colby was born. But she was still pretty.

Nowhere near as pretty as my mom had been, though. Or as smart. Or as nice. Or as anything.

In fact, the only thing she did better than my mom was cook, but I didn't even want to admit that. As if saying so, even only to myself, was cheating on my mother in a way.

"Done with that one?" Marie asked.

I refocused and nodded, handing her the rinsed-off plate to place in the dishwasher. We'd had baked ziti and garlic bread, one of my favorite meals. Colby was happily watching SpongeBob in the living room. Now was the time.

"Can I talk to you about something?" I asked, rinsing the last plate.

Marie took it from me, bent down to put it in the dishwasher, then straightened up again, wincing as she placed her hand on her lower back. She looked tired. I wondered if the new nursing job was harder on her than her old one had been.

"Sure, what is it?"

Now that the time was here, my throat felt like it'd been filled with sand. I fiddled with my hair, tucking it behind my ears. But stalling wouldn't make the words any easier to say.

"Colby told me that he sees a girl in the house. A girl who glimmers . . ."

I told her every detail. About the cold rushes of air I'd felt. The pendant that had been placed on my clothing. How Colby talked to her and felt her emotions. How she was scaring him. How sure I was that this was the ghost of Kayla Sloane.

Marie was serious and somber throughout my entire monologue. Absorbing each word. Not interrupting me. I was glad. I'd expected hysterics since Colby was involved, but she seemed to be handling it seriously.

When I finished, I rubbed my sweaty hands on my jeans and waited for her to speak.

She stood staring at me for what seemed like an eternity, then said, "So this is your next tactic?"

My eyebrows lifted. "Excuse me?"

Marie tossed a dishrag on the counter. "I'm impressed, really. It's smart. We won't listen to you, so maybe we'll listen if Colby's in danger."

"Wait, what?"

"You don't want to live here. I get that. But trying to manipulate me by coming up with this story about my son is just low."

"That's not what I'm doing. It's not a story," I pleaded. "It's the truth. Talk to him."

Her face went rigid. "Oh, I'll talk to him all right."

I had an English paper due in a week on *Rebecca* by Daphne du Maurier. I sat at the desk in my bedroom and glanced over the assignment in my hands.

Analyze both the alienation of the main character and the perceptions of Rebecca.

I hadn't even cracked the spine of the book yet. I picked it up and tried to read it while waiting for Marie to put Colby to bed. Despite its wonderful opening line, I couldn't get past the first paragraph. I found my mind drifting and I have to start from the beginning again and again. I needed closure with Marie before I could concentrate on anything else.

Finally, I heard the soft click of Colby's door shutting and Marie's footsteps walking down the hallway toward my room. Then she came in and faced me.

I straightened in my chair, trying to read the emotion on her face and having trouble deciphering it.

"Did you talk to Colby?" I asked.

"Yes, I did." She paused. "My worst fear was confirmed."

I let out long breath. "So you believe me?"

Marie rushed forward, until she was only a foot away, towering over me in my desk chair. "You've been feeding this ghost talk to him, using him in your ploy to get us to move." She was whispering, though it seemed like she was yelling.

"What? No!" I shook my head vehemently. "He started talking about the ghost before you even told me about the girl who died here."

"Before we had our talk, yes, but perhaps after you already learned about it yourself at school."

"No, that's not it at all." I got up, hoping that standing face-to-face would help her see my sincerity. "Listen, Marie, this has nothing to do with how I'm uncomfortable living here. I'm truly concerned about Colby."

"Save it, Jade." She pointed a finger in my face. "Stop scaring my son with this ghost talk or you'll regret it."

I opened my mouth, but she interrupted. "I'm not going to tell your father. But if you speak one more word about this nonsense, I will have no choice but to let him know."

She stormed out of the room, and I flinched as the door slammed behind her. Marie already had her mind made up that I was a liar. So she'd gone in there, armed with questions, ready to manipulate Colby into answering the way she wanted. The truth never stood a chance.

I dropped my face into my hands. What could I do now? Tell Dad? Marie would manipulate him, too. Tell him I was making it all up and forcing it on Colby as part of my evil scheme.

No, I was on my own.

I booted up my old desktop, which ran about as well as my car. After seven minutes, it was finally up and running and connected to the Internet. *Rebecca* would have to wait another day. I had research to do.

Searching for "ghosts" and "hauntings" brought up too much information, most of it broad and useless. But I lost myself in it, continuing to read more and more, not even realizing how much time had passed until a creak behind me pulled me out of my trance.

I looked behind me. Nothing was there. It was probably just one of those normal house noises, but it still made my heart race.

I turned back to the computer. The clock showed midnight. My eyes felt dry and scratchy from staring at the monitor for so long. I needed to go to bed, but I hadn't learned anything practical yet. I typed in the most specific query I could come up with:

"Cause of haunting, why spirits stay, getting rid of ghosts"

The first link was a website for some ghost society in England. I clicked on it and was brought to their FAQ page.

Q. Why do some spirits linger in our world?
A. A spirit sticks around if he or she has unfinished business. Especially if the person has died a violent death.

The phrase "violent death" made me grimace, but it gave me another thought. That might have explained why my mother never came around. Her death was too early, but it was a natural one and she died with the peace of mind that Dad would take good care of me.

Kayla, however, may not have been so lucky. I continued to skim the questions until I came to:

Q. Is it possible to get rid of a ghost?

A. Once spirits become attached to a place, it is
   nearly impossible to get rid of them. You can ask the
   spirit to stop bothering you. If she's an enlightened,
   positive spirit she might. But if you have a negative
   spirit in your home and the strange phenomena
   seem to be escalating, you're in trouble.

Q. What are the steps involved?

A. Do not show fear. In fact, try not to show
   any emotion at all. The spirits feed off strong
   human emotions and get energy from them.
   Tell the spirit to follow the light. The light is good.
   They should not be afraid of the light.

Q. What if I have a negative spirit?

A. Do not attempt to engage a negative spirit. We
   are the only ones who can help you with this. Our
   consultation price range begins at ten thousand —

I shut down the computer with a groan. That whole society might be a scam, and I certainly didn't have money to pay them. I stretched out across my bed, physically and mentally exhausted.

I was going to feel quite stupid doing this, but I had to try. The instructions were simple enough. I kept my voice firm and unemotional.

"Please leave this place," I said, hopefully loud enough that Kayla would hear me, but not so loud that it would wake Marie. "You have passed on and it's time to follow the light."

My neck blushed, even though no one was there to witness my embarrassment. I felt silly, but I continued, "You are able to move beyond your earthly troubles. You will be happier if you do. Do not be scared of the light. It is a source of love and forgiveness."

I lay in silence, all my senses attuned, waiting for any response. The house made its usual creaks and groans, each one sending a shudder through me. But after a while my eyelids closed involuntarily. I was suddenly overwhelmingly tired. All I could do now was hope that my little speech worked. And that Kayla was a positive entity. Because if she wasn't, all that was for nothing. And then I'd have to think about why she was sticking around.

What did she want?

And what would she do if she didn't get it?

From the Diary of Kayla Sloane

So I was in the teachers' lounge, attempting to slip a mild laxative into the coffeemaker, when I heard footsteps and had to hide in a closet. And lo and behold, guess who two old hags were talking about? Yours truly. I only caught a snippet of conversation. They came in to grab something quickly and left. But here's what I heard.

"Kayla Sloane is aggressively ambitious and competitive, even socially."

Socially aggressive? Whatever.

And then the other Depends-wearing blue-hair clucked in agreement and added, "She's the worst bully in the school."

Really. A bully? Please. Bullies are stupid, powerless oafs who torture kids to make themselves feel better about being so dumb. Not me. I can be hard on others, but those are the rights handed to you when you're at the top.

It's funny. If 14, 12, or 16 all of a sudden stopped asking how high when I told them to jump, I'd actually have some respect for them for once. But I'd also be pissed and probably ruin them.

And, yeah, I'm spoiled by my parents and, yeah, I'm used to getting what I want. But I work hard for it, too. Sure, some things are handed to me. But others take time and effort. The difference between me and losers is that I don't quit. That's why I usually end up getting my way.

But why am I mean? Simple.

Because I can be.

chapter 8

The next morning, my jewelry box was open and I could have sworn it was closed when I went to bed. But I didn't want to read too much into it. I slid my garnet pendant out and closed the lid. I even put a book on top of the box, though I didn't know what I expected to accomplish with that.

I rubbed my finger over the deep red stone, a deliberate choice for today since garnet was known to increase your energy when you were tired. One look in the mirror at the bags under my eyes told me it didn't have an instantaneous effect. I used the makeup tricks Faye had taught me to cover up both the bags and my fading bruise.

In school, my eyes constantly scanned for Donovan, hoping to catch a passing glance in the hallway. Even though I knew he'd only be shuffling along, his head down, gliding through the halls of school like a ghost himself.

I cruised up to my locker midway through the day to exchange my morning books with those I'd need for my afternoon classes. Only a few more hours and it would be the weekend. I elbowed the locker closed and looked up to see Kane Woodward standing there, smiling, his hands in the pockets of his Woodbridge Lacrosse windbreaker.

"How's it going, new girl?"

Faye's warning shot through my head. *He'll be all over you . . . but only because you're fresh meat.*

"The name's Jade," I said flatly.

He frowned, not expecting my unenthusiastic response. Most girls probably giggled and twirled their hair when he called them a nickname.

"I know your name," he said with a nervous chuckle. "We talked in the library, remember?"

I met his eyes. He didn't look predatory. In fact, he looked . . . earnest. Maybe I shouldn't just take Faye's words at face value, maybe I should judge for myself.

"Of course I remember," I said, giving him a smile now. "I was just teasing."

Confidence flowed back into his posture. "So how is Woodbridge treating you so far?"

I tucked my books in the crook of my arm. "Pretty good. The people are nice. The teachers are tough, but fair."

"And the guys?" He waggled his eyebrows.

"They're . . . interesting."

Kane beamed, but he didn't know that the moment I said that, my mind wasn't there with him anymore. It had flitted to an image in my head. Of a boy standing by a window, thinking about the girl he'd loved and lost.

I forced my mind back to the boy talking to me here and now. I was about to start walking out with him, but Kane reached across and rested his hand on my locker, drawing himself closer to me. A random girl walking by actually gasped.

From the wide-eyed stares I was getting, I should have been swooning. Close to fainting. And maybe I would have been if Faye hadn't talked to me about Kane. But I wasn't. It seemed too cliché. Like a well-practiced, slick move.

He leaned over a bit, making up for our height difference, and started talking in a low voice. Something about a party. But all I heard were Faye's words again.

If he decides you're next, he'll pursue you hard, get what he wants, then drop you.

My eyes slid across his arm and focused on his hand. He must have realized I was uncomfortable, because he stopped talking and pulled his arm back down to his side. I took a tentative step backward, reclaiming my personal space.

A barely stifled laugh rang out from behind us. I turned and spied Donovan across the hall. He clearly found my snubbing of Kane amusing. Kane followed my line of sight and his eyes narrowed. If looks could kill, Donovan would be a rotting corpse right now. Apparently those two weren't friends.

Kane returned his attention to me. "What's the matter?"

Half of me thought I was crazy. Any girl in her right mind would enjoy this moment. Stand here and bathe in his attention. But what if what Faye said was true? What if this was some game he played, girl after girl after girl?

"I'm not your fresh meat," I said in a small voice, and hurried past him.

Uncertainty nagged at me on the way home. Had I been too hard on Kane? Was he being skeevy like Faye had predicted or was he only being nice? I didn't have enough personal experience to judge without a doubt. Yeah, the "arm on the locker" thing was a little overconfident but all I'd heard him say was something about a party. And now, here I was, heading home to a weekend empty of any plans.

I let out a long sigh as I stopped at a red light. I always prided myself on not caring about cliques or surface impressions. I liked to get to know people and decide whether or not I liked them by what was inside. Faye could be right about Kane, but I should see for myself, not rush to judgment again. If I could have kicked myself without driving off the road, I would have.

I'd never been so excited for an empty house as when I pulled into the driveway. Marie and I had barely said two words to each other at breakfast. I'd had my max of awkward for the day, thank you very much. I kicked my shoes off, grabbed an apple from the kitchen, and headed up to my room.

My backpack slid off my shoulder as I tossed the apple up in the air and caught it. I tossed it up again, higher this time, but my attention went elsewhere and it landed on the floor with a dull thud.

My jewelry box was open again.

When I'd found it open this morning, I wasn't 100 percent sure I'd closed it the night before. But this time I was positive. I'd even put a book on top of it, and that book now lay on the floor under my desk chair.

This was a message.

The shaking started in my fingers, then spread until my entire body was shuddering. First from fear, then anger. I lashed out and slammed the lid of the box down. Then I twirled around, fists clenched, and yelled at the empty air.

"Why are you still here? It's time for you to go. Move on!"

My chest heaved and I struggled to breathe. It was like the air in the room had suddenly thickened.

"Leave my brother alone," I said through gritted teeth. "I know you're excited that he can see you, but you're scaring him. Just let him be and go away."

The tiny blond hairs on my arms stood at attention. But I didn't have goose bumps. It was like static electricity. The light in my ceiling flickered on and off. I rushed over to the switch, put my hand on it, and yelped as a blue shock lit up my fingers.

Rage built up inside me, quick like a flame. "Just get out, okay? Your time is over. This is not your house anymore! This is not your life!"

I ran into the bathroom, slammed the door, and leaned over the sink. I fought off the urge to cry and splashed cold water on my face until my breathing calmed. I was doing everything those websites said I shouldn't. Getting emotional. Letting her get to me. She could feed off my energy. I had to remain calm.

I took twenty deep, slow breaths until I felt back in control. Then I opened the door and strode back into my room.

And stopped short.

My blood froze in my veins.

The room was wrecked. My made bed was rumpled up. Clothes were pulled down from their hangers. My jewelry box was upended and gems were strewn across the floor. A cold wave of fear washed over me, threatening to drown me in the panic. If Kayla wanted to send a message, this was loud and clear:

I'm mad, and I'm not leaving.

So I turned and ran from my own house.

chapter 9

I had to come back home eventually, had to try and sleep in my room. But I didn't know what to do. My options had dwindled. I'd tried telling Marie about the house and that had blown up in my face. I'd taken it upon myself to get rid of the problem, and failed. Defeated and depressed, I had a new plan: to stay out of the house as much as possible, try not to think about it, and hope it went away on its own. Brilliant, I know.

But that was how I found myself in the school parking lot Sunday for the open house.

Harried parents with their lost-looking freshmen children headed toward the main entrance, where they would meet the administration, tour the classrooms, and other stuff Dad and Marie wouldn't be interested in doing. I headed straight for the open double doors of the gym.

My eyes widened. This was more like a college fair than a "please join our club" thing. Balloons hovered above and spirit posters adorned the walls. A large booth in the center sold Woodbridge tees and sweatshirts. All the clubs' tables lined the walls, each one staffed with one or two people. As I started to slowly walk past a few, I noticed many had fliers and even plates of cookies and swag.

My ambling stride had apparently looked like interest to one booth and a peppy girl called out, "Interested in the ecology club?"

"Um, no thanks," I mumbled and quickened my step. It wasn't like I *wasn't* interested in the ecology club. I like the environment fine. I was just so overwhelmed with all the choices and knew that I'd end up signing away all my free time to the first one that drew me in.

I skimmed over the signs on each table, trying to see which club was right for me. I didn't have an athletic bone in my body. My voice was a danger to glass-paned windows and I didn't play an instrument. I was way too nonconfrontational for debate team. I sucked at art. So many of the clubs seemed geared toward kids who knew what they wanted to do with their lives. Journalism club, science, math, technology, robotics. I had no idea what kind of career I wanted.

The noise level in the gym seemed to amplify as I brought a shaky hand to my forehead. Coming here was supposed to be a respite from scary feelings, but I suddenly felt so overwhelmed I wanted to turn around and leave.

"Sour Patch Kid?"

I turned and found Donovan seated behind a table, holding up a bowl of candy. I nodded eagerly and plucked a yellow one out. The sour punch interrupted my panicked thoughts and by the time I was done chewing, I already felt better. Sugar was like medicine to me.

"You looked pretty freaked out there for a second," Donovan said, giving his head a shake to get the hair out of his eyes.

Normally, I'd smile and come up with some empty platitude to make the uncomfortable moment pass, but for some reason the truth leaked out of me. "Sometimes I think I'm the only one here who doesn't have her whole life mapped out."

Donovan nodded knowingly. "Don't worry. Even the most put-together kids here have moments of panic."

I nodded, feeling somewhat better. "How am I supposed to know what I want to do with the rest of my life? I'm seventeen."

He shrugged. "Who says you have to know now?"

I raised my hands up and motioned to the chaos around us as my answer.

"That's what this is for," Donovan said. "Play around with anything you're even slightly interested in. Do a little here and a little there and eventually something will click."

I hadn't even stopped to think of it that way. That people weren't committing to anything, they were only trying stuff out. "Is that what you do?" I asked.

"Sure. Art's not my only thing. I also love graphic design, gaming. I might end up in software design. I'm dabbling in it all right now."

"So which one is this?" I gazed down at the sign-up sheet and found myself surprised. "Book club?"

He grinned. "Like I told you. Try it all."

"So what book are you guys reading?"

"We'll vote on one at our first meeting. And if you don't

like the book we're reading that month, skip the month. Participate as much or as little as you want."

That didn't sound so bad. In fact, it sounded kind of fun. I bent over and scribbled my name and e-mail on the sheet. My pendant swung forward, getting in the way, so I tucked it under my shirt.

"What's that gemstone called?" Donovan asked, pointing.

I straightened. "Technically, this one's not a gem. It's fossilized resin." *Stop being a dork, stop being a dork.* "But, anyway, it's called amber."

"Amber." Donovan repeated. "It's cool because it's the same color as your eyes."

Heat flooded my neck. *He knows the color of my eyes.* Not only that, but comparing the amber to them was just so unbelievably cool. I tried to remain calm so the embarrassing blotches wouldn't come. I realized my mouth was open but words weren't coming out. Donovan began to look slightly uncomfortable.

"Um, yeah," I blurted out, then immediately wanted to bash my face into the table. *Really, Jade? Out of all possible responses, I go with the lamest one. Why not, "Thanks and yours look like blue topaz." Which they do! Ugh.*

My neck was going to burst into flames.

"See you at the meeting," I said, hurrying away. I didn't even realize until I was outside that I'd stolen the book club's pen. Hopefully he had another one for the sign-up sheet.

Why had I freaked out? All he'd done was make an observation. After all, his heart still belonged to a dead girl.

I stared at the accidentally filched pen in my hand for a few moments, until I felt eyes on me. I cast a glance to the side and caught Kane watching. He turned away quickly, almost scared, and my insides squeezed with guilt. He probably thought I was a psychopath after my behavior in the hallway.

"Hey," I said, stepping over to him.

"Oh, hey." He pretended to notice me for the first time.

"Listen, about Friday . . ." I paused as I tried to find the words to explain my behavior.

"Yeah, what was that about?" he said shaking his head. "Fresh meat? I don't understand."

I shuffled my feet. "Someone sort of warned me about you."

"Warned you?" His brows knit in confusion. "About what?"

"That you're this big player and that you're going to go after me because you've already burned through all the girls in school."

He snorted. "Let me guess. Faye Bettencourt told you this."

My jaw dropped. "How'd you know?"

"This is going to sound totally conceited, but there's no other way to put it. Faye and I dated briefly, emphasis on the briefly, a long time ago and she's still not over it. I try to be friends, but I don't think that's enough for her sometimes. She thinks she owns me."

"She saw us talking that day in the library," I said, almost to myself. Everything made more sense now.

"Yep. That's probably what caused it."

"Wow, I'm really sorry. I should have —"

"No." Kane put his hand up to stop me from apologizing. "I don't blame you for believing her. You're new here. You don't know who to trust."

"Still, I feel like a jerk. Is there any way I can make it up to you?" I realized, as soon as the words left my mouth, that they could be construed in a more forward way than I'd intended. But I didn't regret it. This would put Faye's theory to the test at least.

"Actually there is something you can do," Kane said, brightening.

I waited.

"Could I have a ride home?" He flashed an easy smile and put his hands together in a begging gesture.

Only now did I take in the fact that he wasn't exactly dressed for the open house. He had his lacrosse uniform on, a giant equipment bag on the ground next to him, and beads of sweat along his hairline.

"You just had a game?" I asked.

"No, our games are in spring. I was just practicing with some of the team. My mom went to my sister's field hockey game and I said I'd grab a ride with a friend, but everyone scattered so quickly after that I . . ."

"Say no more." I jangled my keys and waved him forward.

I popped the trunk for his equipment, then settled into the driver's seat. He squished into the passenger side, which didn't have a lot of legroom for his tall frame. As I started to drive, he looked around the car with barely concealed surprise.

"What?" I said, feeling slightly defensive. "Expecting a shiny little sports car?"

Kane shrugged. "Yeah, I wasn't expecting you to drive some old car with a hundred thousand miles on it. But there's nothing wrong with that. I just assumed, you know . . . everyone in this town has money . . . and you live in a big house."

"A house we could only afford because it had been heavily discounted due to its macabre history," I said. A house I was purposefully avoiding because a vengeful ghost had trashed my room.

"What I'm trying to say is that I understand." He paused. "I have no car. I have no *house*. Ellie and I live in an apartment with my mom. No father. No money. The apartment is already more than Mom can afford, but she insists we live in this town because the schools are so good. All she cares about is our education. So we can break out and have a better life than she did."

I stopped the car at a red light and he slid me a look. "So it's nice to finally come across someone who might understand a little bit of that."

My mouth twitched. First I'd pegged him as a dumb jock, then a typical Woodbridge rich kid. "Sorry. I seem to jump to all the wrong conclusions about you. Again and again."

"It's okay." He gave me a light jab in the side. "But if you don't turn left here, you're going to miss my road."

I'd been so busy being defensive I hadn't even asked him where he lived. I tightened my now-sweaty hands on the steering wheel. I thought about reciprocating. Telling him that my family wasn't so picture-perfect, either. But that would involve talking about my mother. And I couldn't do that.

Of course everyone back home knew about my mother's death. But here, no one did. First off, it didn't just come up in conversation in a natural way. "Hey, my mom's dead. What are you up to tonight?" And second, I hated when it had come up in the past. People always saw me differently, after. They got this patented painfully concerned, pitying look on their faces. And I knew I wasn't Jade Kelley anymore. I was the girl whose mother had died. And I didn't want to be defined by that here like I'd been at home.

Kane gave directions along the way and I followed, lost in my thoughts, almost on autopilot. As I reached his apartment complex, I slowed. He pointed toward his door and my eyes were drawn to the defined muscles in his forearm. Then up to the blond stubble on his neck and chin. The masculine angles and edges to his face. I could see why the girls went crazy for him.

"Thanks for the ride," he said.

"No problem. I'm sorry again about all the misunderstandings."

"Forget it." He opened the car door and stuck one leg out, then stopped. "Has anyone shown you around town yet?"

"Not unless my dad counts."

"Does your dad know where to get the best Boston cream pie? Or which pizza place is open the latest?"

"He does not possess this secret and useful knowledge," I said, smiling.

"How about I show you around some night next weekend? I can use my mom's car." He stopped, worry creasing his face. "Oh wait, I don't mean like —"

"Not in a fresh meat way," I said. "Don't worry. I'd love to see the sights."

"Great! Saturday night, then. See you in school."

He grabbed his equipment bag from the trunk and cast one last wave over his shoulder. I watched as he strode up to the door, this gorgeous, nice, charming guy, who defied all my assumptions.

And I wondered why, instead of feeling delight at the idea of spending time with him, my thoughts kept returning to a broken boy.

From the Diary of Kayla Sloane

I took 28 to a party at the clearing tonight and, of course, it made waves. 7 was giving him dirty looks all night. 14 was relieved. (Not that it will help her case any.)

I knew what everyone was thinking. Why him? She could have anyone and instead of someone approved — someone "in" — she plucks this guy out of obscurity.

I'll tell ya, at first it was just the idea of being unpredictable. Plus those eyes. God! Those eyes could bring about world peace. But now . . . it's more than that. I'm surprised. I might keep him longer than I'd planned. I . . . like him. A lot.

28 isn't like the other guys, who seem mostly interested in sloppy groping in darkened corners of house parties. 28 is different. He can talk about books, art, current events. When he asks questions, it's like he's probing your mind. He's truly interested in the answer.

Sometimes it scares me, though. Sometimes I think he's trying to see into my soul.

And I'm scared he won't like what he finds.

chapter 10

I spent the next few days tiptoeing around the house and my family. Kayla wasn't gone. I still walked through cold spots, felt the tingling of unseen eyes on my back, came home to find my stuff moved around. But I didn't play. I ignored her, like you would a child misbehaving for negative attention or a dog that you didn't want to sense your fear. I gave her no emotion or energy to feed from.

I noticed Colby doing the same thing. He was less hyper and energetic and watched a lot more television than usual, curled up in the corner of the couch. Both of us seemed to be sapped of our personalities. We went through our daily motions mechanically, walked through the house like zombies. Hoping that ignoring the problem would make it go away. If we didn't think or talk about it, it wouldn't be real.

Marie was either too tired to notice or stuck in so much denial that she didn't want to look into why. Dad was home Monday and Tuesday, which was nice. But he still had to work, even while not traveling, and spent much of his time on conference calls in his office upstairs.

I stood outside his door Tuesday night for ten minutes,

considering spilling my guts. But fear held me back. What if he didn't believe me? What if he sided with Marie again? I knew, deep inside, that if Dad chose Marie over me one more time, that would be it for us. Something inside me would break and possibly never heal.

I didn't want to lose Dad. I adored him. So rather than give him the opportunity to make that wrong choice and cause that break, I backed away from his office door and went back to my room. And kept silent.

School became my safety net. I loved the routine of my classes and homework, craved the normality of it against the abnormality of what was going on at home. I'd been going in early, mostly to get out of the house as soon as possible. Maybe a little bit to see if anyone else was in the art room. But each morning it was empty. I sat there, studying, my heart racing anytime I heard footsteps approaching the room, and sinking when the footsteps continued on past.

Wednesday morning, I slid my ancient-mobile into a spot at the same time Faye was getting out of her little silver convertible. She closed the door, her eyes taking note of me, and then stood there, waiting. I thought about fishing through my backpack for five minutes or pretending I had an important text to type out, but decided against it. I had to go to school with Faye all year. Yeah, her personality was borderline, but it couldn't hurt to be on the good side of it. And I hadn't talked to her since last week when she helped me with my makeup.

"How's it going?" I said, swinging my bag up over one shoulder.

"Ugh," Faye click-clacked over on heeled boots. Her hair was pulled up tightly in a high ponytail and cleavage spilled out of her low-cut sleeveless sweater. She sighed. "Murph's party was so lame last weekend. There was, like, nothing to do but watch the lacrosse team stalk the freshmen girls. Then the neighbors called the cops because we were too loud and it was broken up by ten."

I didn't really know what to say so I just nodded sympathetically and mumbled, "That stinks."

"Way to start out the school year," she sulked. "Daisy Britton used to throw the best parties, but she's off to college now. If this is how senior year is going to be . . ." She rolled her eyes at the horror of it.

"Where were you, anyway?" she asked, as if suddenly realizing I hadn't been there.

I didn't want to say no one had invited me, though Kane probably had when I was half listening to him in the hall. "Was it Friday or Saturday?" I asked, squeezing between two cars in the front row of the lot.

"Friday."

Good. I could just tell the truth and not seem so lame. "I had to babysit my little brother Friday night."

"Suckage," she groaned, hopping up onto the curb. "Your parents go out or something?"

"No, my dad travels a lot and my stepmom works Friday nights."

Faye shot her arm out across my midsection, stopping me from entering the school. Some guy, whose eyes were superglued to Faye's bobbing boobs, held the door open for us for a few more seconds, then gave up and went in.

"Hold up," Faye said. "Does that happen every Friday night?"

"Only when my dad's gone."

She stared at me. "Is he going to be gone *this* Friday night?"

"I think so, yeah."

"We can party at your house, then!" Her face lit up like a slot machine on a win. "We can do it right. Only invite the seniors. None of those underclassmen wannabes."

I grimaced, thinking that was probably a bad idea. Not only was it not cool to throw a party while my parents were out, my house was also freaking haunted. I opened my mouth, readying an excuse, but at that moment Kane and his sister came up behind us. Ellie stayed a few steps away, but Kane put a hand on each of our shoulders. "What's up, ladies?"

His eyes took in Faye's short skirt, high boots, and the slice of white thigh showing in between. I looked down at my jeans and felt completely frumpy. But, hey, this wasn't a competition. Kane had made it clear he was just friends with Faye. And I wasn't interested in Kane.

Right?

"Hi, Ellie," I said over his shoulder.

Kane's sister gave a little wave, then motioned to Kane that she was going inside.

Faye rubbed her hands together excitedly. "Jade and I were just planning a party at her house this weekend."

I was about to pipe up that we were doing no such thing, but Kane was immediately overcome with an attack of the stupid and announced, "I hope it's not Saturday because that's when I'm taking you out."

Faye looked sharply at me. I shook my head. "No, not like a date, he's just, um, showing me around town a little," I bumbled.

I looked back at Kane, hoping he wasn't insulted by my half retraction, but he had an amused grin on his face. "The party was for Friday," I explained to him. "But it's not happening."

"Of course it's happening." Faye grabbed my hand and squeezed it.

I pulled my hand away. "I can't. My little brother will be there."

"Sleeping upstairs," Faye said. "Close his door and we'll be reasonably quiet. It'll be fine."

"I really don't think —"

"It does sound fun," Kane interrupted. "It would be a great way for you to get to know more of the kids at school."

I could invite Donovan, I thought suddenly. It would be an excuse to spend time with him. Plus, I had been wanting to make more friends, get to know more people, hadn't I? And being in the house alone at night — just me, Colby, and Kayla — was nerve-wracking. It would be nice to have other people around.

"Maybe just a small gathering of like ten kids," I offered.

"Thirty," Faye countered.

I hadn't realized this was a negotiation. I looked back and forth between them, their eyes eager. "Twenty. If you promise not one more."

Faye clapped and bounced from foot to foot. "Awesome! I'll take care of everything."

"I'll make sure it doesn't get out of control," Kane said. "I'll be your bouncer." He fake-flexed his muscles and Faye threw her head back in exaggerated laughter.

I followed them into the school and broke off to go to my locker, where Alexa was waiting.

"What's up with you?" she said, noting my wary demeanor.

"I think I just agreed to have a party at my house Friday night."

"I've never been to a party before," she noted with a frown. "Not my thing."

I twirled my locker combination and swung open the door. "Well, you're coming to mine."

Her shoulders sagged. "Do I have to?"

"Yes."

I needed one person there I could trust.

Thursday, I walked around school with a giant grin plastered on my face. Every afternoon, I'd been hiding in the library after classes let out. But today I had somewhere else to be. The first book club meeting was this afternoon.

I'd seen Donovan here and there in school all week, but mostly with his head down. I would have felt weird just walking up to him and striking up a conversation. But he'd be at book club. And I was looking forward to having a real reason to talk and maybe start to figure out why I couldn't stop thinking about him.

Between classes, I saw Ellie Woodward heading to the cafeteria. I shouted out her name. She turned and smiled shyly.

"Hey," I said, catching up. "I don't know if Kane told you yet but I'm having a party Friday night. You're invited if you'd like to come."

"Oh no you don't." Faye came up behind me, her eyes narrowed. "What are you doing inviting sophomores?"

"She's Kane's little sister," I explained.

"I don't care who she is. We're throwing a party, not opening a day care."

I gave Faye an exasperated look. "We?"

"Yeah. We. You're providing the house, I'm providing the clout. So, we." With that, Faye stomped off, thinking she'd won the argument.

I turned to Ellie, feeling absolutely horrified, even though I hadn't been the one to act like snobzilla. "Don't listen to her. You can definitely come."

Ellie nervously shook her head, making her blond hair tremble. "No thanks."

"Don't let Faye bully you. She's not the boss of everyone. It's my house and I'm inviting you."

"No, it's not that." Ellie paused, selecting her words carefully. "I appreciate you asking me and all, but I really don't want to go. It's just not my thing."

She thanked me again and walked away, but I still felt bad about the whole confrontation. Once this party was over, I was done with Faye. I'd given her a couple chances, but she wasn't the type of person I wanted to hang with. That was clear now.

Each of my final three classes seemed to last longer than the previous one. By seventh period, I swore the clock was ticking backward. When the bell finally rang, I dashed to my locker, then to the bathroom. I fixed my smudged eyeliner, put a fresh coat of gloss on my lips, flipped my head upside down, and shook my hair around to give it a little body.

Yeah, I was really excited to vote on a book.

The hallways were nearly emptied out by the time I reached the classroom the club had reserved. I figured after all the time I'd wasted in the bathroom that I'd be the last one in. But only Donovan was there, sitting alone at a desk, his shoulders hunched, his eyes staring out the window. He looked so sad and hopeless, my heart cinched.

I claimed the desk beside his, my eyes taking in the paper he had ready, with the word *Nominations* written at the top. His expression softened when he noticed me.

I smiled sheepishly. "Where's everyone else?"

His Adam's apple slid up and down as he swallowed. "I guess there is no one else," he said tightly. "Last year the group was bigger."

That made no sense. "Why would no one from last year show up?"

Donovan looked down at his clasped hands. His hair flopped forward, covering his eyes. He didn't have to say it. I finally realized why no one had come to his meeting. He was exiled. Because of Kayla's death.

His chair scraped across the floor as he stood up. "So no club this year."

"Wait," I called out. "We can just . . . hang out for a little while. I really . . ." Now it was my turn to look away. "I don't want to go home yet."

He hesitated for the longest second of my life, then settled back into his seat. "What are you wearing today?"

The corner of my mouth rose. "No pendant today." I lifted my hair up to show my earrings. "Opal studs. It was believed that opals could render you invisible."

He smirked and whispered, "They're not working."

"Not in school hallways. More like invisible in battle."

"Like a ninja stone." He chuckled. "How come you know all that? Why are you so interested in all the stones?"

I shifted in the hard chair and told him what I hadn't told anyone in town. "Most of them were my mother's. She was a jewelry designer."

"Was?" he said softly.

I closed my eyes and let out a deep breath. Normally I hid this side of me, but it had just . . . come out. I kept my eyes down as I spoke, not wanting to watch the change come over him. The uncomfortable, awkward mask of pity that would slide over his features. "She died when I was nine. Cancer. I have a stepmom now." I shrugged. "She's okay."

"Are you following in your mother's footsteps?" Donovan asked. "Designing jewelry?"

I made myself look up and braced for the expression on his face. But it wasn't there. His eyes were engaged, not pitying.

"No," I said. "I tried, but I don't have her talent."

"Tell me about her." His voice was soft but steady, and he met my eyes directly. He wasn't just making conversation. He truly wanted to know.

"Mom always smelled like jasmine. It was probably just a perfume she wore, but it seemed like more than that. Like it was part of her being or something." I paused and took a long, slow breath. "She had a delicate touch. I loved seeing her create a beautiful piece out of nothing. I'd watch her hold the tiny instruments, place the gemstone into the setting with the steadiest hand."

I couldn't resist a small smile at the memories. Usually, talking about my mother was almost painful for me. But Donovan made me feel at ease.

I continued, "She told me what each gem was, where it was mined, its meanings, its ancient uses. People think I just wear the gemstones because I like jewelry. But it's more than that. When I wear them and touch them . . . I still feel connected to her."

Donovan was watching me closely. I was surprised by both my honesty and the fact that my neck wasn't on fire. This should have been the most uncomfortable conversation of my life, but I felt fine. Relieved, actually.

"What about your name?" he asked. "Isn't that a gem?"

I nodded. "That's why she chose it."

He cocked his head to the side. "What does it mean?"

"Jade protects children from harm and encourages people to become who they really are."

"That's fitting," he said quickly.

I raised one eyebrow. "How so?"

"You're the most *you* person I've ever met." He grimaced. "Wait, that didn't make much sense."

I suppressed a smile as he fumbled for words.

"You're just . . . unfeigned."

My neck flared now. I could feel the red blotches forming. "Well, there's an SAT word for you," I said, rubbing the skin around my collarbone.

"I'm sorry, I just —"

"No," I stopped him. "I like it. Unfeigned. That's a nice compliment."

He fiddled with his pen, twirling it up and over his knuckles nervously. "So do you believe in all the gemstones? What they're supposed to do?"

"Of course not," I answered quickly.

"How come?"

I held my hand in front of my neck, though I'm sure the blush had spread all the way up my cheeks. "Because that would just be . . . silly."

He stopped twirling the pen and shrugged.

"What . . . you believe in them?" I scoffed.

"Not necessarily," he teased.

"Then what are you saying?"

He paused and lowered his face, his hair flopping down over his eyes. "I'm saying that it doesn't hurt to believe in a little magic now and then."

I don't know what possessed me to do what I did next. I reached up with one hand and brushed his hair from his eyes. "You shouldn't hide those," I said.

I looked into his pale blue eyes, full of bottomless tenderness. Those were not the eyes of a killer. He had gone through something terrible. Lost someone he loved. And what the kids at school continued to do to him, by shunning him, blaming him . . . they were killing *him*, too. Except instead of one big push, it was a thousand tiny daily deaths.

I blurted, "I'm having a party tomorrow night. Would you like to come?"

His eyes widened. "At your house?"

Oh no. My house didn't exactly hold happy memories for Donovan. I wanted to facepalm myself. "I'm sorry," I backtracked. "I shouldn't have even asked."

"No, it's okay." He hesitated, blinking quickly. "I'll think about it."

That meant no. He began to fidget. I thought about any way I could save the conversation, get our moment back. I didn't want him to walk out now. Not like this.

"It wasn't even my idea. Faye Bettencourt talked me into it." I forced a little laugh to lighten the mood, but Donovan heard the name and just shook his head sadly.

"Faye's trying so hard," he said.

"To do what?"

He gripped his pen tightly. "To replace her best friend."

I hated to even say her name in front of him, but for some reason, I had to know. "Kayla? She and Faye were best friends?"

"Yeah, but it wasn't an equal thing. More like a leader and follower. Kayla was royalty and Faye was her minion."

"So now that Kayla's gone," I pressed, "Faye's trying to be the queen bee?"

"She tried to slip right into Kayla's empty throne like it'd been handed to her. But everyone else seems to realize something Faye doesn't."

"What's that?"

His eyes turned icy. "She's no Kayla."

And then it was me who mumbled an excuse and hurriedly left the room.

chapter 11

I was nuts if I thought Donovan was going to show up at my party. It was obvious he still had feelings for his dead girlfriend. Alexa told me he hadn't dated anyone since. Yeah, most of the school avoided him now, but even if they didn't, he wouldn't look at another girl anyhow.

Thursday night, up in my room, I did it. I shouldn't have done it, but curiosity had been needling at me for days and I couldn't take it anymore.

I logged on to Facebook. Donovan didn't have a page, and if Kayla had, it had since been removed. But it was easy enough to find pictures on other classmates' pages. Lots of Kayla playing soccer. A few of her at parties. And one of her with Donovan, his arm draped over her shoulder, hundred-watt smiles on both their faces.

Alexa's voice echoed through my head. *He doesn't smile anymore.*

I swallowed a lump in my throat as I examined the picture. I had to admit, they complemented each other well. Her glossy black hair, his startlingly blue eyes. The model and the artist.

I tried to picture myself in the photo, Donovan's arm around me. His smile meant for me. And I knew it was nothing but a pipe dream. Hearing about Kayla and how she was so smart, great at sports, popular — the girl who had it all — that was bad enough. But seeing the evidence made me sure. The idea that Donovan would go from her to me? Laughable. In every picture she looked naturally gorgeous. Even in close-ups and from strange angles, her eyes found the lens and she was effortlessly sexy. If I tried that pouty-lipped pose, I'd look fake and awkward.

I shut the computer down and climbed into bed. I slept fitfully, tossing and turning, rearranging the covers and pillows. Eventually, I slipped into a deep sleep, but dreamt about the party.

My living room filled with kids from school and I knew they were there because they wanted to be my friends. The front door opened and Donovan drifted in, his blue eyes ablaze. He was there to get closer to me. I knew it. I felt it. My heart soared. This was all going to work out okay.

I took a step toward the crowd and stopped. Something had me trapped. I could see everyone, but some kind of glass wall kept me from them. I banged on the glass and got no reaction. I yelled but no one heard me. Frustration ate at me. This was *my* party, but I couldn't join in. No one seemed to notice me, trapped behind the wall.

Suddenly, all heads turned. All eyes focused on a figure descending the staircase. Kayla. Beautiful and full of life. She said something I couldn't hear and everyone joined together in laughter. She slipped through the room and all the faces followed her, like snakes to a charmer.

Then she slowly turned to me, and I realized she could see me while the others could not. She smiled. A sly, teeth-baring grin that said, "This is *my* life."

I woke up, panting, and knew. It would never be mine.

Word about the party had gotten around. At school on Friday, people who hadn't so much as looked at me last week were stopping to chat in the hallway, giving me nods in class. I had no idea who was on the guest list and who wasn't. Faye was handling all of that.

I thought I'd feel guilty at dinner Friday night, making small talk with Marie while knowing I was throwing a secret party after she went to work for the night. But she was in a nagging mood, picking on Colby and me for little things. So any guilt I felt was replaced with irritation.

Marie left for work and I led Colby upstairs for bedtime. He asked if he could sit on my lap in the rocking chair while I read him a story. He was starting to weigh too much for that, but I couldn't say no when he asked in his cute, tired voice.

I read his favorite book, twice, as the smell of baby shampoo wafted up from his curls. Toward the middle of the story, his head lolled to the side and rested on my shoulder. By the end, his breathing had slowed and I knew he'd fallen asleep. Grunting, I picked him up and laid him on his bed. Then I covered him with his blanket and backed out of the room, closing the door.

A slow dread built up inside me, some tingling of intuition, telling me this party was a bad idea. But I pushed the feeling away.

It was too late to back out now.

Faye said she'd bring everything we needed, so all I really had to do was get dressed. I wore my favorite jeans and a purple flowy top. I tied my hair up and put in my sapphire drop earrings. Sapphire — to keep worrying thoughts away.

It wasn't working.

Kayla hadn't been too bad the last few days. Only a few cold touches here and there, minor things moved around. But I'd still feel better when I wasn't sitting alone in the living room.

Alexa arrived first. I had mentioned the party would start around nine and she showed up at nine on the dot. Not that she had been looking forward to it, she just valued punctuality.

She sat on the couch, as stiff as her white, ironed blouse, and looked around. "I can't believe you're making me sit here with these people."

"Alexa, no one's here yet."

She crossed her arms. "But they will be."

I sat beside her and put my feet up on the coffee table. The tightness in my muscles was loosening now that I had someone with me. "You act like making friends is torture."

"Is that what you think you're doing?" she scoffed. "They aren't coming here to be your friends."

"I know." I waved my hand. "They'll go anywhere there's a party."

Alexa looked at me like I had four brain cells. "It's about Kayla."

I stared at her. "What do you mean?"

"They want to walk around in *her* house. Look at the staircase she fell down. Stare at the spot on the floor where she died. None of them would admit that, but that's why they're coming. Morbid curiosity."

I would have rebutted her, but inside I knew it was true. They were using me. For the party and for access to Kayla's house one last time.

"I just can't get away from it," I said with a sigh. "The adoration of Kayla Sloane."

"Adoration?" Alexa laughed derisively. "Half the kids probably hated her, the other half feared her."

I pulled my feet off the table and sat up. "Wait a minute. I thought you said she was the girl who had everything?"

"Yeah, but I never said she was nice."

"Kayla was a mean girl?"

Alexa sat up straight and jutted her chin out. "She was crafty, manipulative. She could be very mean. Even cruel. But she was so smart and gorgeous that she got away with it."

I hesitated a moment. "Was she mean to you?"

"I was a target," Alexa admitted. "But so were many others. It's not a big deal."

I had the feeling, though, from the hard look in her eyes, that it *was* more than that.

The doorbell rang four times quickly and before I could

scramble to the door Faye let herself in, followed by a burly looking boy carrying a giant box filled with food and drinks.

"You only invited twenty people, right?" I said, following them into the kitchen.

Faye ripped open a package of chips. "Don't worry about it." Easy for her to say.

People started pouring in after that, walking straight into the kitchen for a red plastic cup like kids to the Pied Piper. Kane brought a few guys from the team and Faye's friends followed them around, giggling.

I lifted myself up onto a counter in the kitchen and sat there, swinging my legs and fingering my turquoise pendant (for good luck), while people came up and talked to me, one after the other. Their tongues got looser as the night went on, and my little corner of the kitchen turned into a confessional.

"One night, I actually prayed for Kayla's death," one girl tearfully admitted. "I felt so guilty after it really happened. My therapist had to convince me that I didn't compel her to fall myself."

The more the night went on, the more these strangers wanted to talk to me about Kayla. They told me stories, some good, some bad. They shared their opinions. It was like — now that she was gone — it was finally safe for them to be honest about her.

One of Kayla's self-professed best friends (there were so many I lost count) started a dreamy-eyed monologue on Kayla and Donovan's relationship. That was the last thing I wanted to hear about, but for some masochistic reason, I couldn't tell her to stop.

"Kayla and Donovan seemed like polar opposites," she said, swaying in place. "He was deep where she was shallow. She was all parties and the popular crowd while he was all art and gamers. She could've had anyone at school. But I never once wondered what she saw in him. I knew what it was."

I leaned forward, nearly falling off the counter. "What?"

"He was different, kind, special."

I wondered why she spoke of him in the past tense. Like he wasn't still all those things.

"And those eyes. When their intensity was focused on you, you felt like the center of the universe." She suddenly snapped out of it, embarrassment shining on her face. "But he totally killed her. We all know that."

She wandered off and I wondered how much of her insistence on Donovan's guilt was merely bitterness that he never wanted her like he wanted Kayla.

"So are you, like, dating Kane Woodward?" Keith, the burly boy who'd come in with Faye, asked.

"No, we're just friends," I answered loudly, hoping to dispel that myth in case Faye was within hearing distance.

"But you're going out tomorrow night," Keith said.

"Yeah, I guess." I didn't want to get into the nuances of it with him.

"Hey." He leaned in closer. "Did you ever, like, see the ghost of Kayla here?"

I fought to prevent a reaction from showing on my face. The answer caught in my throat and I had to force out the word, "Nope."

I had no desire to tell the truth to people I barely knew. They might call me crazy, say I was making it up for attention. I didn't need a reputation at school after only two weeks.

I'd only even mentioned the possibility of a ghost to Alexa, and she wasn't talking to anyone. In fact, she'd told me an hour ago she was going to look at my book collection, and I hadn't seen her since, so she'd obviously snuck out.

I didn't really blame her.

I finally realized that if I stayed in the corner and listened to stories about Kayla all night, I'd be driven loony by midnight. I excused myself from Keith and walked into the living room. But I didn't know who to talk to. They were all chatting about people I didn't know or making inside jokes I didn't get. I wished I could really *talk* to someone.

Suddenly, all the loud simultaneous conversations ground to a halt and a chorus of whispers rose from the silence. I followed the collective line of sight to the front door, where Donovan stood half in, half out, like he was making the decision to stay or run at the last second. I held my breath, silently chanting: *stay, stay, stay.*

He crossed the threshold and closed the door behind him. His eyes made a quick sweep of the room, perhaps thinking back to the way Kayla's family had their furniture arranged, or maybe remembering moments he spent with Kayla here, cuddled on the couch, laughing . . .

"Why is *he* here?"

I looked sharply at Kane, shocked by the intensity of the venom with which he spoke. "I invited him," I said.

Donovan saw me and I swore his eyes lit up. He wore jeans and a pale blue polo — the only time I'd seen him wear something other than black. And he'd gotten a haircut. His eyes weren't hidden anymore.

I wasn't the only one who noticed. A few girls were giving him sly looks over their shoulders, and not in a negative way.

Did he do all this . . . for me? I wondered.

I was shocked enough that he'd shown up. But he'd freshened his look. He even seemed to be carrying himself differently, not staring down at the floor, but instead looking right at me as he threaded his way through the crowded living room.

I cleared my throat, trying desperately to think of something cool to say, but my mind was racing and my heart was pumping wildly. He'd almost reached me when Kane stepped between us.

"Returning to the scene of the crime?" Kane asked.

Donovan's face darkened and his fists clenched. My vague worry about a fight at the party had just turned into a real possibility. I pushed myself between them and put my hands on Donovan's shoulders, forcing him to look into my eyes.

"Go upstairs," I whispered.

I turned to Kane next, grabbing him by the hand and dragging him into the downstairs bathroom.

"What is wrong with you?" I said, closing the door behind us.

He raked his hands through his hair. "I'm sorry. I don't want to make a scene at your party. That guy . . . he just gets to me. Why did you even invite him, anyway?"

I faltered. "Are you . . . jealous? You know tomorrow night isn't a date." I wanted to make sure that was very clear.

"No. Just protective. I don't trust him. I don't want anything to happen to you."

I paused. "You don't *really* think he killed Kayla, do you?"

"Only he knows what happened. He was the one who was here that day. And he gave a statement to the police, but never spoke a word of it to anyone else. So what does that tell you?"

"That if he did it, the police would have arrested him."

"Maybe he did do it, but they couldn't prove it," Kane countered.

"Or maybe he didn't and you guys are torturing him for nothing." My jaw tightened. I shouldn't have felt so defensive. I barely knew Donovan. But after our talks, I'd grown to feel protective of him. If other people wanted to torment him over Kayla's death they could . . . but not in my house.

"I don't want to talk about this anymore." Kane stepped closer and put a gentle hand on my arm. "Let's not let Donovan O'Mara ruin your party."

I stiffened. "He's not the one who nearly did."

I left Kane behind and made a quick loop through the kitchen and living room, looking for Donovan, but he wasn't there. Hopefully he'd gone upstairs like I asked and hadn't left. I frowned at the crowd in the living room. There were at least thirty kids in there, plus more in the kitchen. Shockingly, Faye hadn't kept her word.

The front door opened as more kids readied themselves to come in. I darted up to it and slammed and locked it closed.

Faye stomped over. "What are you doing?"

"You said no more than twenty people. No one else is coming in."

Faye rolled her eyes. "Loosen up, Jade. I let you bring in Robot Girl and Killer Boy."

Righteous anger burned through my veins. Who did she think she was? This was *my* house and *my* party. And though Faye had deluded herself into thinking she ruled the school, she certainly didn't rule me. I didn't know what kind of girl she was used to, but I cared more about my dignity than popularity. I swelled up with confidence and spoke firmly, "Faye, I'm going upstairs for a minute. When I come back, there'd better be ten less people in this house. If there aren't, the whole party ends."

I went straight up the stairs and didn't look back, but enjoyed imagining the shocked expression on Faye's face. I felt exhilarated after standing up for myself. But when I reached the landing, my elation evaporated. I never could cross the top step without thinking of Kayla.

My thoughts muddled again, I turned down the hallway. For some reason, I'd expected Donovan to be waiting in my room. But instead he was standing outside Colby's closed door. The old Donovan was back — shoulders hunched, sad aura pulsing from him.

And as I stepped up to him, I realized why.

"This was her room, wasn't it?" I said gently.

"Yeah," he said, staring at Colby's door. "She had framed black-and-white photos all over the walls. There was always a stack of fashion magazines three feet high on the floor next to her bed." He looked at me quickly, then away again. "I imagine it's different now."

"Yeah, take all that away and replace it with Star Wars."

Donovan gave me a curious look.

"It's my little brother's room," I explained. What I didn't say out loud was that now I knew why Kayla's ghost appeared most often in there. Colby's room had been hers.

Donovan turned away from the door and faced me. "Sorry about downstairs."

"You're not the one who needs to apologize," I said. "And the party was kind of sucking, anyway. The only reason people even came was because this was Kayla's house." I groaned. "I can't escape her."

My hand flew to my mouth. Fantastic. Here he was mourning and I'd basically bad-mouthed and complained about the girl he was missing so much. Normally, I'd have more tact, but I felt so comfortable with Donovan that the truth kept slipping out before I could stop it.

I was about to apologize, but Donovan gazed into my eyes and said, "I know how that feels. When people see me, they don't think, 'There's Donovan O'Mara.' They think, 'There's the guy who may have killed Kayla Sloane.'"

"I'm sorry," I said. "About your losing her."

He shook his head. "I'd already lost her."

I scrunched my forehead in confusion and he added, "The day she died, I came here to break up with her."

The front door slammed so forcefully, the house shook. Raised yet muffled voices drifted upstairs. Then the door opened and shut again.

I clenched my jaw. "I have to go deal with this before they wake my brother up." I gripped the banister tightly as I descended the stairs, mostly out of anger that my time with Donovan was interrupted.

When I reached the bottom, a girl with a horrified look on her face shouted, "I'm leaving, too," as she tore out the front door, slamming it behind her.

What was going on? I'd asked Faye to thin the crowd, not rile them up. I turned the corner into the living room and stopped short.

Less than twenty people remained now, but they were all clumped around the coffee table. The recessed lights in the ceiling had been turned off and the room was instead lit by candlelight.

"What's happening?" I pushed myself through the crowd and gasped.

A Ouija board was centered on the coffee table. Faye sat cross-legged on the rug beside it. She placed the pointer on the board, then looked up at me, grinning wickedly.

"We're going to contact the ghost of Kayla Sloane."

chapter 12

The air held a mixture of almost-nauseous foreboding and palpable excitement. A few kids backed away, shaking their heads. But even more stepped forward, eyes wide with anticipation.

"No, you don't mess with those things," a guy said, pointing at the Ouija board like it was on fire. "My grandmother told me stories. Those things can open doorways."

"It's made from Hasbro," Faye snapped. "Grow a pair."

The crowd erupted into debate.

"What if it works?"

"Those things aren't real."

"Who brought all this stuff?"

"Who cares who brought it? Let's do it!"

"This isn't cool."

"We shouldn't do this."

"It's just for fun."

Eventually all eyes turned to me. It was my house. I was the deciding factor.

The board was plastic. The top was just stickered on in a factory somewhere, not carved by a witch. I'd played with a Ouija board in a barn back home once with Nicole and Elizabeth. Nothing had happened.

But things were different here. My house was haunted. I knew that. These kids didn't. Maybe nothing would happen. Kayla had been quiet all night.

But she wasn't gone.

And I wanted her gone.

Maybe we'd play with the board and nothing would happen. Or maybe — I felt a spark of hope — this could be the way to end it all. Kayla had trouble letting go of her life. That was obvious. Maybe all she needed was to communicate with her friends one last time. Have the good-bye she was never allowed before. This could be the answer I'd been looking for.

"Let's do it," I said with finality.

A gasp came from close behind me. I turned to see Kane, his eyes reflecting deep disappointment.

"This isn't right," he said, backing away.

I reached out for him, but the crowd closed the circle around me and all I saw was a glimpse of his back as he went out the door.

"So who wants to be on the pointer with me?" Faye asked.

Murmurs rippled through the crowd.

"I'll do it," Donovan said, stepping forward and surprising everyone. He eased himself down on the rug on the opposite side of the coffee table.

"We should have one more," Faye said, looking right at me.

"Fine." I sat cross-legged on the end corner and took a closer look at the board. It was in shades of brown, the alphabet in the center, a row of numbers beneath that, and the words "YES" and "NO" in the upper corners.

"Okay," Faye said, reveling in being in charge. "Put your hands on the planchette."

Donovan and I complied. He looked intense, his mouth drawn tight. Faye shushed the room into silence and then said, "Are any spirits here with us tonight?"

Everyone, whether standing or sitting, was stiff, with eyes wide. The light from the candles flickered and distorted their faces.

The pointer began to inch its way across the board.

YES.

My breath was loud in my ears. I was shocked that the board had worked so quickly. It seemed almost too easy. I stared at Faye and Donovan, wondering if either of them was pushing the pointer.

Faye said, "Are you willing to communicate with us?"

The pointer slid back to the center of the board, then back up.

YES.

"What's your name?" someone in the crowd called out.

Faye's eyes cut to the talker, angry that her MC job had been snatched away, but immediately returned to the board as the pointer moved again. People called out the letters as the planchette stopped on each one.

"K! A!"

It wasn't smooth. The pointer jerked a bit as it stopped and started between letters. I felt like I was being pulled along.

"Y!"

"Oh my God!"

"L! A!"

"It's Kayla. She's here," Faye said.

But she wasn't. I'd gotten to know when Kayla was in a room. I felt it in my bones. Something wasn't right.

"You're moving it," Donovan shouted at Faye, and he pushed the planchette off the board.

Faye caught it before it fell to the floor. Then she laughed guiltily. "Come on," she said. "It was funny."

The crowd groaned. I gave Faye a look. All the other people here just wanted a bit of entertainment. But this wasn't a game to me. I needed this. I wanted Kayla gone.

"Do it for real," someone called.

Faye placed the pointer back in the center of the board. "I'll stop."

"No, you're out," Donovan said.

"No, I promise. I won't push it again," Faye insisted.

He inhaled deeply and looked at me. I nodded. Faye wouldn't be stupid enough to fake it twice.

"Fine," he relented.

"We each put our index finger on it this time," Faye said. "Only one finger. A light touch. And we'll know it's not being pushed."

I wiped my sweaty palms on my jeans and returned one finger to the planchette.

"Is someone there, for real?" Faye asked.

Several long seconds passed. No one spoke, nothing moved. But the air seemed to thicken. I knew there were at least ten pairs of eyes on me, but I felt something larger looming around us. Something unseen but watching our every move. Waiting. Leaning forward with anticipation.

The pointer vibrated, sending a tingle up my finger. Faye paled and I knew she'd felt it, too. Donovan's eyes widened. We all held our breath.

The pointer slid almost effortlessly.

YES.

"Is it you? Kayla?" Faye's voice changed. She was no longer the loud leader.

The pointer doubled back, then returned.

YES.

The sudden fear in Faye's eyes was unsettling. This was no joke anymore. The air morphed, felt almost alive and electric. The crowd quietly leaned closer. The candle flame flickered, making our shadows dance along the walls.

I flinched as the pointer began to move beneath my finger. No one had asked a question.

"Someone write down the letters," Faye ordered.

I heard the rustling of a bunch of people pulling out their phones, the clicking as they transcribed.

IM

STILL

Too many people were calling out the letters at once. "Shut up," Faye said tensely. I tuned out all the noise and concentrated on spelling the words myself. The pointer slid to the next let-ter and the next.

HERE.

"I'm still here," I translated.

Adrenaline surged through me. A small cry rang out from the crowd.

I tried to keep my voice even, unemotional. "Why haven't you moved on?"

The pointer darted again, swiftly. I watched the letters intently.

DID NOT FALL.

A rush of breath came from the gathered crowd. I inhaled deeply through a twinge of anxiety.

"Then how did you die?" I asked. Faye was shocked into silence; she didn't even seem to mind that I'd taken over.

The pointer slid around the glossy cardboard, stopping briefly between letters.

PUSHED.

"Who pushed you?" I asked. The tension rose in the air like a swelling wave.

"Stop!" Faye yelled. "This isn't right. We have to stop."

We pulled our hands away as Faye began to sob hysterically. Donovan frowned at his fingers like he'd touched something dirty. I wanted to keep going.

The pointer shuddered back to life and began to swirl slowly around the board.

With no one touching it.

Faye crab-walked backward, away from the table. Donovan

ducked his head underneath, looking for the trick. Searching for how this could be happening. I stayed completely still on the floor. I knew what was going on. Kayla was really here. Really talking to us.

DID NOT SEE WHO PUSHED ME.

"Was it Donovan?" a voice from the back of the crowd yelled.

A sort of vibration went through the room, a slight rumble coming from the floor and pulsating up the walls. I exchanged a horrified glance with Donovan — he'd felt it, too.

The pointer charged over to NO.

"How do you know it wasn't Donovan if you didn't see?" a skeptical voice said.

The pointer angrily shot off the board.

I choked out a cry as my throat tightened. The floor beneath me trembled and I clambered to my feet. Everyone jumped and twisted around, reaching for each other. The board itself was shaking. Energy swirled through the room like a tornado, rushing at all our faces. My breaths came fast and shallow, leaving me dizzy. The lights in the room that had been off turned on, almost impossibly bright. Static electricity charged through the air. Long hair lifted, short hair literally stood on end.

Donovan stared, mouth open. Faye raked her fingers down her cheeks. I had only one thought: run like hell. But I couldn't move.

The light got brighter and brighter until the bulbs burst and shattering glass fell from the ceiling like rain. As hands and arms rose up for protection, the candles blew out, plunging us into complete darkness. Screams of terror, male and female, echoed off the walls. The front door crashed open and people nearly trampled each other in an effort to get out.

My muscles ached. Burned to join the others and run from the house. But I fought against the instinct. I couldn't leave Colby alone. I stayed, my feet bolted to the floor as the energy quaked around me. Then, the trembling that had started in the floor seemed to climb up the walls and in a vast whoosh rose up to the ceiling and disappeared. Like a door closed against the wind. It just . . . shut off.

My heart thumped so hard it hurt. I clutched at my chest, willing it to calm.

Silence fell over the house. But, in a sickening moment, I realized it shouldn't have. Colby should have woken. He had to have heard the smashes, the screams. He himself should be screaming and terrified.

Something was wrong.

I ran up the stairs, taking two at a time, not even faltering at the top like I usually did. Colby's door stood closed, as I'd left it. Was it really possible he hadn't heard any of the commotion? I drew a deep breath and reached out for the knob. The brass was icy cold. It almost burned against my overheated skin. I turned the knob slowly until I heard the click of a release, then let the door slowly sway inward.

Colby's night-light cast an orange glow over the room. I padded up to the side of the bed, my eyes focused on the lump under the blankets. Colby's whole body was covered, even his head. I reached out, grasping the comforter in my hand and slowly pulled it down to reveal Colby's face. His mouth was open slightly. After a quick paranoid thought, I put my hand, palm out, under his chin. He was breathing. He seemed hot, which was no surprise, after being completely under that thick blanket. But he was fine.

I backed out of the room. Right into someone.

Clutching my heart, I turned to face Donovan. He stood waiting in the hallway. He hadn't run like the others. He'd stayed.

"Everyone else is gone," he said. He motioned to the bedroom. "Is your little brother all right?"

My throat was so tight and raw, I couldn't speak. I only nodded.

Colby was safe. It was over.

My emotions released like a busted dam. Tears flowing, body shaking. Donovan pulled me into his arms and I collapsed willingly onto his chest, so thankful that he'd stayed behind.

We went downstairs. Donovan helped me sweep up the broken glass. I tossed all the cups and the half-eaten bags of food into the trash. I pointed Donovan toward where we kept our stepladder and lightbulbs, and he replaced each shattered one. I didn't know what I would have done if he'd left me behind, too.

Neither of us spoke. Perhaps it was trauma that silenced us, or not knowing where to start. Whatever the cause, it was an unspoken, mutually agreed-upon silence. Fix. Clean. Keep moving forward.

My thoughts wandered to the days ahead. Would all of us band together in silence like this? Or would tonight's details be passed around school like any other party tale? Would we rush to compare notes or fear acknowledging what had happened? Would I even still go out with Kane tomorrow night? Tomorrow seemed so far in the future. I couldn't even figure out what I was going to do in ten minutes.

After we'd finished cleaning up, I walked Donovan to the door. His tired eyes scanned my face for a moment, then he pulled me into a hug. I sucked in a long, slow breath. I didn't want to let go of him and lose the comfort he brought me.

He released me with a kiss on the top of my head. "I'll call you."

The house felt terribly empty when he was gone. I reminded myself that empty was good.

I trudged back upstairs and stared at my bed, wondering how in the world I was going to sleep after tonight's events. But as I burrowed under the covers, a complete and utter exhaustion washed over me like a wave and pulled me under. I felt no fear. Only the glimmer of hope that when the house shook and the lights burst it had been Kayla's exit from this plane. Maybe, wherever she was now, she could get some peace.

I slipped into a mercifully dreamless sleep, only stirring when a shaft of icy air wafted over my face with a feathery touch. Someone must have opened a window during the party. I only hoped it was open and not smashed. But I was too tired to get up and close it, wherever it was. Way too tired. I pulled the comforter higher and tighter, tucking it under my chin. But instead of getting warmer, I felt like a layer of ice was settling in around me like fog. I opened my eyes.

Colby stood beside the bed, his unblinking stare fixed on me.

I recoiled, startled by the sight of his face only inches from mine.

"What is it, buddy?" My voice wasn't sleepy. A rush of adrenaline jump-started my whole system. Colby had never sleepwalked before, but that seemed like what he was doing now. Standing there, silent, unmoving, staring at me.

"Did you have a nightmare?" I asked.

Finally, movement. His head tilted slightly to the side. One word. "No."

But it didn't sound like Colby's voice. Not at all.

"Colby?" My voice trembled.

He smiled. Slow and wide, his bright white baby teeth glistening in the murky gloom.

"No. Not Colby."

chapter 13

I cy fear encased my heart and my chest heaved with quickening breaths. *This isn't happening,* I thought. *It's a dream.*

I dug my fingernails into the skin of my arm and winced in pain. But what hurt more was the sharp, terrifying realization: This was real.

"The door was opened," Colby, but not Colby, said. "So I can do this now. Use him. Anytime I want."

"Please," I begged with a quivering voice. "Just leave him alone. He has nothing to do with any of this."

Not Colby smiled, pleased with my reaction. "I've got your attention now, don't I?"

I scrambled up to a sitting position and huddled back against the headboard, my legs pulled up to my chest. "You're mad that I ignored you these last few days, I get that. I'll . . . give you all the attention you want from now on. Just leave Colby alone."

"It's not attention I want."

"I'll never talk to Donovan again. I'll stay away from your friends. They're all still yours. They're not mine."

He cocked his head to the side. "You think this is as simple as jealousy? I know I'm dead. I know I can't come back. They're not what I want."

"Then what *do* you want?"

Not Colby blinked once. "To know who killed me."

"I — I don't know that," I stammered.

"You'd better figure it out, then. You're my best chance. You're in my house. Walking around with my friends." The whites of Not Colby's eyes glowed. "Wanting my boyfriend."

"People think it was him," I said.

"It wasn't," Not Colby snapped.

"How do you know?"

"Because Donovan left. I watched him walk out the door and then a second later someone came up behind me. Someone who'd already been there. Waiting."

My body was trembling violently, teeth chattering. "I don't know how to find out who did it."

"You'd better figure it out. This will be unpleasant for him," she said, gesturing down to Colby's small frame. "But I'll keep doing it until you get me what I want."

I made myself speak. "Please, Kayla. I know you're angry. You have every right to be. But he's just a little boy."

Not Colby made a mockingly sad face. "So very small, yes. It would be a shame if he . . . fell down the stairs in the middle of the night."

I put my hands up. "Please! Don't!"

"Promise me!" Not Colby demanded.

I was willing to say or do anything to make this stop. For her to take that gleaming stare and surreally terrible voice out of my sweet Colby.

"I'll do it. I promise. I'll figure out who did it."

Not Colby smiled one last time. Then his eyes rolled up and he crumpled to the floor like a dropped doll.

I jumped out of bed and knelt down beside him. He was limp, asleep. I picked him up into my arms and carried him back to his room, trying not to panic. I laid him on his bed and put my hand on his chest. His heart beat quickly under my hand. His breathing seemed regular, if not a little fast.

I curled up in the rocking chair beside his bed.

I watched him breathe all night.

Marie came home from work at dawn, and I came up with a quick lie.

"He had a nightmare," I whispered. "So I came in here. I must have fallen asleep in the chair."

"Poor thing," Marie said, exhaustion showing on her face. She still had her blue scrubs on. "Poor you, too," she added. "I hope you're not too sore today from sleeping in that chair."

"I'll be fine. And Colby . . . it was one of those night terrors, so he might not even remember it."

Marie leaned down over Colby's sleeping frame and gave him a kiss on the forehead. Then she gasped.

"What?" I stood up from the chair quickly, my knees and back cracking.

She placed the back of her hand on his forehead for a few seconds. Then she pulled the blanket down, pulled his pajama top up, and put her hand on his chest. "He's got a fever. Possibly a very high one. Get the thermometer."

I dashed into the bathroom and riffled through the medicine cabinet until I found it. When I got back to the room, she had Colby up on her lap. His eyes were open but the sheen of sleep was still on them.

"What time is it?" he asked sleepily.

Colby's voice — so familiar, so vulnerable — made my heart cinch with both relief and worry.

"We're going to take your temperature," Marie said, grabbing the thermometer from my outstretched hand. "Open up. Under your tongue. Okay, keep it closed. Don't bite it. Keep it under your tongue."

A minute later, the thermometer beeped and Marie read it. "One-oh-three."

"Is that . . ." I was going to say "dangerous," but I didn't want to alarm Colby.

"We'll have to keep an eye on it," Marie said. "Get some fever reducer into him." She growled. "Those kids at school aren't good about washing their hands. They share viruses like toys."

I backed up and stepped out into the hallway. Marie was busy blaming every other kid in town, when I knew the truth. But what was I supposed to say? *Colby's sick and feverish because apparently those are the after-effects of being possessed by a dead girl. And, oh yeah, she can do it again anytime she wants to. But don't worry, I vowed to find out who killed her. To keep Colby safe.*

That would elicit more than a stern talking-to and getting

my phone taken away. Yeah, that was a one-way ticket to the closest nuthouse.

I retreated to my room. There was nothing I could do here for Colby. Sitting in his room and worrying wouldn't help, long-term. Marie was best equipped to treat him today. But I'd be the one to make sure it didn't happen again.

I grabbed my phone. It was time to confirm my plans with Kane and get this thing rolling. I had to insinuate myself even deeper into Kayla's crowd.

I'd learned a lot about Kayla yesterday. She wasn't the picture of perfection like I'd imagined. She may have been beautiful and smart and gifted, but she was also deeply flawed. Maybe because things came so easily to her, who knows. All I knew was that she'd been a mean girl in life. And now she was bullying me in death. I didn't blame her for being vindictive. Getting murdered could bring that out in anyone. But she'd threatened the life of an innocent child.

I didn't want to be Kayla's puppet. But all I had to do was look at Colby and I knew I had no choice. I was committed. I would find out who pushed Kayla Sloane.

And then I'd put her to rest for good.

14 spent the afternoon sobbing in my room because she's still upset 7 dumped her two freaking years ago. Every few months she does this. I don't know what kicks it off — seeing 7 with someone else, probably. But get over it already. Seriously.

I told 14, "He's a player. He only wanted you freshman year because you'd just moved to town and were fresh meat. Forget about him."

But do you want the ugly truth, Diary? 7 DID like 14 her freshman year. Not in the temporary, surface way he'd felt about other girls. But in the real way. A little too real for my taste because I'd always enjoyed his puppy-dog-like attention.

So I got him to dump her.

Yep, here I was today patting her back and saying all the right things while I knew that I was the one who broke them up two years ago.

One day freshman year, I told 7 I'd gotten a Facebook message from an old summer camp friend. Someone who'd seen online that 14 and I had recently become friends.

"So?" 7 said.

"Well," I said. "This person went to her old school and filled me in on something you should know . . ." I trailed off and buried my face in my hands as if I really didn't want to tell.

"What, Kayla?" 7 said, nervous now.

I peeked between my fingers. "You have to promise to never tell. If you decide to break up with her, don't mention this. Just say you're not feeling it."

"Fine, just tell me what it is!"

I had him basically panting for the news now.

"Well, she still has a boyfriend back in her old town. She hasn't broken up with him. She's planning on secretly dating you both. She's playing you."

I paused a moment to let that settle in, then added, "I didn't know what to do when I found out. She's my friend so I didn't want to betray her, but I also didn't want you to get hurt." I traced a finger down his arm with a feathery touch. "I chose to tell you."

In that split second, I saw that 7 and 14 were over. He'd soon be returned to the spot I kept for him in my back pocket. 14 would be fine. She'd find someone else. And just in case, before 7 left, I reminded him, "Remember, this stays between us. She can never know this is why you're breaking up with her. Swear on it."

His face darkened. "I swear on your life."

chapter 14

Colby was sleeping his fever off, and Marie was napping with him. Dad was due home in the afternoon, but for now the house was quiet and still. After realizing I hadn't eaten in about twenty hours, I managed to make myself lunch and sat at the kitchen table to force it down.

The only way for me to deal with the trauma of Colby's possession was to move forward with a plan. But that plan — getting in with Kayla's crew, finding out who killed her — required Kane. And after he'd seen the Ouija board and fled last night, I didn't know what to expect from him.

I sent him a text, asking if we were still on for tonight. He replied quickly with an Of course! Pick u up at 7.

I let out a sigh of relief. At least one thing was coming easily.

I cleaned up the mess I'd made cooking lunch and carried the trash outside. I opened the trash can, grimacing at the stench, and tossed the bag on top. The bag underneath crumpled easily under the weight. Mostly, as I knew, because it was full of plastic cups. The only physical evidence of my party. I was happy to be covering it up with more trash. The truck would come Monday and take it all away.

I was wrestling with the top of the can, trying to fit it back into the metal grooves, when a voice said, "Big party last night, huh?"

I whipped around, holding the metal lid in front of me like a shield.

"I'm your neighbor, Mr. Tucker."

I knew who he was, though we'd never spoken or stood this close. I usually only caught glimpses of him through his window. And he'd obviously been standing by that window last night, watching the comings and goings. I was toast.

But then I looked again. At his hunched-over frame, the hand he dragged through his scraggly white hair, the forlorn look on his acne-scarred face. He didn't seem like an angry neighbor. Just a sad man. He was probably in his fifties, though from a distance you'd think he was older.

For some reason, I felt a tiny sting of pity. But I pushed it away. He was creepy, always watching from that window of his. And now he'd startled me and was obviously playing with my head, trying to scare me.

I figured I'd get to the point. "Are you going to tell my parents about the party?"

He hesitated, then answered with a firm, "No." But before I could relax, he added, "Be careful, though, who you befriend."

Um, okay. I was pretty much done with this awkward conversation, but he stood, waiting, as if he needed something.

"I will," I said, my sweaty hands gripping the lid tightly. "Thank you, Mr. Tucker."

He nodded then and lumbered over the landscaping that divided our yards.

I tossed the lid on the trash, not even caring anymore if it was perfectly closed, and hurried back inside.

If being creepy was enough to make someone a murder suspect, I'd just filled in number one on my list.

Marie and Colby were both awake by the time Dad got home. Colby's fever had broken, but his face was still pasty. The bags under Marie's eyes were so dark it looked like she'd been sucker punched. Dad had his usual stunned, jet-lagged look to him. And I radiated guilt. Combined, we must have looked like four circles of hell.

I was in my room, searching my closet for clothes for my non-date, when a knock came on the door.

"Come in," I called.

Dad bent over as he cleared the doorway, then straightened when he was safely in my tall-ceilinged room.

"What are you up to?"

"Finding something to wear," I said as I pushed a few hangers to the side.

"Are you going out with new friends tonight?" His voice was filled with hope, as if me having friends was the answer to all our problems.

"One friend. He's going to show me around town."

"A boy?" Less hope in his voice now. "Like a date?"

I smirked. I complained about his protectiveness to his face, but inside I actually didn't mind. That's what dads were for. To worry about boys and proclaim each one unworthy of his daughter.

"No. It's a non-date," I said, and I could practically see the relief in his neck and shoulders.

"Oh. Good." He pulled my desk chair out and sat down, though he looked kind of silly. The small wooden chair was definitely made for someone of my size, not his. "So how are things?"

Oh no. I didn't expect a talk. I didn't want a talk. Not now. Not after the last twenty-four hours I'd had.

"They're fine, Dad. But I have to figure out what to wear."

"Is something going on?" he blurted.

I gripped a shirt tightly in my fist. "No . . . why?"

"You don't seem like yourself. I know it can't just be that story about the girl dying in the house. You've been avoiding me all afternoon and I barely saw you all week."

"You're busy. I'm busy." I faced my closet again so he wouldn't see the lie on my face. Even Faye's makeup trick that I used to cover my dark circles couldn't cover that.

"How's the new school?"

"It's great. Much better than my old one."

"And the kids? They're treating you okay?"

"I'm fitting right in."

He paused, as if the next question was harder to ask. "Did you and Marie argue about anything?"

"Dad, Colby's sick. You should really be with him."

"I know he's sick. But right now I'm worried about *you*."

My heart squeezed. I never doubted my father's love for me.

I never once thought that he'd forgotten about me or anything like that. But still . . . it was nice to be reminded.

Even if I didn't want to talk.

I turned around slowly, with a smile I hoped looked real enough. "I appreciate it, Dad, but I really have to get ready."

"For your non-date."

I smirked again. "Yeah."

He rose from the chair and hiked his chinos up. "I'll leave you alone now, on one condition."

"What's that?"

"We have one of our Daddy-Daughter outings some night this week. I've been traveling so much and I really want to hear about school and your new friends. We can go out to dinner, just the two of us, and catch up. How's that?"

We used to do that all the time when I was little. A Daddy-Daughter outing could be the movies, bowling, ice cream, my favorite pizza place back home. I'd always loved it.

"Deal."

Satisfied, Dad smiled and left the room, watching his head on the doorway.

I hoped I'd have the answers Kayla wanted by then, so this nightmare would be over and I wouldn't have to spend the dinner lying to him.

chapter 15

Kane pulled into the driveway right at seven, and I rushed outside as he was getting out of the car. I didn't want him to come in and have to face one of my father's interrogations.

"I was going to come get you," he said motioning at the front door as I breezed by him.

"That's okay." I opened the passenger side door. "Let's go."

He got back in and slid me a look. I tensed, wondering if he was going to ask questions about last night. I didn't want to start the non-date with a big talk about what had really happened. And I certainly wasn't going to tell him about Colby. I needed to pretend this was a normal night out.

"You didn't even let me open the door for you," he said.

I blinked. He did realize this was a non-date, right?

"I guess you don't want the flowers I got for you, either?" he pouted.

My mouth opened in shock, but then he burst out laughing. "You should have seen your face."

"You were joking?" I asked, stating the obvious.

"Yeah. You made it quite clear this wasn't a date date." He

grinned wickedly and added, "But if you change your mind, this can turn into a real date any moment you want."

I felt my neck blushing, which made him smile more as he backed out of the driveway.

"So where are we going?" I kept my eyes on the houses passing by as we drove down my street.

"First, I thought I'd give you a drive-by tour of the important places in town. Then we'd go for the best Boston cream pie in the world. Then we'd go to the clearing."

"The clearing?"

"Where kids from school hang out."

"Sounds great." I started to get excited for a night of fun, then remembered it was more than that. I had a purpose. Someway, somehow, I had to find out who pushed Kayla Sloane. Colby's life depended on it.

The tour of town ended up being more of a tour of Kane's life. He pointed out his elementary school, the field where he hit his first home run, the street that always gave the best Halloween candy, the bench where he got his first kiss (in fourth grade, the little player). But some of his favorites were good to know. A bookstore I foresaw myself spending a lot of time in. The place he called "the best pizza joint in town" that I would suggest to my dad for dinner.

Before long, we stopped at a diner that was the size of a trailer. But Kane insisted the food made up for the lack of atmosphere. We slid into the last available booth and Kane ordered us each a Coke and a slice of Boston cream pie.

"I hope this lives up to my high expectations," I said.

"Oh it will." He beamed and tugged on his Woodbridge Lacrosse windbreaker. I didn't think I'd ever seen him not wearing it.

"Do you sleep in that thing?" I teased, motioning at the jacket.

He blushed a bit. "It's tough when you don't have the money to shell out for designer duds. I don't have a polo in every color of the rainbow or a limitless amount of authentic team jerseys."

I hadn't even thought of that. He couldn't afford a lot of clothes, so he probably wore plain T-shirts every day and tossed the windbreaker over them. *Great job making him feel like a total loser, Jade.* I tried to shrug it off. "I think it's cool. Team pride."

"Yeah right," he said, calling my bluff.

"School's not a fashion show, anyway," I insisted.

"Tell that to everyone else."

He was right, but thankfully the pie gods chose that moment to bestow upon us our order. I do not exaggerate and neither did Kane. With the first bite, I let out an embarrassing moan.

Kane said proudly, "I didn't do you wrong."

"Not at all. This is wonderful."

We ate in silence. Part of me wanted to scarf the whole thing down as quickly as possible and the other part wanted to savor each bite as long as I could. I compromised with a medium pace.

"I'm sorry I bailed on your party last night." Kane wiped his mouth with a napkin. "I just thought the Ouija board was in poor taste."

"I understand." And I did. The whole thing was obviously the worst idea ever. It opened some sort of door that allowed Kayla to possess Colby at will. If I had listened to Kane instead of going forward with it, things wouldn't have gotten as bad as they did. "I don't even know who brought the thing."

"How did it go?" Kane smirked. "Did you all communicate with the dead? Did Kayla give everyone the answers on the next Calc test?" He wiggled his fingers in the air and laughed.

"Actually," I said, while fiddling nervously with my fork, "something did happen."

He stopped laughing. "Are you serious?"

"Kayla came through," I said. "Faye and I asked questions . . . about that night."

Kane paled. "What did she say?"

"She said she was pushed."

His eyes widened. "By who?"

I scraped at the last bit of pie. "She didn't know."

Suspicion clouded his face. "Did she give you any indication that it was really her? And not just someone moving the pointer thing?"

"Yeah. She got really angry when someone suggested it was Donovan who had pushed her. The lightbulbs burst, the house shook." Despite the warmth in the diner, I shivered at the memory.

He shook his head. "Someone was messing with you."

"No, Kane. It was real."

"It was Faye." He dropped his fork, and it clanged loudly on the table. "She's mad that we're going out tonight. I bet she brought the board and orchestrated the whole thing somehow to get back at you."

"No, Faye was terrified."

"Faye's an actress. Lying comes second nature to her. It was faked."

He seemed unyielding on the topic, so I didn't press. After an awkward silence, I said, "I'm sorry about your sister, by the way."

"What about her?"

They seemed so close, I'd just assumed she would have told him. "I invited her to the party," I explained. "But Faye had this hissy fit right in front of her. Clinging to some idea that it was seniors only. I told Ellie to ignore Faye and come, but I think the damage was done."

He waved his hand. "Don't worry about it. Ellie wouldn't have come, anyway."

"Why not?"

"I don't think she'd want to be in the house. Kayla's death really affected her."

"They were friends?" I asked, surprised.

"No, Kayla wouldn't publicly hang with underclassmen," he laughed. "But Kayla and I had been friends since kindergarten and she'd been over at my house hundreds of times. Ellie used to follow us around and try to play with us. I never let her. But Kayla was always nice to her. I think part of it was an ego trip, because Ellie worshipped her. But Kayla genuinely liked her. Ellie looked up to her as this sort of model of perfection. So Kayla would give her advice now and then, toss her a bone, you know. When Kayla died, Ellie was brokenhearted."

Well, there's one person who was. What I'd learned at my party, however, was that there were dozens of others who weren't so sad about Kayla's turn of events.

And I had to find out which one of them was the cause of it.

Kane pushed his empty plate to the side of the table. "Ready to go to the clearing?"

I brightened. "Absolutely."

Ten minutes later, Kane stopped in a gravel parking lot beside a playground. A few other cars were there, but the park was empty.

"What are we doing here?" I asked, feeling a little anxious.

"This is how we get to the clearing." He killed the engine and pointed out the windshield toward the woods beyond the playground. "There's a path in there that leads to it." The corner of his mouth lifted up a little. "You're not scared, are you?"

I *was* a bit unsettled. I fingered my red agate pendant and remembered that the Romans had used the stone to protect against bug bites.

I rolled my eyes playfully and said, "Only of mosquitoes."

He laughed and we got out of the car. The playground was surprisingly creepy at night. The slides were empty. The swings still. No playful shouts of children rang out as they ran, their little feet kicking up mulch.

"Hey," Kane said, lightly grabbing my arm. "Let's sit for a minute before we go in." He gestured at the swing set.

"Sure." I settled onto a swing, wondering if this would be when his flirty banter would turn serious. I gripped the swing's chains tightly and steeled myself for a bad moment. He was cute and all, and I liked his attention, but I didn't want him to make a move. This wasn't romantic for me. This was about saving Colby.

Don't lean in for a kiss, I prayed.

"I want to talk to you about Donovan O'Mara."

Well, that was unexpected. "What about him?"

Kane stretched his long legs out in front of him and planted his feet so the swing wouldn't move. "I don't want to fight with you again, but I'm also not going to ignore the alarm bells going off in my head. So I just want to say my piece and then that will be it, okay?"

I lifted my feet under the swing and kicked them out forward, pumping lightly, enjoying the breeze across my face. "Sounds fair."

"I know that you and Donovan are . . . friends. And no one can tell you who to be friends with. But be careful, Jade."

Jeez, first Mr. Tucker and now Kane. Two warnings in one day. Way to make a girl feel safe.

Kane continued, "Some people, myself included, really and truly think he had something to do with Kayla's death. And I know he's trying to convince you otherwise, but please keep a clear head on this and consider both sides."

"But even Kayla herself said it wasn't him last night."

He gave me a look that said *oh please*.

"If there was any evidence, the police would have done something," I said.

"There was a witness."

I dragged my feet on the ground to stop the swing. "Someone saw him push her?"

"No, some neighbor saw him go into the house with her and walk out alone. Around the time the fall would have happened."

"Mr. Tucker?"

"If you mean the creepy guy that likes to watch young girls out his window, then yeah."

"So your credible witness is the neighborhood perv?" I kicked at an empty juice box on the ground.

"Hey, he's always watching out that window. If anyone else walked in the house, he would have seen it. Even if they used the side door, that's facing his property."

And maybe that's why reclusive Mr. Tucker crossed the yard boundary today to talk to me. Because he'd seen Donovan at my house last night. I dropped my hands from the swing's chains to my lap.

"I'm not going to turn against him like the rest of the

school," I said, jutting my chin out. "Innocent until proven guilty."

"But?" Kane said hopefully.

"But I'll be careful and keep my mind open."

He nodded solemnly. "That's all I ask. I never want something like that to happen again."

There was grief in his eyes. Not fresh, but deep. "You and Kayla were close, weren't you?"

"Yeah, we'd been friends since we were five."

"Did you ever date?"

He averted his eyes. "No." Then looked back up at me. "But not for my lack of trying."

So he'd liked Kayla, maybe even loved her, and she'd only thought of him as a friend. No wonder he and Donovan shot fireballs from their eyes whenever they saw each other.

A crunch of gravel caught my attention, and I looked over Kane's shoulder.

A shadow approached from the parking lot.

From the Diary of Kayla Sloane

Hung out at 7's today, like old times. He got all mad at 8 for following us around (seriously — just like the old days), but I didn't mind. In some ways, 8 reminds me of a younger me. When I leave WHS, maybe I'll pass my crown to her. I already gave her some tips on handling boys and friends. Told her to trust no one. Keep her secrets to herself and her diary.

But then 8 took off to hang with her friends and 7 and I were alone and it was . . . different. That 7 wants me is a constant fact . . . like the sun rising, like 11 being a robotic nerd, like 1 spending 2's money, like 9 being creepy. You get the point.

But 7 was in a sad mood. Kind of mopey. I know it's about 28. I've dated guys before, so I don't know why 7 is so bitter about this latest one.

I said, "You're no fun today," and left. But then there was something else in his eyes, something new.

Something like anger.

chapter 16

The shadow grew in size as it approached, and then separated in two.

"What are you lovebirds doing?" a voice called out.

Kane stood up, laughing, then greeted the guy with some overcomplicated handshake. He was one of the jocks Kane hung with. The second shadow, probably the guy's date, turned out to be one of Faye's friends. I didn't know either of their names, just recognized their faces. The girl hung back a bit. Her eyes went from Kane to me and back again, then she whipped out her phone and started texting.

Great. Within sixty seconds, the entire school would know we were here together in the dark. This might incite jealously in a few girls, Faye included, and it wasn't the best time for me to be making enemies. I wanted to ingratiate myself into Kayla's crew, not make them mad.

"We're heading in now, man." Kane pointed at the woods. "You comin' with?"

"Nah, we'll keep those swings warm for a few more minutes," he replied, with a glint in his eye. That probably meant they were going to slobber all over each other for a little while before joining the group.

"Later, then." Kane put a hand on my lower back, leading me toward the edge of the woods. He lowered his voice. "I'll go first. You can hold on to the back of my jacket if you want. It gets pretty dark in there for a while."

"That's fine," I said with forced bravado.

The path was narrow. We'd have to walk single file unless I wanted to be swept by brush and branches. I followed him onto the trail and after a few steps it was like the woods swallowed us whole. It was darker in there. The thick tree cover blocked the moon and stars.

I stayed close to Kane, my eyes glued to his blond hair, the only thing I could clearly make out. With his black windbreaker and dark jeans, he looked almost like a head with no body floating down the path. I reached out and grabbed the back of his jacket.

"Changed your mind, huh?" I could practically hear the smile on his face.

"Shut up."

The trail seemed to be getting narrower, and a claustrophobic panic started to flutter in my chest. But then voices drifted out of the darkness. And, a moment later, music. Deep bass as rhythmic as a heartbeat. The path opened, and suddenly, we were out in the open. The woods released us and moonlight returned.

The clearing was a perfect square, but the ground was covered in moss. Flames glowed from a small fire pit in the center, ringed by rocks. Over a dozen kids from school, mostly seniors, stood around. A couple girls danced and giggled.

"So this is it." Kane opened his arms wide. "Our hidden spot."

"Very cool," I said, my eyes sweeping the crowd. First I looked for Donovan, but he wasn't there. Of course. Then I scanned the faces, wondering who I should talk to and how I would even go about this. I was no detective. But then I remembered how people had talked about Kayla at my party with little to no prompting. It was like they'd *wanted* to talk about her to me. Maybe because I lived in her house. Took her place.

"Want a drink?" Kane asked.

"No, I'm good. Thanks."

He nodded. "You can go sit down or come with me . . ."

A few of his friends were standing in a circle, talking, and I knew he probably wanted to join them for a while. "Don't worry about me. I'll finagle my way into a conversation somewhere. I don't need a babysitter."

He smiled. "I know you don't."

Kane darted off to his friends and I inched toward a small group of girls who were sitting on a couple boulders. They might have all been at my party, though I couldn't be sure. One in particular was the girl who'd basically admitted she'd been crazy about Donovan. What was her name? Laura? Lauren? Ugh. I was terrible at this.

"Hey, Jade!" She waved me over.

I put on a perky smile. "What's up?"

"Jade, this is Madison and Jessica," she said.

We exchanged a round of "heys," though I still didn't remember the third girl's name. Madison and Jessica seemed nice enough. After a few minutes of small talk, I found that they were all on the soccer team. Which meant they'd probably played with Kayla.

Score.

"This place is so cool," I said.

"Isn't it?" Laura/Lauren said. "It can get kind of insane here some nights. Though not as crazy as *your* party." She waggled her eyebrows, which were already pretty high on her forehead due to her tight ponytail.

"Yeah, that was nuts," I agreed.

"I still don't know what really happened and what my terrified imagination exaggerated."

Madison piped up. "Fill us in, Jade. Laurie won't tell us anything."

Laurie! That was her name. I stopped myself from snapping my fingers.

"Yeah," Jessica said, a greedy look in her eyes. "We know something freaky went on, but only like ten people were still at the party and they're not talking. It's like they're traumatized. Faye wouldn't even come out tonight."

"Well," I leaned in and lowered my voice to a whisper. If they felt like I was letting them in on a big secret, maybe they'd unload some secrets on me in return. "Don't spread this around, but we sort of . . . contacted Kayla using a Ouija board."

They were bending so far forward, I thought they'd fall off the rock.

"What did she say?" Madison whispered.

"She was murdered," Laurie snapped. "I told you guys."

"But," I said, remembering Laurie's bias, "Kayla said Donovan didn't do it. It was someone else."

"Who?" Jessica yelled.

"Kayla doesn't know. Whoever it was came up behind her right after Donovan left."

"What else did she say?" Madison dug her fingers into the boulder.

"Nothing." I shrugged. "That was it."

Jessica crossed her arms and shook her head. "I always knew she was pushed."

Laurie started mumbling about how Donovan did it. Again. Clearly she didn't like getting rejected. Jessica disagreed with her and they bickered back and forth, using almost the exact same points Kane and I had in our argument.

Madison's voice carried over both of them. "I have a theory . . ."

We all stopped talking and gave her our full attention.

She smiled slowly. "And it's a good one."

I shot a glance at Kane, who was still chatting with his teammates on the other side of the fire. He caught me looking and I turned away quickly. He might think I was miserable and needed saving from a bad conversation. But I didn't want him to come over now, not while things were getting good.

"I've thought a lot about it over the past few months," Madison began. "And I think I know who killed Kayla."

Kane was patting a buddy on the shoulder and taking a step back, like you'd do when you were leaving a conversation.

"Well, out with it!" Jessica snapped, pretty much taking the words out of my mouth.

"Alexa Palmer."

But I wasn't expecting those words. I stiffened as a heavy feeling settled into my stomach.

"Robot Girl?" Laurie said. "Why would you think that?"

Madison held up two fingers and counted off. "First — motive. Second — ability."

"We're gonna need more details," Jessica said.

Madison adjusted her position on the rock. "Alexa and Kayla were in a heated competition for the valedictorian spot. A spot that is now clearly Alexa's."

"Robot Girl wouldn't kill someone just for the number one spot," Laurie said.

"Have you met her?" Madison countered. "Hello! That's all she cares about. She has no friends, no life. All she cares about is her test scores."

Suddenly feeling defensive, I butted in, "I'm friends with her, actually. She's more than grades."

They ignored me as Jessica added information of her own. "Plus, Kayla was so mean to her. Kayla's the one who started calling her Robot Girl."

"Then everyone else joined in," Laurie said, clearly remembering.

"Plus," Madison added, "Alexa's . . . off. She's like . . . emotionless. She could totally push a girl down a flight of stairs and not feel a thing."

My insides twisted into knots. Everything they said made sense, but I didn't want it to. Could Alexa be a sociopath? She was awkward, but in a way I found endearing. She was the girl I liked most in the school, *because* she was different and quirky and honest. But my priorities had changed. It was all about finding the truth now. And if I was going to investigate, I had to consider every possibility.

"How's it going over here, ladies?"

I hadn't even noticed Kane make his way over. The girls all sat up straighter, tossing their hair. Kane gave me a confused look and I realized I'd been frowning, stuck on the image of Alexa thrusting her arms out and pushing Kayla from behind.

Kane reached out and grabbed my hand. "I'm going to steal Jade from you. Hope that's okay."

All the girls giggled in response.

More people had shown up, clumping up in circles and groups, laughing and yelling. Kane led me over toward the fire, to an empty spot where we could be alone. We settled next to each other on the ground. I sat cross-legged. He pulled his knees up and rested his arms on top of them.

He edged in a little closer and knocked my knee with his. "You're not having a good time, are you?"

"No, I am. I mean, yes!" I bumbled.

"Yes you are, or yes you aren't?" He grinned.

I gave him a light shove with my elbow. "You know what I mean. Yes, I am having a good time."

His face turned serious. "You didn't look like it over there."

"I was deep in thought for a moment. I'm back on planet Earth now."

"What were you thinking about?"

"Nothing important." How easily the lie slipped from my mouth.

Whether he believed me or not, he didn't press. He picked up a stick and stuck the end of it into the fire.

"We should have brought marshmallows," I said.

"That'll be our second date." He tilted his head toward me with a sly smile and I laughed.

If this *had* been a real date, this would have been the moment when we'd kiss. Snuggled up close, a fire burning in front of us, the chatter of friends around us but still feeling like we were alone. All he'd have to do was lean in a bit more.

I met his gaze. I knew I should have been wondering what kissing him would feel like. But my heart wasn't in it.

Kane must have seen the unease in my eyes, because he turned forward and began playing with the fire again, shoving the brush around with his stick.

Here he was, the most popular, best-looking guy at school, happy to be spending time with me. My heart should have been all fluttery. Why was I holding back when any other girl would have been doing backflips of joy?

I knew why. Because I wasn't completely there. My mind kept returning to Donovan. I thought about his eyes, his rare smile. The way he'd cleaned up his look for my party. I wanted to check my phone to see if he'd texted me, but knew that would be rude to do in this moment with Kane. But I couldn't stop wondering where Donovan was and what he was doing at that moment.

I didn't have to wonder for long.

A dark figure passed through the trees and into the light. His eyes scanned the crowd and stopped on me. My heart skipped a beat as Donovan began walking right toward us. I tensed up, not knowing what to expect. I felt like a girlfriend caught cheating. But why? Donovan and I weren't dating. Kane and I weren't dating. I had no reason to feel guilty.

"Hey, Jade," he said, stepping up next to us. He reached his hands out above the fire and rubbed them together.

"Hi, Donovan." My voice sounded small. I wished Kane and I were standing. I wished Donovan hadn't seen us sitting next to each other on the ground.

He looked down at Kane and nodded. "Woodward."

Kane pointed his stick toward Donovan in acknowledgment. "O'Mara."

They were only saying each other's last names, but for some reason it came out sounding like the filthiest insults.

What's that smell? Oh yeah, testosterone.

"O'Mara!" Someone actually happy to see Donovan called out from the crowd. I recognized him as a fellow gamer dude he sat with at lunch.

Donovan waved and wandered over without even a look back at Kane and me. My first thought, when I'd seen him appear from the woods, was that he had come for me. The gossip vine had reached him and he came to see if I truly was here with Kane Woodward. But now I saw that he was meeting a friend. He probably didn't mind who I was here with.

I picked up a stick that still had one leaf attached and held it in the flame, watching the leaf curl up, wilt, and disappear into ash.

chapter 17

Word about the Ouija incident got around school. To most of the upperclassmen, anyway. Reactions varied. Some thought we were making the whole thing up, like a senior prank. Others thought we'd all suffered from some mass hysteria. A few believed. You could tell who they were from their slanted, apprehensive looks. One thing was sure. No one wanted to use me for a party anymore. Even Faye was keeping her distance. Which, for once, was unfortunate because I had an important question for her.

At lunchtime, I snagged a slice of pizza and carried the tray toward my usual spot next to Alexa.

"Jade!"

Kane was waving me over. I felt a bit of apprehension approaching the popular table, but it couldn't hurt to say hi. I scanned the faces for Faye, but she wasn't there. It was like she was hiding from me.

"How's it going?" I said. Everyone at the table stopped chatting and stared at me.

"Not bad for a Monday," Kane replied. "Hey, why don't you sit and have lunch with us?"

"Sure," I said with a smile. "Let me go get Alexa."

Two guys laughed and one of Faye's girls muttered something about the nerd patrol.

"The thing is," Kane said, "there's only room for one more."

"Oh." I stood for a long awkward moment. "No problem."

Kane smiled and moved his tray to make room for mine, not realizing until I turned away that I had chosen Alexa over him. I'm sure things like that didn't happen to him often.

"What was all that about?" Alexa asked as I sat opposite her. "I thought you were ditching me."

"Of course not. Just saying hi." There was no need for me to tell her the truth and hurt her feelings.

I scarfed down my pizza as Alexa dutifully cut her chicken patty into small, equally sized bites.

"How was the rest of your party?" she asked.

I opened my mouth to say with surprise, "You haven't heard?" But stopped myself. Of course she hadn't heard.

"It was . . . interesting. Someone brought a Ouija board and we contacted Kayla's ghost. She wants me to find her murderer."

Alexa didn't even look up. She frowned at a piece of chicken that was bigger than the others, halved it, and stabbed it with her fork. "So who pushed the pointer thing? You?"

Well, that wasn't exactly a guilty reaction. As usual, she had nearly no discernable reaction at all. I ignored her question and asked my own. "Why did you leave the party, anyway?"

She put her finger up for me to wait until she finished chewing. "You know that's not my scene. I came because you asked me to. And then when you got busy I left. You're not mad, are you?"

"Do I look mad?"

She considered me for a moment, then brought her eyes back to her chicken. "I don't know."

"No, I'm not mad."

I wanted to steer the conversation to Kayla and their history together, but it would seem too forced. *By the way, I heard you had every reason to want Kayla dead. And you and emotions don't seem to be in lockstep. Are you, by any chance, a sociopathic killer?*

"So do you want to hang out together after school?" I asked instead.

"Sure!" The hint of a smile appeared at the corners of her mouth.

"Today?"

"No, I'm much too busy today. Tomorrow after school will work better. You can come to my house."

"Deal." I smiled and looked down at my tray. My pizza was long gone. I wanted another slice, but a quick look at the wall clock told me it was too late. I also spied someone standing in the doorway to the cafeteria. Faye.

"I'm going to get a head start to my next class," I told Alexa. She nodded, probably thinking that was a great idea.

Faye saw me walking purposefully toward her. Her eyes widened and she bolted out the doors and into the main hall. I sprinted to catch up and put my hand on her shoulder.

She shrugged it off. "Jade, I'm in a hurry."

"Are you avoiding me?"

"I'm not." But she didn't slow her "had to be uncomfortable in those heels" pace.

Small talk wasn't going to get me anywhere but brushed off. I had to get direct. "Faye, did you bring the Ouija board?"

She stopped and stared down at her chipped nail polish. "Yes," she admitted in a quiet voice. "I brought it. But I didn't expect anything real to happen. I was just messing around." She looked up at me with frightened eyes. "It *was* real, wasn't it?"

"Yes. That was Kayla."

"Is she . . . haunting your house?"

I nodded. "She won't rest until she knows who killed her."

Faye's eyes scanned the hall, back and forth, and came back to rest on mine. "Are you going to try to find out?"

My first instinct was to lie. Faye would spread whatever I said across the whole school within twenty minutes. But then I reconsidered. If word got around that I was trying to figure out what happened to Kayla, the killer might get spooked enough to make a mistake or get smoked out of hiding.

I straightened my shoulders and said confidently, "Yes. I am. I want my house back."

Faye wrinkled her small, upturned nose. "Well, leave me out of it."

The bell rang and students poured from the cafeteria into the hallway as Faye clomped away.

"Faye's upset, huh?" Kane said, stopping beside me.

"Is she ever not?" I joked.

Kane chuckled. "Hey, I'm sorry about lunch. The table was just too crowded."

He seemed sincere, though I'm sure he would've made room for someone other than Robot Girl. But I wasn't about to abandon her for more popular friends. She'd been the first one to talk to me at school, to show any interest that didn't involve my house or Kayla.

"No problem," I said. Figuring the conversation was over, I started walking slowly toward my locker, but he stayed with me.

"Did you have a good time Saturday night?"

"Yeah, it was fun. Thanks for showing me around."

"Maybe we could do it again this weekend."

I was taken aback. I tried to make my mind work, to come up with the answer I wanted, but it was like the spinning wheels on an upside-down car. Kane could get me closer to Kayla's friends, to getting the truth. And he'd been a complete gentleman Saturday night. I had no reason to say no. But there was something there, just under the surface, that made me not want to trust him. Sometimes he looked at me in a not-friends way. Sometimes he looked at me like I was someone else.

At that moment, Donovan walked by, in seemingly slow motion. Like he needed to talk to me, but didn't want to interrupt. Our eyes met and then he moved on.

"What do you think?" Kane prodded.

"Um, I have to check with my parents. Can I let you know later in the week?"

Kane either couldn't or didn't bother hiding his disappointment. "Sure."

I watched his blond hair disappear in a sea of people, then made my way upstairs and to my locker. Donovan was standing there, waiting for me.

"Hey," I said. My instinct was right. He had wanted to talk to me. "What's up?"

"If you're not busy, can you meet me after school?"

My neck burned. I forced myself to dial down the enthusiasm that suddenly rushed through me. "Sure. Is there something you need to tell me?"

He hitched his black bookbag up higher on his shoulder. "I haven't been able to stop thinking about —"

A bunch of kids walked by, pushing themselves in between us.

He couldn't stop thinking about what . . . me? Wanting to be with me? That he'd hated seeing me with Kane? That it had made him realize he was over Kayla and ready to move on?

"Sorry," he said when the kids were past and we could talk again. We were only a foot apart now. His intense eyes bored into me.

"You were saying?" I said.

"Yeah. Since your party and everything that happened, I haven't been able to stop thinking about what Kayla said."

To say my heart sank would be an understatement. More like it sank in a puddle of quicksand and was then covered with cement.

Donovan would never get over his ex. And I just couldn't

compete with a dead girl. Especially one who was prettier than me, smarter than me, more popular than me. More everything. There wasn't any use in even trying.

"So can we talk after school?"

"Yeah," I said with a catch in my voice. "Sure."

I drowned my sorrows in a chocolate milk and three peanut butter cookies during free period. It didn't make me feel better. I felt drawn to Donovan. And there were moments when I wondered if he felt the same way, but they were fleeting. He was broken. Maybe beyond repair. I had to accept it and move on.

I had to trash any romantic thoughts about Donovan and focus on finding Kayla's killer.

I caught up with Kane after last period. He and Ellie were walking out together. Always the gentleman, I thought. Walking his sister home.

"Kane!" I called out.

He and Ellie stopped and waited for me to catch up to them by the exit.

"About this weekend," I said.

"Yeah?" He braced for my answer.

"I texted my dad and he's fine with me going out. I don't have to, um, babysit or anything."

His eyes lit up. "Great! We'll figure out what to do later, okay?"

"Sounds good."

I watched him and Ellie stroll away and waited for my heart to feel better.

ᘓ
From the Diary of Kayla Sloane
ᘔ

*In Math last week, the top three high scorers on the test were
posted on the board. (Damn, this school knows how to create an
atmosphere of competitiveness!) Anyway, I came in number two.
One guess as to who came in on top: 11, natch. And that's fine
and dandy except when 11 found out, she turned around and
looked right at me with this smirk on her face.*

Big. Mistake.

*But this is why I'm one of the great ones. The simpleminded
will lash out immediately with whatever unplanned, hasty hate-
bomb they can scrape up at the moment. I'm patient. I bide my
time. I wait until the moment is right and then unleash my revenge.*

*So I waited until today. Our English papers were due in sixth
but I share a study hall with 11 in third. When she went for a
bathroom break, she left her laptop and bookbag unattended. I
slipped her English paper out of her bag and — to make sure she
couldn't print out another copy — I quickly logged into DOS and
formatted her hard drive, wiping out her paper and anything else
that was on there.*

*When she came back and sat back down, I briefly caught
her eye.*

And I smiled.

chapter 18

Donovan texted me our meeting place: the gazebo on the green next to the school. On one of those beautiful, sunny fall days, the green would have been full of classmates. Girls lounging around and gossiping. Guys tossing a football. But today was cool and gray, and as I walked toward the center of the green, the only other person there was the shadow in the gazebo. Donovan sat on the bench, head lowered, staring at his clasped hands.

"Hi," I said, no doubt dazzling him with my superb conversational skills. But I didn't have to worry about trying to impress him anymore. I was finished with that.

So then why was I still bitter?

"Hey." He stood up and shoved his hands in the pockets of his jeans.

"So," I said dryly. "You can't stop thinking about Kayla."

"About what Kayla said," he corrected, giving me a confused look. "At your party."

I paused. "What about it?"

He motioned to the bench. "Want to sit?"

I slipped my backpack off my shoulder and leaned it up

against the side. The wooden bench was painted white, same as the gazebo and the latticework. It was pretty and could've been a romantic setting if the conversation weren't so morbid. I swept a fallen leaf off the seat and eased myself down.

Donovan settled in next to me. "I never thought she was pushed."

I kept my voice neutral. "Why not?"

"Because I was there. It was just us. We argued. I left. And she was crying really hard. So I thought she fell because she was so upset." His voice tightened. "I could almost picture it. Her eyes were closed, her hand over her mouth, doubling over sobbing. Then losing her balance, and . . ."

I cocked my head to the side. There had been more to Donovan's sadness than I'd known. Despite his innocence, he actually blamed himself for her death.

I watched him with a calm stare. "You thought it was your fault."

He gave a slight nod. "I thought . . . if I hadn't left . . . if I'd stayed until she calmed down . . . she wouldn't have fallen."

Maybe he wasn't the broken boy because he still longed for Kayla. He was the broken boy because he felt responsible.

"But now, it looks like she didn't fall after all," I said.

"Not that that's any better. The end result is the same. But . . ."

But, in some way, it *was* better. For his conscience. She hadn't fallen in distress over their argument. Someone else did this to her.

He sat up straighter and met my gaze. "So what I'm trying to say is that — because of what happened at your party — I believe now, that she was pushed."

I wished I could tell him that I knew it for a fact. I'd heard it from Kayla herself, through my brother. But a small part of me worried that he'd think I was crazy. So I only said, "Me, too. And I want to find out who did it, but I barely know where to begin. It could have been anyone."

"No," he said, angling toward me. Our knees touched, sending a spark up my leg, and I had to force myself to concentrate on what he was saying. "It was someone she knew. A random killer doesn't wait in a random house for a random person and push them down a flight of stairs."

"What's strange, though," I said, "is that it seems planned, since the person was probably there, waiting for you to leave. But it also seems unplanned. They didn't bring a weapon and couldn't have known Kayla was going to be standing at the top of the staircase. So maybe the person didn't plan to kill her, but was . . . overcome. What do they call that?" I knew I'd read the term in a mystery novel or two, but couldn't recall it.

"A crime of passion." His eyes narrowed. "That's a good point. I mean, think about it. They probably didn't even know if she was dead or not. A fall down a flight of stairs, even hardwood, isn't an automatic kill."

"You're right," I agreed. "It was someone who knew her. Someone we know."

"The person was probably at your party," Donovan said.

"I'm thinking more like someone who wasn't there." I thought again of all the crime novels I read. "Sicko serial killers love going back to the scene of the crime, but someone who didn't mean to kill her? Someone who felt guilty about it? They probably wouldn't want to go."

Donovan countered, "But if they had known Kayla, they'd have to go or risk the appearance of guilt. Maybe they'd make an appearance and then leave."

Like Alexa, a voice in my head added.

"They certainly wouldn't have stayed once the Ouija board came out," Donovan added. "Just in case Kayla really could finger her killer, they'd get out of there fast."

My thoughts turned to Kane. His sudden fierce reaction to the idea of us contacting Kayla. Or Faye, who'd been avoiding me ever since and wanted no part of finding out who killed her supposed best friend. My mind was spinning. There were so many possibilities.

Donovan rested his hand on my knee, causing my mind to still and a wonderful electric shock to race through my body.

He said, "If we want to do this, we have our work cut out for us."

We? Do what?

His sky blue eyes turned steely. "I know you want to find out who killed her. I do, too. I want to clear my name, once and for all."

He cleared his throat and that vulnerable look returned. "And I was wondering if you'd like to team up."

☙

Back in my room, I opened a fresh notebook and wrote down the names of anyone who could be a suspect. I started with the major players, then listed anyone from Kayla's old group. All the people I'd met at my party and at the clearing. I put them all down.

When I was done, I stared at the long list and sighed. That overwhelmed feeling was starting to creep over me again. The idea of having Donovan to talk things out with had temporarily sated the doubt monster, but it returned in full force now. It leaned over my shoulder, whispering, *You can't do this. You'll never figure it out. You won't be able to save Colby.*

I slapped the notebook closed and pushed my chair back from my desk. My jewelry box called to me from the top of the bureau, so I brought it over to my bed. The bedsprings squeaked as I sat in the center, opened the box, and started my ritual.

Sometimes, in the months after my mother's death, this was the only thing that could calm me. Though I relied on it less now, I felt my anxiety begin to wane as I touched the first gemstone and whispered its name.

"Rose quartz." I rolled the smooth gem between my fingers and remembered its origins. It's a pink, romantic stone used to both attract new love and heal old love's wounds. It fixes the fissures of a broken heart.

I replaced the quartz and picked up another. "Watermelon tourmaline," I said, in barely a whisper. It helps you see the silver lining in every situation. The stone was pink enfolded in green, just like a sliced watermelon. But much more expensive. This had been one of my mother's favorites.

I picked up my amber pendant, the one Donovan said reminded him of my eyes. I ran my finger across the polished amber, the smooth sensation calming me. I closed my eyes and smiled.

But before I could pick out the next stone, my eyes snapped open. The energy in the air had changed. I wasn't alone anymore.

I straightened and looked around the room, even though I already knew, from the thickened, charged air, that it wasn't a family member in here with me. It wasn't anyone that I could see. Just feel. I'd gotten good at sensing when Kayla was around, watching. And she was here now.

A cold breeze tickled the back of my neck, like someone was right behind me, lips pursed, lightly blowing air on my exposed skin. I shivered and rubbed it.

"I'm working on it," I said to the empty room. "Leave Colby alone. I'm getting you what you want. I have a . . . list of suspects and I'm working on it."

After a moment's pause, the hostile energy drained from the room. Warmth immediately returned to my goose-pimpled skin, like someone had taken a blanket from the dryer and draped it over me. All was back to normal.

I got the message.

Back to work.

chapter 19

When my mother died, I laughed.

Dad and I were in the hospital waiting room, surrounded by family and friends, waiting to hear something, anything about the surgery. Time had never passed so slowly and it had taken far too long. When the surgeon came down the hallway, I should have known just by looking at him. But I figured, he was a surgeon — that serious, somber expression was probably permanently etched onto his face.

Then he said those terrible words. And I laughed. I didn't think it was funny. Not even amusing. Just absurd. My mind couldn't make sense of it. Couldn't process an appropriate response.

I was as shocked as everyone else when this fake, almost insane-sounding cackle bubbled up out of me. Before I knew it, I was doubled over. The laughs became gasps as I couldn't catch my breath. I tried. In and out. Faster. Faster. But I wasn't getting any air.

Someone said, "She's hyperventilating," and then arms were around me, leading me toward a chair, but I didn't make it. I woke up sometime later on the rug, hoping I'd only been dreaming. I hadn't been.

So I know all about poor reactions. Sometimes your mind goes a little berserk and produces an unexpected and completely inappropriate reaction to the situation at hand. It's understandable.

What scared most people away from Alexa wasn't so much the inappropriate things she sometimes said, but her reactions — or lack thereof — to people. Madison wasn't the only one who suspected Alexa was capable of pushing Kayla. Now that my little detective project was public, a couple more people whispered to me in the halls on Wednesday that I should look into Alexa. Apparently, Kayla had bullied her to the point where any other girl would be nothing but a bucket of tears, but Alexa had kept her steely eyes down and ignored her each time. This cold, nonemotional response seemed to frighten the other girls.

But I respected it.

As I followed Alexa's car in my own after school for our planned "hang out time," I thought about how hard that must have been for her. To be the target. To have no one else backing you up. To feel so alone.

I wished I had been here back then to protect her.

But I reminded myself to be on guard. Just because I liked Alexa and her quirky personality, that didn't mean she was innocent. I had to keep my mind open and not let my personal feelings cloud the facts. Alexa had a motive. A real one.

Her car signaled right and took the turn. I followed — onto a road filled with the most gigantic houses I'd ever seen. I was glad we weren't in the same car, because I couldn't hold back my audible gasp.

Did Alexa *live* in one of these?

She took another right. I followed her down a long driveway. The middle door of the three-car garage opened as Alexa's car approached.

She lowered her window and yelled, "You can park in the circle!"

I followed the winding drive as it circled around a fountain. I parked near the front door and got out onto the clay pavers. I'd never been anywhere near a house like this before. I looked down at my hoodie and jeans and felt underdressed. Though I had no reason to. Alexa wore a simple white button-down blouse and jeans herself. She was so unassuming. I never had any idea she was a gazillionaire. I knew rich people. Rich people carried giant thousand-dollar handbags with tiny dogs in them and wore oversized sunglasses, even at night.

"What's wrong with your mouth?" Alexa asked when she reached me.

I realized my jaw had been hanging open like I'd taken a punch and was physically unable to close it. "I was not . . ." I managed. "I wasn't expecting your house to look like this. I mean . . . you drive a regular compact car."

"This," she pointed to the cascading fountain with one hand and the double doors with the other, "is my parents' taste. Not mine."

"Oh" was all I could muster.

"Now you understand why it wasn't worth my while to fight the athletics requirement for the Bodiford Scholarship."

Ah, yes, the scholarship she'd ranted about because it wasn't just based on academics. It went to whoever had the highest class rank *and* made all-state in a sport.

"It's not a need-based scholarship," Alexa continued. "But they do have a maximum family income and we surpass that."

By a lot, I guessed.

I followed her inside, feeling the need to remove my shoes before I stepped on the gleaming floors. But since Alexa didn't take hers off, I kept mine on. We passed a living room that looked like no one had ever lived in it. For one, it didn't have a TV. Just stiff-looking furniture and a glass coffee table. Maybe that's what a sitting room was. Someplace you just . . . sit. We passed several closed doors and another room marked by white floor-to-ceiling columns. Alexa didn't stop to give me a tour or explain what anything was until we stopped at one of the closed doors and she opened it.

I was expecting her bedroom, but there was no bed. Only a computer desk and bookcase after bookcase. "You can drop your bag in here," she said.

"Is this your dad's office?"

"No, this is my office. My mother's is the next room and my father's is after that."

They each had their own office. I let that percolate as I dropped my bag on the floor.

"So do you want to watch TV in the theater room or get a snack in the kitchen?" she asked.

The theater room sounded amazing but if we were watching something we wouldn't be talking. And I needed to get her talking. "Yeah, let's head to the kitchen."

My first thought when I entered was: Marie would love this kitchen. Not Mom, she wasn't a big cook. But Marie was. And this place had countertops for miles. A kidney-shaped island that could seat more people than our dining room table was centered in the room beneath a hanging iron pot rack.

I climbed onto a stool at the island while Alexa rummaged through the fridge. "Soda and grapes sound okay?"

"Sure," I said.

"One healthy, one unhealthy." She smirked. "It's all about balance."

Alexa placed a porcelain bowl of grapes and two sodas on the countertop.

"How's the essay for MIT going?" I began.

She shook her head, almost angrily. "I wrote a draft and it was terrible. I scrapped it and have to start again."

"You're probably being too hard on yourself, Miss Perfect SAT Score."

She smiled. "What was your score?"

"Not perfect." I shrugged. "But I did get the highest of all my friends back home." *All two of them*, I added silently.

"What'd you take? Kaplan? Princeton Review?"

"Nothing. We didn't have places like that in my old town."

Alexa gaped at me like I'd told her we didn't have running water. "Then how do students prepare?"

"They mostly just . . . take the test. I suppose we could take a course online somewhere. I bought a book. A study guide." I nearly laughed at the horrified look on Alexa's face.

She could probably talk academics all day, but I needed some segue into a different conversation. A framed photo was centered on the island. I pointed at it. "You and your parents?"

"Yes. From a vacation in DC." She picked up her soda and started chugging it.

I gazed down at the picture. The three of them stood together in front of the gates of the White House. They stood stiffly, smiling without showing their teeth, each parent with one hand on a much-younger Alexa's little shoulders.

I replaced the photo, let my eyes wander the room, and sighed. "I still can't believe you live like this. It must be like waking up in a beautiful dream every morning."

Alexa's finger trailed along the outline of a tile over and over, making the same square. "Yeah, sure, we have money but there are drawbacks."

"Like?"

"Impossibly high expectations. Stress. Inherited perfectionism." Her finger stopped retracing the pattern. "Sometimes I wonder. What if I didn't *want* to go to MIT? Or any college, for that matter. What if I loved art and I wanted to move to the city and live a bohemian, artsy lifestyle? I truly think my parents would never speak to me again."

"Well, *do* you want to?"

She shook her head. "No way. I hate art. I love numbers. I love to memorize them, manipulate them, play with them. I want MIT so bad I dream about it almost every night."

"If you and your parents want the same things, then what's the problem?"

"It's the 'what if,' I guess. What if somewhere down the road, I *do* disappoint them?"

In my old school, I was smart. Not Alexa smart. But probably one of the top three smartest girls. Here, I was average and I knew it. But Dad and Marie never pressured me. I imagined for a moment what it must be like to be Alexa. To feel the weight of those expectations on your shoulders.

"Would they be mad if you didn't end up graduating valedictorian?"

"I don't have to worry about that," she answered point-blank.

"Why not?"

"No one else is close enough to catch up with me now."

The little hairs on my arms rose. *Now.* As opposed to then — when Kayla was alive.

"So Kayla was your only real competitor?" I asked innocently.

Alexa tensed and risked a quick glance at me before she returned her eyes to the tile. "Yes. But she was a cheater."

I rested my elbows on the counter and leaned forward. "She cheated on tests?"

"Not every time. She was very smart and could do fine on her own. But sometimes she got too busy with soccer or parties or whatever. So she'd cheat now and then. Or she'd sabotage other people's —" Alexa stopped herself. "I didn't like her very much."

Here it was. All I had to do was push a little bit more. "I heard that she gave you a nickname."

Alexa's face closed down and she waved me off. "I don't want to talk about her anymore. Let's go to the theater room."

She picked up the bowl of grapes and started walking. I followed, knowing I'd reached a wall. What was beyond it, I didn't know yet, but I wasn't getting past it today.

chapter 20

I took Dad to the pizza joint Kane had suggested. It was actually a cute little Italian place that had more than just pizza. The smell of garlic wafted in the air, making me salivate. Each table had a plastic checkerboard tablecloth, a tiny vase with fake flowers, and a little metal spice rack that held crushed red pepper and Parmesan cheese.

Half the tables were empty, probably because it was Tuesday night. I could picture it packed on weekends. We were seated right away. I nearly tripped as we passed a stack of wooden high chairs.

"I should have named you Grace," Dad joked.

"Grandma should have named you Shrimp," I shot back with a grin.

The waitress handed us laminated one-page menus, but I already knew what I wanted. A big heaping plate of spaghetti. My favorite comfort food. I ordered that and a soda. Dad ordered chicken parm and a light beer.

"We haven't done this for a while," Dad said. "I'm glad you still have time for your old man."

"At least until I leave for college and never come home to

visit again," I joked. We slipped right back into our routine of teasing each other. I loved it. It made things feel normal.

The waitress arrived with our drinks. Dad refused the glass and took a sip from his bottle. "How's school going?"

"Good. Some of the classes are more challenging than back home, but it's okay."

"The kids treating you well? Mom said you were at a friend's house this afternoon."

I bristled when he referred to Marie as Mom. Dad noticed and looked down at his silverware. I didn't get mad, though. This was my hang-up, not his. And he was so used to calling her "Mom" in front of Colby.

"Yeah," I said. "Her name's Alexa. She's the smartest kid in school. A little unusual. I like her."

"I'm glad you've made a friend so quickly."

If he only knew how many new "friends" had been at his house last weekend. I was glad Mr. Tucker hadn't told on me, but part of me wished he had, because the guilt I felt was almost as bad.

"And how was your date the other night?" he said teasingly.

I spun my straw in the soda, making the ice cubes clink against the glass. "Non-date, Dad. We're just friends."

"So how was your non-date?" Dad wore a half-amused, half-concerned expression.

"It was fun. We're going to hang out again this weekend."

He dropped the amusement. "Another non-date or a real date?"

I paused. "Non-date."

"Because you know if it's a real date, I want that boy to have some manners and come in the house so I can meet him."

"He wanted to come in the house last time, but I ran out to save him from the Daddy Inquisition."

Dad threw his head back and laughed. "I'm not that bad."

"You can be!"

"But you're my little girl and I —"

"Oh, Dad, please stop."

Thankfully, the waitress came with our food. Dad dumped so much Parmesan cheese on his it looked like it'd snowed on it. I spun the spaghetti around on my fork and took a big bite.

"Mmm," Dad mumbled.

I agreed. This tiny hole-in-the-wall had great food. Colby would love this place. I pictured all four of us coming here. Maybe making it a regular thing once a week. I felt peaceful for a moment, picturing us like a normal, happy family. Then I remembered the giant cloud hanging over us. The threat. Kayla could destroy my family at any time.

Dad's fork clanged as he dropped it on his plate. "There it is again."

"What?" I was surprised by his sharp tone.

"That look on your face that I've been catching now and then around the house. You're worried. Something's wrong."

"There's nothing wrong, Dad." *Nothing you can help me with.*

"Are you being bullied at school?"

"No, Dad. It's nothing like that."

"So what is it?"

I looked up into his hazel eyes, the same as mine. The protectiveness I felt for Colby was the same as what my dad felt for me. But at least I knew the problem I was dealing with. Dad was in the dark and that might be even worse. Maybe. . . .

I sucked in a deep breath and took a chance. "Do you believe in ghosts?"

Dad raised his eyebrows. "Where did that question come from?"

I'd been pretty sure Marie hadn't told him about our little talk, but from the shocked look on his face I was now positive. She'd kept her word.

I gave a shrug. "I was just curious."

"No, I don't," he said warily.

"You've never seen, heard, or felt anything weird?"

"In our house?" he asked.

"Anywhere."

He picked up his knife and fork and began cutting the chicken. "Well, sure, weird stuff happens, but I assume there are real explanations for it. A noise is the house settling. That sort of thing."

I dropped my gaze and started twirling another forkful of spaghetti around and around. Even if Dad had experienced anything in the house, he was such a skeptic by nature, he'd never believe it was something supernatural. Plus, he'd spent the least amount of time in our house out of all of us. What had I expected? That he'd confess he thought the house was haunted, too? That I could share what happened to Colby with him and he'd have some miraculous solution to our

problem? There were only two solutions I could see: move —
which Marie would never allow — or find Kayla's killer and
put her ghost to rest.

"There's another reason I don't believe," Dad added in a
softer voice. "If ghosts did exist, Josephine would have come
through."

My heart skipped a beat at my mother's name. He barely
spoke it anymore. I understood why he brought her up, though.
She'd been my first thought, too, after I'd realized this ghost
stuff was real.

"Maybe we've never heard from her because she's at peace,"
I said. As opposed to Kayla, who was clearly *not*.

Dad's shoulders tensed. He spoke quickly. "I just think if
any of that were real and there were any possibility, she would
have found a way to come through. To at least say good-bye."
His voice was rough, but etched with grief. "And I don't want
to talk about this anymore."

He dug into his food and I figured something out for the
first time. He still wasn't over her. Not any more than I was.
He just hid it better.

CR

From the Diary of Kayla Sloane

ဆ

28 and I had a fight today. The usual. I said a few choice words to 11 as we headed into class. 28 told me that was unnecessary. I reminded him that it was. That 11 and I were neck and neck for valedictorian so I liked to throw her off her game before a test. It's no different than athletes trash-talking between plays.

But 28 got this sort of disgusted look on his face. He said, "Every single thing you do is calculated." And then he ignored me the rest of the day.

We made up — also as usual — but I was a little worried that this would be the time I couldn't fix us with a smile and a kiss. And then I was mad at myself for worrying about this. I'm Kayla Sloane. I could have another guy within five seconds. And I've never given a moment's thought to what anyone thought about me before. Why do I care so much about what he thinks?

chapter 21

I loved the art room in the early morning quiet. Before people started arriving and the school stirred to life — lockers slamming, people rushing, bells ringing, the day starting once again. But for now, it was only me.

"Hey."

And Donovan.

My stomach fluttered at the sight of him. He wore what I figured by now were his favorite dark jeans and a blue tee with a cool swirling pattern on it. I realized, after a moment, that I'd been staring. "I like your shirt," I said.

He pulled on the end, straightening it out. "Thanks. I designed it myself."

He dragged a stool next to mine and sat down. "How are things in the house?"

"Eerie now and then. Nothing as crazy as what happened at the party." And what happened *after* to Colby, which I still didn't want to share with anyone.

"Do your parents know?"

I shook my head. "My dad is a huge nonbeliever. I tried to tell my stepmom and she accused me of lying."

"Things are rough with her, huh?"

"Now they are. But we don't usually fight much. Mostly because I hate confrontation, so I tend to keep negative feelings inside and deal with them by way of silent snark."

He grinned. "I've heard that works well."

"It's one tactic." I smiled. "What about you? Divorce? Stepsiblings?"

"No, I'm an only child. My parents are cool. They get along great. My home life is actually pretty nauseatingly functional. It's my life outside of home that's a mess."

His gaze settled on me and I would've given anything to know what he was thinking. Did he feel the same attraction to me that I felt toward him? Or was he still hung up on Kayla? Was he just using me to help him clear his name? Or was he using Kayla's death as an excuse to get close to me? I wished I had the guts to tell him how I felt. I wished I were the type of girl who could come right out and ask him if he was interested, instead of playing all these guessing games.

I opened my mouth, hesitated a second, and said, "So let's talk about Kayla."

Something — disappointment? — flashed across his face. "Okay, where do you want to start?"

"You probably knew her better than anyone. Tell me what she was like."

He paused for a long moment. "Driven. Ambitious."

"At my party, you mentioned that the day she died . . . you broke up with her?"

He picked up a dry paintbrush and ran his finger over the bristles. "Yeah."

"Why?"

He shrugged. "That's not relevant."

"Tell me, anyway." I shifted in my seat. "To be honest, I can't believe you even dated her to begin with. You seem like opposites."

"At first I was running on pure flattery." He smiled sheepishly. "When the most popular girl in school asks you out, you say yes. But then, you know, reality set in."

"The reality that you were dating a soulless evil demon girl?"

The side of his mouth twitched. "Not that, no."

"Then what?"

He hesitated, like he was trying to find a way to translate his thoughts into words. "I think people, by nature, want to believe that there's good in everyone. That if you peel back the layers of the onion you'll find an explanation, an excuse, a justification. The bully is bullied by his own father. The bad girl is ignored by her parents and just wants attention, even if it's negative. So I had this romantic notion that if I dug deep enough, I'd find goodness at Kayla's center. And I'd fix her. Help her to become the person she *could* be."

"And what did you find at Kayla's core?"

"Nothing." He rubbed a hand across his forehead. "Maybe I didn't dig deep enough. Or maybe the conventional theory is wrong, and some people really aren't any deeper than their outside layer."

I gave him a long look. I couldn't help feeling that Donovan was holding something back. Some key piece of information.

But why would he do that? Especially now when we were working together?

"I have a game plan for this afternoon," he said, changing the subject.

"And what's that?"

"I think we need to talk to this witness. The man who told the police I was the only one who went inside the house that day."

"Mr. Tucker?"

"Yeah. Your creepy neighbor. He always gave Kayla the willies."

"He has that effect on me, too. Okay, let's meet after school."

From the increased decibel of the noise in the hallway, I knew it was time to get to homeroom. I swung my bag over one shoulder. Donovan motioned for me to go before him through the narrow doorway. The hall was packed and a group of guys ambled toward me, arguing in loud voices about some trade the Patriots made.

Donovan placed his hand on the small of my back, protectively, and steered me around them. I stiffened at the shock of his touch, and he quickly drew his hand back, probably thinking I hated the feeling of his hand on my body. But I didn't. Not at all. And, for a long time, while my first-period teacher lectured us about something I should have been paying attention to, all my mind could think about was Donovan's hand on me. And how I wished it were still there.

ᘒ

"The heroine of the novel comes to her new home and finds that her husband's dead first wife still has a hold on the house. The so-called ghost of Rebecca and the villain of the story, Rebecca's loyal servant Mrs. Danvers, pose a threat to both our heroine's marriage and sanity."

I shifted uncomfortably in my chair in last-period English as Mrs. Mayhew lectured about *Rebecca*.

Mrs. Mayhew paced the front of the classroom. "The heroine feels that she'll never be as satisfactory to her husband as Rebecca was and she worries that her husband is still in love with his dead wife. But by the end of the novel, what do we find out?"

Some boy in the back answered, "She wasn't all that."

"Correct." Mrs. Mayhew smiled. "Despite all the wonderful things said about her and her undisputable beauty, Rebecca was — underneath — quite an evil person."

Everyone else was feverishly copying Mrs. Mayhew's words into their notebooks, but not me. The parallels to my life were disturbing. The four walls of the classroom seemed to be closing in. I needed air. I needed to get out.

Thankfully, just as I was about to bolt, the bell rang. As soon as I reached the hallway, the pressure on my lungs lifted. I took a deep breath and calmed myself.

I went to my locker to grab my things. Donovan and I were supposed to meet in the parking lot. So I was surprised when I felt a hand on my shoulder.

"I thought we —" I started, spinning around. But then

stopped. It was only Faye. She wore a tight pink shirt and a short skirt. She'd curled her hair into long corkscrews.

"Sorry to disappoint you," she said at the look on my face.

"I'm not disappointed, Faye," I lied to spare her feelings. "I was just expecting someone else."

She crossed her arms tightly. "How's your little investigation going?"

I turned back to my locker and pretended to look through the books, even though I'd already taken out everything I needed. "Fine."

"I heard Donovan O'Mara is helping you. Isn't that like asking the defendant to investigate his own case?"

I sighed heavily. "Donovan didn't push her. Kayla herself said it. You were there."

"She might have been confused. Maybe he came back in after he left."

I spun around to face her again. "Donovan broke up with Kayla that day. Why would he kill her if he didn't want her anymore?"

Faye's face turned a fiery red. "He didn't break up with her," she said through clenched teeth.

"Why do you say that?"

"Because she was above him," Faye spat. "She was prettier, more popular. Above his station. Why would he put an end to that?"

Well, hello, Mrs. Danvers. "Maybe she wasn't as perfect as you think."

Faye shook her head so hard the curls trembled. "No one dumps Kayla. Plus, he never told anyone he broke up with her. That makes no sense."

Except me. Why would he tell only me? I suddenly got the feeling that this was a secret I should have kept to myself. "I must have heard him wrong," I said. "Don't tell anyone. It's . . . it's bad information."

"You're damn right it is," Faye said indignantly.

Despite her poor attitude, part of me respected Faye's defiant defense of her friend, even in death. Faye took a few steps away, then stopped. Her head turned slowly back in my direction, taking in my outfit. My non-designer jeans and Interpol T-shirt. Not exactly Faye's taste and I could see that on her face.

"So," she said, "your whole 'playing hard to get' thing seems to be working on Kane."

Not this again. "I'm not playing hard to get. We're really just friends and that's it."

"Don't deny it. I'll admit, it's smart. The boy who can have almost anyone always wants the one he can't have." She took a step closer to me. "But who does the girl want? Donovan or Kane? Kane or Donovan?" She twirled a curl around her finger. "It's the age-old question." When I didn't respond, she curled her lips and hissed, "He's only using you to try to feel closer to her. It's sick."

I stiffened as she put into words the worry I'd had about Donovan in the back of my mind all day. But I wouldn't give her the satisfaction of knowing she'd gotten to me. I lifted my chin and pulled my shoulders back. "Donovan isn't . . ." But my voice trailed off as a smug smile came over her face.

She sneered. "I'm not talking about Donovan."

chapter 22

Faye had unnerved me at my locker. But I put that information in a little box and shoved it into a dark corner of my mind so I could focus on the task at hand.

I pulled into my driveway. Donovan parked his little black car behind mine. I walked up as he lowered his window.

Donovan looked out at Mr. Tucker's house. "So . . . should we go knock on his door?"

"There's no need for that," I said. "Just wait."

A moment later, a face appeared in the window on the side of Mr. Tucker's house. Like clockwork. I straightened and waved at Mr. Tucker, motioning for him to come outside. Then the face disappeared.

I leaned back down. "He's coming out."

As creeped out as I was by Mr. Tucker, I still knew I had to talk to him. He was the only other person around the afternoon Kayla died.

"Does he always do that?" Donovan grimaced toward the window.

"Yeah. Every day when I come home, seconds later, his face appears at the window. He's always watching."

"He's even creepier than I thought." Donovan reached for the car handle.

I held a hand up. "No, wait in the car."

He paused and looked up at me. "Why?"

"He might be less forthcoming with his answers about that day if the last kid he saw leaving the house is the one asking him the questions."

"Touché."

I left Donovan and walked to the property border. Mr. Tucker ambled over a minute later.

"Good afternoon, Mr. Tucker. Could I talk to you for a minute?"

"Sure." He eyeballed the shadow in the car. *Did he recognize Donovan from here?*

"Mr. Tucker, the morning after my, uh, party, when we talked . . . why did you tell me to be careful?"

He shifted his weight. "Because those kids at your party were the same kids who paraded through that house last year. And we both know how that ended."

"Do you think Kayla was pushed?"

He looked past me at the house and the yard. "I watched that girl grow up doing cartwheels and flips in the backyard. Her father even fashioned a balance beam for her from a plank of wood. I can't imagine someone with her athleticism and grace perishing from a simple fall." His focus returned to me. "That's why I was forthcoming with the police. About the boy I'd seen coming from the house. The same boy who's staring at me from that car right now."

I looked over my shoulder. Donovan's face was poking out of his car window. He was eavesdropping, and not very subtly. I turned back to face my neighbor, trying to sound braver than I felt. "Mr. Tucker, Donovan is my friend. And I'm sure that he didn't push Kayla."

"How can you be sure of something like that?"

I couldn't exactly tell him it was because Kayla herself had told me. "You'll just have to trust me."

"Then trust me and watch yourself, because no one else went in that house except Kayla and that young man. And he was the only one who came out."

He turned and began walking away with a slight limp. I knew if I followed and badgered him with more questions, I'd risk him telling my parents everything — about the party, my new friend Donovan, me asking about Kayla. So, with a heave of my shoulders, I returned to Donovan's car.

"I assume you heard all of that?" I said.

"Sorry if I ruined it," he said sheepishly.

"Nah, I don't think he knows any more, anyway." I paused, wondering what to do next. I didn't want Donovan to leave yet, but we were done with our plan for the day. I kicked at a leaf on the ground. "Um, do you want to come in for a while?"

Marie and Colby were at one of their Mommy and Me classes. Dad had left at dawn for his next business trip. So we had the house to ourselves.

Unless Kayla showed up.

I hadn't thought of that. But now the offer was out and I

couldn't exactly retract it. And I wanted to spend time with him. And Kayla wasn't around *all* the time . . .

Donovan gazed at the house, then back at me. "Sure."

He followed me up the walk and stepped into the living room, almost as hesitantly as I did. I took a moment to feel the energy in the room. But this, thankfully, seemed like one of the times when she was . . . wherever it is ghosts go when they're not haunting people.

"Are you okay? Being in here?" I asked as Donovan's eyes swept the room.

"Yeah, sure." He flashed a quick smile. "I was here for the party, remember?"

"I know, but still. If you're uncomfortable you don't have to stay."

He reached out and took my hand. I felt a blush spread down my neck like a stain. "Jade, it's fine. With your parents' furniture and being here with you . . . it's like a different house."

I was able to push out an "okay" from my tightened throat. He let go of my hand.

"Want to go over what we've learned?" he said, motioning toward the couch.

I didn't know if I'd be able to concentrate sitting next to him. I wanted to suggest the dining room, with a giant table between us, but that would be weird. So instead, I said, "Sure. Let me get us some sodas."

I returned from the kitchen a minute later and found him sitting comfortably. I settled beside him on the couch, not too close, yet not suspiciously far away, and placed the glasses on the coffee table.

"What do you think about what Mr. Tucker said?" he asked, pausing to take a sip. "About how I was the only other one in the house?"

I shrugged. "He only usually starts watching when I get home, so he probably wasn't watching the house all day when it was empty. Maybe someone went in before you and Kayla arrived. Someone who was already there, waiting in the house."

"But if he heard someone arrive," Donovan argued, frowning, "he would have looked out the window, thinking it was Kayla."

A disturbing thought flashed through my mind.

"There is one other explanation . . ." I aimed a thumb in the direction of his house.

Donovan looked slightly surprised. "Mr. Tucker?"

"What better way to cover his own tracks than to be the helpful witness who talks to the police? Maybe he saw you leave, knew no one else was home, went in, and killed her himself."

"But why?"

"Maybe he was obsessed with her, who knows. He watches me constantly from the window; I assume he did the same to her." I shivered at the notion.

"Yeah, he did," Donovan muttered. His fingers trailed along his chin as he thought. "But I always got a harmless old dude vibe from him."

"Vibes aren't evidence." I'd been reminding myself of that a lot lately. My thoughts turned to what Faye had said at school and I blurted the question out. "Why didn't you tell anyone you broke up with Kayla?"

"It's no one's business," Donovan said, clearly startled by my sudden question. After a moment he added quietly, "We broke up and then the next thing I hear is she's dead. Her parents were destroyed. They'd always liked me and were very kind to me. I wasn't about to tell them, 'Oh, by the way, I dumped your daughter.' So I decided not to tell anyone." He paused and gave me a long look. "Until you."

I wanted to ask why, but the words wouldn't come. My throat had dried up. I fiddled with my pendant nervously.

Donovan's eyes went to it. "What's that one?"

I looked down and back up at him, at those intense eyes. "Red garnet."

The gem is used to heighten romantic feelings, but that was the last thing I needed help with at the moment. Just being this close to Donovan, alone with him, was more powerful than any magic stone. I racked my brain for the gemstone's other meaning. It was on the tip of my tongue, but I couldn't grasp it. All I could see was Donovan's face, his eyes, his mouth.

He smiled. "You're so funny with all your gemstones."

The fever coursing through my body suddenly iced over. That's what he thought of me. I wasn't sexy and intriguing like Kayla. I was funny and quirky. I'd be his cute little friend. Nothing more.

"Yeah, I'm weird," I said, and before I could stop myself I added, "Not like Kayla."

He inched closer, maybe sensing he'd hurt my feelings. "The thing about Kayla . . ." He stopped and rubbed his cheek. "Yeah, she was pretty and, yeah, sometimes I enjoyed the ego boost of having the school's most popular girl on my arm, but there were also times when I was disgusted by her and the way she treated people. She could be very cruel. Day to day, you never knew which Kayla was going to show up. What I like the most about you is that you're you — all the time."

My brain wanted to stop and examine every word he'd said, but I forced myself to pay attention so I wouldn't miss anything. I'd have time to overanalyze the entire conversation later.

"You're different, Jade." He reached up and tenderly tucked a strand of hair behind my ear. "You strolled into our school out of nowhere. You don't really fit in with any clique and you don't care. You're dating the most popular jock and you're friends with the weirdest, most unpopular girl. You're interesting to talk to. You don't care what anyone thinks about you, but not in a defensive or aggressive way. Just a natural way."

He stopped and dropped his gaze, a blush rising to his face. Then he looked slowly back up at me and said, "I've honestly never met anyone quite like you."

My breath hitched. That was the nicest thing anyone had ever said to me. Unfortunately, I couldn't respond. I felt paralyzed from the throat up. I couldn't blink, talk, or even swallow.

Donovan opened his mouth to speak again. I couldn't tear my eyes from his slightly parted lips. Heat spread through me. My neck smoldered. I felt like my skin was on fire. I was going to spontaneously combust any moment, I knew it.

"I'm not dating Kane," I mumbled. There was so much more I wanted to say but those were the only words I could muster at the moment.

Donovan moved closer. There were only a few inches between us now and I felt each one. He leaned in and whispered in my ear, "So it's okay if I do this?"

He kissed my earlobe, then his lips trailed down my neck, then back up to my cheek. He stopped at my lips, and I realized he was waiting for a response.

"Yes," I breathed. "That's okay."

His soft lips brushed lightly across mine as if he were testing things out. I closed my eyes and kissed him back, loosening up and letting go as he deepened the kiss.

The guessing game was over. He did want me. As much — if not more — than I wanted him. He stroked my face with both hands. I trailed my fingers up his back, his neck, and locked them in his hair.

I wanted to go on like this for hours, days. All my worries evaporated as I lost myself with him. I was blind, with closed eyes, but my other senses were overloaded. His kiss, his taste, his scent, his moans, his hands. I never wanted it to end.

But then I felt something else. First a small tingle on my skin, like a warning. Then the cold. It wasn't possible for me to be cold right now, not in this moment. Unless . . .

I stiffened. Donovan pulled back and looked into my wide eyes. "What's wrong?"

"I think she's here," I whispered.

We sat frozen for a few moments, not even breathing. Just waiting for something to happen. If Kayla had made the whole house shake before, I almost expected it to explode now. I braced myself for the fury, so tightly wound my muscles ached.

But it never came. The energy drained out and disappeared, and the temperature returned to normal. It was like she'd watched us for a moment, and then left. Was she giving us privacy? Or planning to kill me in my sleep? I didn't know. All I knew was that my perfect moment was over.

"You should go home now," I said softly.

And I would wait to see just how angry Kayla was.

chapter 23

I barely slept Wednesday night, tossing and turning, my consciousness on high alert. At any movement of air, any creak or slight sound in the house, my eyes snapped open and my heart pounded loudly in my ears. I expected the worst, but nothing happened.

Maybe Kayla wasn't mad. Maybe she was glad Donovan was happy and moving on.

Or maybe she was just biding her time . . .

In class on Thursday, Kane asked if we were still on for Saturday night. I told him yes and suggested the clearing again. I needed something decidedly friendly and not "datey" and somewhere Kayla's friends would be.

As weird as I felt making plans with Kane after what had happened with Donovan, I had to keep focused on my main goal: solving Kayla's murder.

Donovan was standing against my locker after last period, waiting for me with a crooked smile. It was clear that our kiss had changed everything. I'd been so aware of him all day, like my entire being was attuned to his proximity. In the cafeteria at lunch, I felt his eyes on me while I was chatting with Alexa, and I couldn't stop grinning. In between periods, we passed each other once in the hall, and I felt electricity shoot through my body. My pulse quickened, my temperature rose, my mind raced. No one else had ever had that effect on me before. It was wonderful and intoxicating but . . . the timing was wrong.

Romance could not be the focus of my life right now. Protecting Colby was my top priority. So finding Kayla's killer had to come before everything else. Donovan had texted me that morning that he had an idea for our "project" that he'd tell me about after school. Unfortunately, I also had something to share with him. Something I didn't know how he'd react to.

I reached my locker and felt the spark from being near him again. He leaned forward and gave me a quick kiss on the cheek. But I involuntarily stumbled back a step and looked around to see if anyone had seen.

Uncertainty flickered in Donovan's eyes, then went away. He probably figured I was against PDA. "So," he said, choosing to ignore the awkward moment. "Ready to hear my idea?"

All I could feel was the invisible mark on my cheek where his lips just were. I wanted to throw my arms around his neck and repeat yesterday's make-out session, right there in the hallway. But we couldn't. And I had to tell him that.

"Sure," I said, my voice barely audible.

He shifted his backpack from one shoulder to the other. "I think we should pay a visit to Kayla's parents."

I had to admit, I'd thought of that. But the idea gave me a rotten feeling. "They moved," I said.

"Only a couple towns away. I found their new address online. We can head over there and ask them some questions. See if they can think of anything that might help us."

"I don't know . . ." My voice trailed off. It seemed dirty to be interrogating Kayla's grieving parents. And I wasn't about to tell them she wasn't at rest — they didn't need to hear that after what they'd been through.

"The only thing is . . ." Donovan paused. "I don't think it's a good idea for us to . . . you know . . . act like a couple in front of them. I haven't seen them since the funeral, and they probably still think of me as Kayla's boyfriend and —"

I put up a hand and stopped him midsentence. "I agree." I took a deep breath. This was the conversation I'd been dreading all day. But now that it had come up naturally, I had to just say it. "Actually, I've been thinking we should keep our . . . keep . . . *us* . . . a secret for now."

His eyes met mine, and there was no mistaking his disappointment.

The last thing I'd wanted was to hurt him. I started babbling. "Just until we find out the truth about who killed Kayla. After that, she can be at peace and we can . . . move on."

He tilted his head to the side. "You're scared of what she might do?"

"Yeah." *Among other things.*

Donovan scratched the back of his neck. "I guess I'm okay with keeping it a secret for now."

Our talk was going easily so far. Might as well get it all out.

"And there's one other thing." I shifted my books into the crook of my arm. "I'm supposed to hang out with Kane again Saturday night."

He shrugged. "So cancel it."

"I kind of don't want to."

Donovan's features fell. He looked nearly shattered. So I spoke quickly before I hurt him even more. "Not like that. I want to go so I can learn more. For our project. Kane can give me access to her old group. Her friends."

He took a moment to let this sink in. "That's why you went to the clearing with him before," he said with tentative relief.

I nodded quickly. "I don't have feelings for him. But he and I, hanging out together, could give us the answers we need."

Donovan lightly blew out a long breath. "For the record, I don't like any of this. Hiding. Going out with Kane."

"It's temporary."

"I know." He reached up to push his hair out of his eyes, out of habit since his hair wasn't even long anymore. His fingers instead raked down his cheek. "Just promise me one thing. When you go out with him, go somewhere public. Don't be alone with him."

"Why?" I cracked a smile. "Jealous?"

He didn't smile back. Worry lines creased his forehead. "I just don't completely trust him."

Donovan and Kane obviously had no love for each other. But on my drive to Kayla's parents, Donovan's warning stuck in my head and made me start thinking. Could Kane have pushed Kayla? It didn't feel right. Despite his player reputation, Kane had been nothing but a gentleman with me.

But we were only starting to hang out. He and Kayla had known each other since they wrote with crayons. A relationship like that runs deep. And, perhaps, after years of always getting whoever he wanted — except Kayla — Kane couldn't stand it anymore. He seethed every time he saw her with Donovan. And figured if he couldn't have her . . . no one could.

And then Faye's words echoed in my head. About Kane only hanging with me to feel closer to Kayla . . .

I gripped the steering wheel tighter and forced myself to focus on the road. That line of thought wasn't giving me any answers, only the willies. I stopped at a light and looked down at the crumpled paper on my lap. Donovan had scribbled down directions he'd gotten online to the Sloanes' new place. I decided it was best to go alone, but I didn't even know what I was going to ask them yet. Or how I'd even bring it up.

Hi! I'm Jade! I'm living in your dead daughter's house. She was a bully in life, and guess what? She's still one in death, and she's forcing me to solve her murder. Can you help?

I sighed heavily. This was a bad idea.

The light turned green, and I took a left. The drive was only twenty minutes, but the town seemed a world away. It was more rural, a bit run-down. I actually laughed out loud when I saw a pickup on blocks in someone's side yard, because it reminded me of my hometown.

Why did the Sloanes move from Woodbridge to here? It seemed like a strange choice.

I finally reached their road and squinted at the number on the first house. My foot lifted off the accelerator and the car slowed while the numbers counted down. As 129 Gillums Road came into view, the car coasted to a stop, and I threw it into park.

This had to be a mistake.

I looked down at the paper and back up at the house before me. It was a rental. One half of a duplex. From what I'd heard from kids at school, the Sloanes weren't exactly known for their humble living. They were downright materialistic. From Kayla's clothes to Mr. Sloane's luxury cars to Mrs. Sloane's beautifully appointed, grand colonial home.

It *was* only natural for Mr. and Mrs. Sloane to want to leave the house their daughter had died in and, yeah, now that it was only two of them they could downsize. Buy a cute smaller place in a different neighborhood. But this wasn't downsizing. This was downgrading. The paint was peeling, weeds reached out of cracks in the driveway. Donovan must have given me the wrong address.

The front door opened and I slunk down in my seat. Mr. Sloane lumbered down the two cement stairs and bent over to pick up the bundled newspaper on the driveway. His hair was greasy and forked out in all directions. His open robe barely concealed the fact that he was only wearing boxers underneath. It was late afternoon and he wasn't even dressed. I recognized him from some pictures online, but he was like a different man. In those pictures, with Kayla and her mother, he was always wearing a suit and looking well put together.

My heart sank as I realized what happened. He must have quit his job. Her parents were so overtaken by grief they were unable to work. They couldn't afford another house like their last one because they couldn't gather the strength to go to a job every day.

I rested my head on the steering wheel and closed my eyes. *What was I doing here?* I wasn't walking up to that door. Kayla's parents were a mess. My conscience wouldn't let me add to their grief. I'd have to figure this thing out without them.

With one last glance, I put the car into gear and pulled away.

During the drive home, the sky turned from a light gray to a dark, metallic color. The clouds were sweeping past quickly, a sign that it was going to pour. I parked in the empty driveway, wondering where Marie and Colby were. They should have been home from his swimming lesson by now.

A big gust of wind shook the trees. Leaves rained down around me as I walked up the path to the front door. I used my key to get in and closed the door behind me. As usual, I felt the air with my senses, checking for Kayla's energy. Something wasn't right. It didn't feel like Kayla, but the house felt unnatural. Probably because it was too dark for the late afternoon, due to the encroaching storm.

I flipped on lights as I made my way to the kitchen. There was a note from Marie on the table:

Went grocery shopping.
Please put the lasagna in the oven at 4:00.

I glanced at the clock. It was already four thirty. Whoops. I hit the preheat button on the oven and wandered back to the living room.

The sky had darkened in only minutes, like someone had slipped a veil over the world. The wind moaned, rattling the windowpanes. I gazed outside. Rain would soon start pounding. Maybe even one of those rare fall thunderstorms. I leaned in and pressed my nose against the cool glass.

And jerked back when I heard a muffled thump from upstairs.

I froze and held my breath, listening hard. A creak, followed by a soft scrape — movement. Marie never would have left Colby home alone when she went to the store. I dashed to the bottom of the staircase and called out, "Hello?"

Silence. I peered up at the landing. Because of the darkness, I expected to see the glow of the bathroom nightlight casting an orange radiance across the hallway. But there were no lights on.

I thought I saw shadows collecting in the gathering dark, forming a person, a girl. It looked real, too real. I dug the heels of my hands into my eyes. I was driving myself crazy, putting my imagination into overdrive. Kayla wasn't at the top of the stairs. I just thought she was because I half expected her to be.

I waited motionlessly for a few moments until another sound filled the void — a loud snap, like wood splintering. It came from the direction of Colby's room. Kayla's room. Panic swelled inside me like a wave. Kayla must have finally been delivering retribution for my kiss with Donovan.

My heart pounded harder and harder as I took the stairs up, one by one. I imagined tendrils of black reaching out for me, waiting at the top, readying to push me. I pressed on, grasping the railing in a death grip, tighter and tighter the higher I rose. I reached the landing and immediately scurried to the right, away from the gaping hole of the stairwell.

Cold air swirled down the hall. Not icy, like the usual blasts I felt now and then. It was refreshing, actually, since I was covered in a sudden sheen of sweat. Colby's door was closed. My hand hesitated over the knob for a moment.

I steeled myself for what I would find inside. Some poltergeist-like trick with the furniture? Or perhaps just a traditional room trashing like she'd given mine. I turned the knob and gently nudged the door open with my shoulder, ready for anything.

But the room wasn't trashed. I should have felt relief, but I was only confused. The closet door Colby always kept closed was open and so were some dresser drawers, but mostly the room seemed untouched. And the cold? That was nothing supernatural; it was coming in from the open window. I wondered briefly why Colby or Marie would have left it open, but as I stepped over to it, that confusion turned to fear.

It wasn't only the window that was open. The screen was pushed up, too. Like someone had gone *out* the window. But no one could do that — unless they could fly. This was the second floor.

I leaned my head out, looked down, and my throat tightened. There *was* a way to get in and out — without the gift of flight. I stared at it and wondered why it hadn't occurred to me before. It was one of my favorite touches to the house: the winding ivy.

Someone had climbed the trellis.

It hadn't been Kayla making noise upstairs. It was a real live person. Someone had broken in and — when he or she heard me — broke back out via the trellis. But why? What did the person want? What had they done here?

I brought my head back in, pulled down the screen and the window, and locked it. I gazed at the woods beyond. We had no neighbor on this side. No one would have seen who it was.

A shiver coursed through me. The day Kayla died, Mr. Tucker swore up and down that he hadn't seen anyone else come in or out of the house. And it made sense — from his viewpoint he could see both our front and side door. But he couldn't see this side. Someone could have snuck in and out by climbing the trellis, and Mr. Tucker never would have seen them. In fact, if that was how the killer got in and out of the house *that* day, there was a good chance that it was that same person who'd done it now.

The killer had just been in my house.

From the Diary of Kayla Sloane

Sometimes I think no one loves me. Not my friends. Not 28. Not even 1 and 2. Not really.

I think the only reason 1 and 2 even had a kid was because a baby was the "in" accessory among their friends at the time. They don't want to be with me much and granted I'm not exactly a ray of sunshine around the house. But maybe they're the reason why.

If I'm sad, they don't ask me what's wrong. They avoid me. They only want to talk when I have good news to share.

If I died today, they probably wouldn't even care. It would just be an excuse for 1 to buy a new Donna Karan black suit.

I wonder what would happen if I just disappeared.

chapter 24

Later that night, Marie plodded into the kitchen, dressed in her scrubs, a coffee mug in her hand. The bags under her eyes were darker than normal, and she still had a full night of work ahead of her. She was in one of her moods, probably exacerbated by the fact that Dad wasn't coming home until Sunday *and* that I'd forgotten to put in the lasagna.

As if I didn't have enough to worry about — like a killer breaking into our house this afternoon. But if I told her about that, she'd ask me for proof. And, of course, I had none. Nothing was broken or stolen. She'd call me a liar again and nothing would come from it but more fighting.

She brought her coffee to the table and sank into a chair. "Guess I'll be working the overnight shift on an empty stomach tonight," she said groggily.

It took all my willpower not to roll my eyes. Yeah, I hadn't had a chance to put the lasagna in the oven before she and Colby returned. But she could make herself a sandwich before she had to go. Plus, I hear hospitals have these things called cafeterias and vending machines. I didn't say any of that, though. I just quietly sat and pretended to do my homework. The sounds of SpongeBob drifted in from the living room.

"You know what Colby's kindergarten teacher said today?" Marie said bitterly.

I shook my head no.

"She said he seems tired during the day and accused me of not putting him to bed early enough. Would you believe that? That boy goes to bed plenty early." Marie rubbed her face. "The only one around here not getting enough sleep is me."

Marie was perpetually tired, no doubt about that. And — despite the defensive Mom act she was pulling right now — I knew she was worried about Colby. I could see it in her eyes.

I thought about giving honesty a second go-around. Twisting a pencil in my lap, I said, "He goes to bed early, but he doesn't always stay asleep." I paused, giving myself one last chance to back out, and decided to go for it. "He's scared sometimes —"

She cut me off. "Don't even start with that ghost nonsense again, Jade." She shot me a look. "I don't want to hear it."

I slammed my textbook closed and stood up. "Fine." And added silently, *Keep your head in the sand.*

Marie pulled her hair back with an elastic band and moved on, quickly pushing aside my attempt at truth. "I need you to babysit Saturday night. The other nurses invited me out."

"I can't," I tossed over my shoulder. "I have plans."

"You'll just have to change them to Friday night. This is the first time they've asked me to come out, and I could really use some friends in this area."

"Well, I have to make new friends, too." Frustration filled my voice. "And I already babysit at least three nights a week."

Anger leaked into my voice. I was sick of being taken for granted. I didn't mind taking care of Colby. I loved that kid so much I'd rearrange the night sky if he wanted me to. And I knew we didn't have the kind of money most families in this town had, so I had no problem pitching in. But it would be nice to be thanked now and then. After all, I was enrolled in Overachiever High and was the sole person responsible for getting rid of a vengeful ghost.

Marie snapped, "I'm sorry your half brother is such a burden to you."

The words were like a sucker punch. My mouth opened and closed, shocked at the venom leveled at me. Marie paled, knowing instantly she'd gone too far. She probably wished she could take the words back, but they were out there, hanging in the air between us. No one had ever referred to Colby as my half brother before. I despised the word. It was technically true, but the insinuation was that we weren't fully connected.

"He is not a burden to me," I seethed. "I love him more than anything. If you even *knew* what I was doing for him . . ."

"Are you guys fighting?"

Both of our heads turned to the doorway. Colby stood wide-eyed, his thumb in his mouth. He hadn't sucked his thumb in three years.

I rushed over to him. "No, it's okay."

He pulled his thumb out. "I heard you."

"It was just a little disagreement." I held his tiny hand in mine. "Want to go upstairs and I'll read you a story before dinner's done?"

He looked at Marie, who must have nodded some form of encouragement over my shoulder. "Okay."

I threatened to tickle him on the way up the stairs, and he giggled as he climbed them. When we reached the landing, I said, "What book do you want?"

He hesitated, staring at his open door. "Can we read in your room instead?"

"Sure, buddy. Why?"

He peeked down the staircase, presumably to make sure Marie wasn't in hearing distance. "The girl was in my room again last night," he whispered. "She was just watching me. Like she wanted something. She didn't even try to talk like she usually does. Then she left. It really scared me, Jade."

I dropped to my knees beside him so I could look him straight in the eye. "It's going to be okay, Colby. I'm working on a way to make her go away. Don't worry."

"Are you sure?"

The little tremble of fear in his voice made my heart ache. Made me hate Kayla for messing with him. And hate Marie for not believing me. But Colby didn't need my anger right now. He needed confidence.

I cracked a smile and did my best Darth Vader voice. "I find your lack of faith disturbing."

Colby cackled like he always did. My Darth Vader was a sure thing.

"Seriously, buddy. I'll protect you. You have nothing to worry about."

I pulled him into a tight hug and rubbed his head. He still had that soft, fine hair. It smelled of baby shampoo and innocence.

I *would* protect him. Whatever it took.

Friday night I put on jeans and a red T-shirt and tossed a hoodie over it. Comfy and not sexy in the least, so Kane wouldn't get mixed messages. I slid a rosy shade of lipstick on and used cover-up on my chin (it always breaks out when I'm stressed). Satisfied, I nodded at myself in the mirror, grabbed my phone and car keys, and left for my non-date.

When I'd first asked Kane to hang out Friday night instead of Saturday, he was a little reluctant and said that he'd planned on going to the football game. But that just happened to be perfect. Tons of people were going, so I'd get to do some research on Kayla and also keep my promise to Donovan about staying in public. I convinced Kane that going to a high school football game was just what I wanted to do, and we made plans to meet there.

I'd sent Alexa a text, inviting her along, thinking the more the merrier. But she replied that she'd rather mentally count prime numbers to infinity, which I think was her way of saying she'd rather watch paint dry than go to a football game.

Kane was waiting for me in the parking lot as planned. He patted his buddies on their backs and shouted a "see you in there" while he walked over to me.

"Hey," I said. "So are we going to win tonight or what?" I smiled awkwardly, hoping my sudden surge of school spirit seemed legit.

But Kane looked as uneasy as I did.

"What's wrong?" I asked.

"Nothing." He shoved his hands in the pockets of his jeans. "It's just . . . meeting at a high school football game isn't really what I had in mind for our second date. I wanted to pick you up and take you out to dinner somewhere nice."

Second date? I almost laughed, thinking he was joking again, but he was watching me intently, waiting for my reaction. He was serious. This wasn't just hanging out to him. He really thought it was a date. That was why he'd been reluctant before.

I panicked, thinking fast. If I shot him down, hurt his feelings, the night would end now. I wouldn't get to spend hours with Kayla's friends, listening to gossip, figuring things out. I needed to be here tonight.

Making a last-minute decision, I grinned and playfully slapped his arm, "Don't be silly. We'll have just as much fun here as we would at a fancy place. That stuff doesn't matter to me."

"It matters to some girls," he said with a bitterness in his voice that made me pause.

I had seen all the girls at school throw themselves at him. His lack of money clearly didn't matter to them. But it had obviously mattered to someone. I ventured a guess. "Is that why Kayla wouldn't go out with you?"

He looked back up, meeting my gaze. "She said it was because our friendship mattered too much, but I knew the real reason was because she loved nice things and I couldn't come through in that department."

Materialistic wench, I thought. "Well, I'm not Kayla. And I think it's a great night for football." I grabbed his hand and gave it a little squeeze, but let go quickly, not wanting him to read too much into it.

It was enough to convince him, though. His demeanor lightened. "All right, let's go in before there are no seats left."

"It fills up?" I said, surprised.

"Not most weekends, but this is the biggest game of the year. We're playing Alton." At my blank expression he added, "Our rival. *Everyone* shows up for this game."

As students, we got in free, but Kane caved to the 50-50 raffle pressure and bought some tickets. We got our hands stamped, and Kane steered me through the crowd toward the bleachers. He wasn't kidding. The place was packed. We slowly climbed the metal stairs, looking for a place to sit. Then, seemingly out of nowhere, Kane placed his hand on my shoulder in a possessive move. I was surprised, until I saw him flash a look at someone.

Donovan sat on the bleachers with a couple of his friends. They'd probably dragged him here, and he looked miserable enough to begin with. But when he saw Kane and me — together — the boredom drained from his features. He turned away before I could see what expression replaced it.

Oh no. Did he think I'd lied to him and made plans with Kane for two nights? I wanted him to look back, so I could send him some sort of message with my eyes. But he didn't.

"Woodward! Over here!"

A few hands waved from the sea of red and black, and as we got closer I recognized the faces. The popular crowd. Kayla's crew. Exactly where I needed to be sitting. The guys moved over to make room for us.

From the row in front of us, Madison turned around and said, "Faye was sitting there. Keep room." But no one paid attention to her. The team had jogged onto the field, and the bleachers erupted in a loud roar of cheers.

After the game preliminaries were done, the crowd settled down a bit. As I saw the adults sit back down, my knees started to bend, but then I realized the student section — everyone around me — remained standing. *Guess we stand the whole game?* I didn't know. I'd never gone to games back home.

After the first play, the guy to my left pushed into me with a "move over." Our row was full enough but apparently someone had insisted on squeezing in on the end. I was shoved up against Kane, who didn't seem to mind.

"Faye's back," Madison said, pointing to the end of the row. Gulp.

I turned my head, expecting to see her standing there, arms folded, foot tapping, glaring at me. But she wasn't. Her eyes didn't even go to mine. They stayed on Kane, longingly. Then she turned away, shoulders slumped forward. Her whole posture reeked of despair. This "second date" of ours seems to have been the nail in her coffin of hope.

A lump formed in my throat. I owed that girl nothing, but still. I don't like to hurt people and pain was evident on her face. I wanted to dart over there and whisper in her ear, "This isn't real. I don't want him." But I couldn't trust her any more than I could trust anyone else in this town.

"Here we go twelve!" Kane yelled through cupped hands.

I leaned toward him. "Who's twelve?"

He pointed toward a big guy on the field. "He's on the team. The lacrosse team."

"Oh! I didn't know you could be on both teams."

"Sure. Lacrosse is a spring sport. A few guys from the team play football in the fall."

"Why don't you?" I asked over the cacophony of the marching band.

"I don't want to spread myself too thin. Academics take a lot of my time and I try to keep focused on lacrosse. I play in an indoor league during the winter. And I make sure I practice every day in the fall. Hit the wall for twenty minutes."

I had no idea what "hit the wall" meant, but didn't want to extend the sports conversation too long by asking. I know nothing about sports, especially football. Sitting there on a chilly Friday night was usually the last thing I'd want to do. I only fit in by copying what everyone else did. I groaned when they groaned, clapped when they clapped, and stood and exchanged high fives when we got a touchdown. And I didn't even erroneously call it a "great goal." Good for me.

By halftime, I was ready to stretch my legs, mingle, and eavesdrop. You know, detective work.

"I'm going to head to the concession stand," Kane said. "You want anything?"

My teeth were chattering and I would have loved a hot chocolate, but didn't want him to get it and come looking for me right away. "Not yet," I said. "Thanks, though." Most girls seemed to be walking toward the main building. "I'm going to head inside for the bathroom," I added.

The metal stairs vibrated as a bunch of us descended at once. The smells of popcorn and hot dogs had my stomach growling, but I ignored my hunger. I had work to do. I kept my ears open while I walked through the crowd. I hoped to get involved in some conversations, try to get people to tell me more about Kayla like they had the night of my party.

I was about to join the line for the girls' room when a shadow farther down the hall waved to me — from the doorway to the art room. I sped down the hall past six other rooms. The door was cracked open, but it was dark inside. I pushed the door open, let my eyes adjust, and smiled. Donovan straddled a chair that had been spun around. His arms were draped over the back, his chin resting on his clasped hands. When he saw me, he stood in one swift motion.

"You came," he said.

I rushed up to him. I knew what I'd said in school about keeping us quiet, but we were alone here in this darkened room, and I couldn't hold back. I threw my arms around his neck, rose up on my tiptoes, and pulled his face to mine, kissing him. He responded instantly, his tender kiss quickly turning hotter. His hands tightened on my waist, drawing me closer to him.

I wanted to stay like this, in this room, all night, but knew we couldn't. I pulled back, and we both took the moment to catch our breaths. He leaned forward, resting his forehead on mine and whispered, "I hate seeing you with him."

"I had to switch nights for the date. I'm sorry I didn't tell you."

"I figured it was something like that."

I had so much to tell him — about Kayla's parents, the intruder, but we didn't have time. "Can you come over tomorrow? I'll fill you in on everything."

"Absolutely. In the meantime . . . please be careful."

"I will. I promise." I paused, hating what I had to say next. "I need to get back."

"After one more kiss," he breathed and our lips joined again. But only for a moment.

Because I heard a click.

Donovan froze, his biceps hardening under my hands. I turned and squinted at the bright light of the hallway. In my rush to touch him, I'd left the door open behind me. No one stood in the doorway now, but that noise had been familiar and distinct. The kind of noise a phone makes — when it's taking a picture.

chapter 25

Donovan dismissed the noise as the click of the wall clock, but I'd been so sure it was the whir and snap of a camera phone. Or maybe I was getting paranoid. That wasn't too hard to do when your house is haunted and you're surrounded by murder suspects.

I really did have to use the bathroom, though. That part of what I told Kane wasn't a lie. But before I pushed the ladies' room door in, my ears perked up. Someone had said Kane's name.

I didn't immediately recognize the girls' voices, and pressed my ear against the door, straining to listen.

"Seriously, your brother is so hot."

"Ew, guys, shut up." Ellie's voice.

"Is he dating that new senior?"

Um, that would be me. They are talking about me.

I listened closer as Ellie replied, "I think so. But I don't know."

The other girl snorted in disbelief. "How can you not know? You two tell each other everything."

"I don't know because *he* doesn't know. They're taking it slow."

Another voice. "I can't imagine living in that house, where Kayla died. Gross."

"Seriously," said the first girl. I guessed there were three in there. Ellie and two of her sophomore friends. "I bet that nasty old man watches her like he watched Kayla. What a perv."

They knew about Mr. Tucker? My mind was processing this as the door suddenly swung inward. I stumbled, making it quite obvious that my ear had been on the wood.

"Oh, hey, Ellie," I said, smoothing my hair and walking past her into the bathroom.

Her two friends continued on out the door, but Ellie hung back. "Can I talk to you?" Her voice was sweet as usual, but her eyes were different. Suspicious.

"Sure." I pretended to primp in the mirror. "What's up?"

"What's going on with you and my brother? I mean, are you into him or what?"

My eyes found hers in the reflection of the mirror, and I felt like she was seeing right through me. I was using Kane and she sensed it. I understood her protectiveness. Respected it. I can only imagine how I'd feel about Colby's girlfriends when he was old enough to date. I couldn't imagine anyone being good enough for him.

I slowly turned around. "We're friends. I don't think either of us is rushing into anything." I smiled to try to set her at ease and hoped that the blush forming in the hollow of my neck didn't betray the nonchalance I was forcing into my voice.

Ellie's posture seemed to relax, but doubt remained in her eyes. "Friends are cool. I just wanted to see if you're on the same page. I don't want him getting hurt, you know?"

Kane was lucky, having a sister like this. I wanted to tell her that. Maybe someday I would. But right now I had one priority and that was saving my own brother. I was doing my best not to lead Kane on, but if I did a little bit — well, that was something I had to live with. But it wasn't like I was completely faking. I did want to be friends with him.

"And one more thing," she said, worry creasing her forehead. "Watch out for your neighbor."

"Mr. Tucker?"

"Yeah. There's something not right about him. The way he watches. And . . ." she lowered her voice. "Kane told me something Kayla said that I've never been able to forget."

I involuntarily stepped closer. "What?"

"That when she first moved into the house when she was little . . . there were weird piles of dirt in his backyard. Like Mr. Tucker had buried something."

Or someone, I thought.

By the time I returned to the bleachers, the third quarter had already started. The conversation about Mr. Tucker had added a mental chill to the already cold air, and I wished I'd worn a coat instead of a hoodie. But when I reached Kane halfway down the row, he smiled and said, "There's my girl!"

I flinched. *My girl.* In front of everyone. We were suddenly but surely *not* on the same page.

He held out a Styrofoam cup. "Even though you said you didn't want anything, I figured you could use a hot chocolate."

I felt a dozen eyes on me, gauging my reaction. If I rejected the "my girl" thing, it would hurt his feelings. And I didn't want to do that, especially in front of his friends. Plus, I needed access to those friends, hopefully only for a little while longer.

I inhaled a deep, wavering breath. "That was so nice." I took the cup from his hands. "Thanks."

I drank a sip and winced as the heat slid down my throat. I tried to swallow my guilt with it.

I went home after the game, a mix of emotions boiling and bubbling in my stomach like a witch's cauldron. I was a good person. Not the type to lie to people, fake my way into a crowd, lead a boy on. I told myself over and over that I was only doing what had to be done.

I crawled into bed and pulled the covers up to my chin, relieved to finally be warm. The night had taken a lot out of me. I hadn't played a game out there on the field, but mental exhaustion can wipe you out just as much. Soon, sleep came over me with a welcoming, warm haze.

But hours later, in the blackest dark of the middle of the night, I was instantly awoken by a sharp cry. I shot up in bed, holding the comforter up to my face as if it could protect me. My eyes took their time adjusting to the darkness, but my ears were immediately attuned. I listened hard for any sound over the heavy beat of my startled heart.

Had I imagined it? Was it a dream?

I had to check on Colby, just to be sure.

As I slipped out of bed, my breath was loud in my ears. I padded quietly down the hall, the floor cool under my bare feet. Hushed murmurs came from my parents' bedroom. I peeked my head in. Dad was gone, not returning until Sunday. Marie had fallen asleep with the TV on. The bluish glow illuminated her sleeping face.

The cry came again. Colby's cry. The sound pierced my heart like a bullet.

I rushed into his room, my quick footsteps almost making me slip on the hardwood floor. He lay in his bed, peacefully at first glance. But as I moved closer, I saw the scrunched up expression on his face. He was having a nightmare.

I was considering whether or not to wake him when a loud thud came from behind me. Colby's prized baseball, one Dad had caught at a Red Sox game, was on the floor. It was always, always on Colby's dresser. I realized, with building trepidation, that it couldn't have fallen off the grooved pedestal on its own. It had to have been nudged.

The temperature in the room plummeted. I started to shiver uncontrollably. I wanted to rub my arms in a feeble attempt to get warm, but my muscles seemed frozen and stuck.

I stared in rapt attention as the ball began slowly rolling toward me. The stitches thumped against the floor as the ball scuffled along. Fear slithered over me, around me, tightening, suffocating.

Colby's nightmare.

The rolling ball.

They were messages. Reminders. Kayla was playing with his toy, but could just as easily play with him. Possess him at any time. Make him do anything.

"I'm working on it," I whispered through my suddenly dry throat. "I promise."

The ball kept on its slow, purposeful roll.

"I made progress tonight. I have a strong suspect. I'm going to investigate him further tomorrow. I have a plan. I'm close, I know it."

The ball stopped.

Kayla was in control. She could lose her patience with me at any moment. And she needed me to know this. Fear and panic clawed its way up my throat, wanting to emerge in a scream. I swallowed it back down, forcing myself to stay strong.

Colby's face had changed back into his usual angelic sleeping expression. His nightmare was over.

For now.

From the Diary of Kayla Sloane

1 and 2 told me a secret today. And, all of a sudden, I have to worry about stuff I've never had to worry about before.

I don't know what I'm going to do.

chapter 26

After breakfast Saturday morning, Marie and Colby left to go to some farm a few towns over. It actually sounded kind of fun. They were going to do tractor rides, go apple picking, all that fall stuff.

Me? I was planning on a little breaking and entering.

I'd told Marie a friend was coming over and we were going to do homework. When she found out it was a boy, she gave me this little smirk and an eyebrow waggle. A full night's sleep and the promise of Dad returning tomorrow had done wonders for her mood.

Donovan arrived fifteen minutes after I texted him. His hair was damp and he smelled faintly of soap. I wanted to pull him into my arms and spend the day drowning in his kisses, but Kayla had made it clear last night that I had no time for that anymore. In fact, time was running out.

I led Donovan into the kitchen, sat him down, and caught him up on everything. That Kayla's previously wealthy parents weren't anymore. That someone had broken into my house, though I had no idea what they'd been looking for. And, finally, that Mr. Tucker might not just be a harmless old guy who spent too much time looking out his window.

"Phew." Donovan leaned back in the chair. "That's a lot to take in." He chewed on his thumbnail for a moment. "I don't know what to do next."

"I do." I sat up a little straighter. "Every Saturday, at eleven o'clock in the morning, Mr. Tucker goes out. I've noticed it two weekends in a row." I glanced at the clock on the wall. "If he does it again, ten minutes from now, I'm breaking into his house."

Donovan's head rocked back in surprise. "Hold up. I don't know if that's such a good idea."

"Why not?"

"Well, for one, it's against the law. Second, what if he comes home earlier than you expect and catches you? If he is the person who killed Kayla, he won't hesitate to do it again."

I smiled. "That's where you come in. You're my lookout. If he comes home, text me and I'll feel the vibration in my pocket and get out of there."

He shook his head. "It's dangerous. I think you're rushing into this. We can look into him more, yeah, but —"

"I *have* to rush," I blurted out. "I have no time left."

His eyes met mine. "What are you talking about?"

I sighed and pulled my fingers through my hair. "The night of the party, after we cleaned up and you left, something happened." I paused, not wanting to say the words out loud because they sounded so crazy. "Kayla possessed Colby."

Donovan's jaw dropped. "Your little brother?"

I nodded. "She somehow took over his body and told me she could do it again at any time and that, if I didn't find out who killed her, she'd kill him." The words sounded so absurd I wouldn't have believed it if I hadn't seen it myself.

"How — how —" he stuttered. "How can that even happen?"

"The night of the party, the Ouija board opened some sort of door and gave her this power. This access to him." I shook my head. "We never should have messed with it."

"Why him? Why an innocent little boy?"

"Maybe he's the only one she can possess. Or maybe she chose him to control me. To get what she wants. She knows I'll do anything to protect him. So she gave me the ultimatum — find her killer or Colby dies. She gave me another warning last night. I have no time to waste, Donovan. She'll kill him. She told me so."

"I can't believe that. I mean, yeah, she's not the nicest girl on the block, but I can't believe she'd kill a little boy."

"She did some mean things when she was alive," I said.

"Yes, she did." His voice took on a faraway sound. "She did some terrible things . . . but that's different from murder."

I wondered again, for a moment, if Donovan was holding something back. "Well, I'm not going to take any chances with my brother's life. I'm giving her what she wants, no matter what it takes. I'm breaking into Mr. Tucker's house. Now. Whether you help me or not."

I slipped in a back window easily enough, but now that I was inside I didn't know what to do. Mr. Tucker's house was dark and musty. Faded, outdated wallpaper lined the walls. Heavy curtains and dark, ornate furniture gave the home a gloomy feel. I first went to the living room window that faced my house. I didn't know what I expected to find. A big note tacked to the wall saying, *This is why I stand sentinel over my neighbors' daughters?* But it was just an ordinary window.

There had to be something to his behavior. It was more than odd. It was almost . . . compulsive. Like he *had* to watch. And it wasn't like he'd had some single-minded obsession with Kayla because he watched me, too. Was he a pervert? Was it some pedophile thing? An involuntary shiver coursed through me. I never got that vibe from him, but would I really know?

I had to find out. I moved from room to room on the first floor. Everything looked normal. No dead bodies in the freezer. Just an old TV in the living room. He had a small den, but no computer, just stacks of books and newspapers. I searched through them and found nothing suspicious or pervy.

I moved to the bottom of the staircase and gazed up. If there were anything to find, it would be upstairs.

The house was a small Cape. Upstairs only had a bathroom and two bedrooms. The bath was plain and clean. The master bedroom held nothing unusual. I even checked his — eww — underwear drawer and under the bed. The only strange thing was that the wallpaper and bedding were more feminine than I'd expected. I moved on to the second bedroom, my last chance at answers.

The door was closed.

Strange, I thought. He lived alone. Why keep a room closed? Unless it was something he didn't want to see every time he walked by. Something he didn't want to be reminded of. Flashes from crime dramas flickered in my brain. Serial killers on TV usually had a room where they let their crazy out. You know, walls covered with psychopathic scribblings, photos of eyes, and newspaper clippings of their crimes.

The hand I held on the knob started to tremble. I wanted to know what was in that room. Needed to know. But I was suddenly terrified.

I closed my eyes and pictured Colby's face, his laugh, his toothy smile. *Focus, Jade. You can do this.*

I turned the knob and gently pushed the door open.

My hand flew up to my mouth. It was a little girl's room. The twin bed had a bright purple comforter. Unicorn figurines, small and large, littered the top of a white dresser. A poster on the wall featured an old cartoon that wasn't even on TV anymore. The room was like a time capsule. A little girl had lived here. One who would be much older than me now, judging by the age of her things.

The only item that seemed out of place was a black, masculine-looking album on the little white desk. If this girl had a scrapbook it would have been pink and glittery. Not like this. I found myself gravitating toward it. I sat on the small chair, pulled the album onto my lap, and opened it.

At first there were only photos. Baby photos, toddler photos, family photos . . .

I froze. My eyes blinked and refocused to be sure. Yes, there was a picture that showed a much younger Mr. Tucker, with a wife and a little baby girl.

He'd had a family.

What happened to them? I thought about what Kayla had seen when they moved in. The dirt pile in the backyard. No. Just no. Mr. Tucker could not have murdered his family and then kept his daughter's room as a shrine to her. I knew in my heart this was wrong.

I kept flipping through the album. Disney World, holidays, first day of school, swimming in a pool, sledding . . . in every picture their eyes were bright and their smiles large. The photos stopped when the girl looked to be around seven or eight years old.

And then came the newspaper clipping.

I read it, with both horror and intense sadness. The little girl had drowned in the inground pool in her own backyard. The mother had been out running errands. The father, Mr. Tucker, had gone in the house to answer the phone. And in those few moments when the girl was alone, something happened, and she drowned. From a quote in the article, it seemed that Mrs. Tucker blamed her husband, calling it an "irresponsible choice to leave our little girl alone." I assumed she'd divorced him.

He was left alone, in this empty house, surrounded by the constant reminder of the family he'd once had and lost . . .

. . . because he wasn't watching.

I understood it then. Mr. Tucker was harmless. Just tortured. And apparently he considered it his penance to make sure no other girl died on his watch. That's why, when he learned that a little girl was moving in next door, he filled in his pool. Covered it with dirt. And watched her play in her yard. Watched her grow up. Even watched the day she walked into her house and never walked back out.

My phone buzzed in my pocket.

I heard the crunch of tires in the driveway.

I had to get out. I returned the album, closed the bedroom door behind me, and dashed down the stairs. As Mr. Tucker turned his key in the front door lock, I slipped out the back window and returned to my home.

Understanding him a little better, but nowhere closer to solving Kayla's murder.

chapter 27

After I told him about Mr. Tucker's daughter, Donovan went back home. We needed to regroup, think of another angle to try. And fast.

In a rare stroke of luck, Marie wasn't feeling well when she and Colby came home from apple picking so she canceled her night out with the other nurses. I wasn't glad she was sick, don't get me wrong, but this gave me another opportunity to get out there and search for answers. I'd found out at the football game that everyone was hanging at the clearing tonight.

I'd tried contacting Kane several times during the day, to see if he wanted to get together tonight, but he wasn't returning any of my texts. So I decided to go on my own. I knew enough of Kayla's friends now that I could just show up, even if Kane wasn't there. It actually might be easier for me if he wasn't. If I found myself embroiled in some good theory-tossing chats again, it would be nice to not have to worry about being pulled away.

A sense of urgency filled me to the marrow as darkness fell. Colby was already sleeping. Marie was huddled under a blanket on the couch with a cup of tea, watching some old black-and-white movie.

"Can I get you anything before I leave?" I asked, inching toward the door.

"No thanks." She sniffled. "I'm pretty sure I caught what Colby had last weekend. Sometimes these viruses lie dormant for a few days. Let's hope you don't come down with it, too."

Post-possession fever? Yeah, let's hope not.

I tossed a "feel better" over my shoulder and headed out into the night.

A bunch of cars were already in the park's lot when I arrived, and I followed the well-worn path through the woods toward the noise and the scent of campfire. As leaves and dirt crunched under my sneakers, I started mentally compiling questions and comments that could segue into fruitful conversations. I ran a thumb over my sterling silver marcasite ring, hoping the tiny filigreed stones lived up to their reputation for bringing about clear thinking. As the orange haze of the fire got closer, my confidence rose. I could do this.

The first thing I saw when I passed the tree line was Kane. With someone else.

This pretty little freshman with a high ponytail and a higher skirt was giggling and telling him some story while he stood with an amused smile on his face. When her little anecdote reached its crux, they both threw their heads back in laughter and she took the opportunity to put her hand on his arm. He didn't move it, didn't flinch. And I wasn't the slightest bit jealous. If she were doing that to Donovan, I'd probably have given her an ice cream scoop to the eyeball. But I was sort of happy, seeing it. I knew that Kane really didn't have his heart set on me. Once this was all over and Kayla was put to rest, Donovan and I could come out in the open, be a real couple, Kane would have no trouble moving on, and there'd be no drama.

I stepped fully into the clearing. Kane spied me over the other girl's shoulder and his faced morphed into an unexpected expression. Not guilt at being caught flirting with someone else. Certainly not happiness at seeing me.

It was rage.

He whispered something in the girl's ear and stormed toward me with long strides.

What was going on?

Laurie and Madison brushed past me, muttering something about trouble. I crossed my arms over my chest defensively. My eyes flicked around the party. Everyone was watching, anxiously awaiting whatever was about to happen.

"What are you doing here?" Kane said in a clipped voice.

I put my shaky hands in the back pockets of my jeans so he wouldn't see how nervous I was. "I'm here for the party. Didn't you get my texts?"

"Those weren't the only texts I got today." He spat out the words with such contempt that I flinched.

"I'm sorry. I don't know why you're mad."

He yanked his cell out of the pocket of his jacket, pulled a photo up, and handed the phone to me.

Someone *had* been there last night in the hallway. They'd snapped a picture of Donovan and me kissing. And sent it to Kane. From the looks on everyone else's faces, it might have gone to more than just Kane.

"Listen," I began.

"I don't have to listen to anything." He started to turn away.

"Wait!" I grabbed his arm. "I never set out to hurt you." My eyes begged him to believe me. But coldness came off him in waves. "I always insisted you and I were just friends," I explained. "I never said we were dating."

Kane's eyes flared. "You were using me! I knew you were investigating Kayla's death. I'd heard that around school and I thought it wasn't a bad idea. But then I find out that you were just using me for information about Kayla, and you were with Donovan the whole time. Him! Out of everyone."

I staggered back a step. "It wasn't just about Kayla," I pleaded. "I want to be friends with you. I always did."

"You're sick!" He jabbed the air with his finger, pointing it at my face. "You're living in her house, trying to get in with her friends, going after her boyfriend. You're mental!"

As he raged at me, I watched the hurt in his face. This was about more than me not wanting to date him. Faye had been right. His interest in me was because of history. Because of Kayla. Maybe hanging with me made him feel closer to her. Picking me up at her house, taking me places he'd taken her. He'd been using me just as much as I'd used him. But bringing that up would only infuriate him even more.

"It's not like that," I said. "Let me explain." But I knew, from the fire in his eyes, that I couldn't make him understand. Not now, anyway, while the wound was fresh.

"No," he said with finality. "I don't want anything to do with you. None of us do."

I glanced around. Everyone stood, clumped in circles, staring at me with contempt. I was out now. Ostracized. Excommunicated from Kayla's world and her friends. This must have been how Donovan had felt when they'd turned on him. One day in, the next day — out.

Panic gripped me as I realized that no one from that crew would talk to me anymore. So now . . . how could I uncover the truth?

I retreated from the clearing, the ire from everyone's eyes burning a hole in my back. But I'd only made it a few steps down the path when someone grabbed my arm.

I pulled it back, defensively, and looked over my shoulder. Faye stood with a finger over her lips. It was dark this far away from the fire, and I could barely make out her features. She jerked her head to the right, motioning for me to move deeper into the woods and away from the clearing. Curious, I followed her.

We were only a few steps off the path and into the thickness of the woods. The party still raged close by. But it felt like we were all alone.

"I need to talk to you," she whispered.

"So go ahead." I expected her to revel in my fall with a smug look on her face. But as my eyes adjusted to the darkness, I saw Faye flash me a guilty, almost regretful smile.

"I was the one," she said.

A branch scraped my neck, and I shoved it away. "The one what?"

"I sent the picture to Kane."

Faye was the person in the hallway? "Why? Why would you want to hurt him like that?"

"You were the one who hurt him," she snapped back defensively. "Not me."

"Then why are you grabbing me in the woods and confessing what you've done?" I asked with mounting anger.

"Because . . . I like you. I think you mean well. I'm sorry about what happened over there. I only sent the photo to Kane. He's the one who sent it to everyone else and went on a rampage. I never expected him to humiliate you like that."

So that's what Donovan had meant when he said Faye was no Kayla. She snuck around, manipulated, and betrayed — but then apologized after. The mean girl, win-at-all-costs persona didn't fit her as perfectly as it had Kayla.

"I just," she hesitated for a moment. "I wanted Kane to know, that's all. I didn't mean for the rest to happen."

We stood there in silence for a minute. I didn't quite know what to say. I understood her motives, but wasn't ready to forgive her. She'd ruined everything I'd worked so hard to put into place.

Faye leaned her shoulder against a tree. "You know, I always wanted to ask Kayla something, but never had the guts. I could ask you, too, since you find yourself in the same position." She waited, as if she needed my permission to ask.

"Go ahead," I said with a sigh.

"If you could have Kane, why on earth would you choose Donovan O'Mara? Not to be rude, but I don't get it."

I tried to formulate my thoughts into words. I could say that I was more impressed by Donovan's integrity than Kane's popularity. That the sensitive, dark, artsy guy made my knees weaker than the athletic golden boy. That, when I looked at them, Kane was a flashlight and Donovan the sun. But my thoughts muddled, and I knew it would make no sense to Faye who — it was obvious to me now — had always loved Kane.

So I only shrugged and said, "We want who we want, right? No matter what other people say. No matter what reason or reality we're faced with. No matter what facts our brains process. The heart's a stubborn organ."

Faye seemed stunned into silence. She swallowed hard, nodded, and stole a look toward the clearing. "Yeah," she said, agreeing and possibly understanding.

I felt for her. It must have been tough, all that time, loving Kane while he only longed for her best friend.

"Listen," I began cautiously. "I know you miss Kayla and this is hard, but if there's anything you know that can help me . . ."

She started shaking her head before I even finished the sentence. But I tried again.

"Faye, you were her closest friend. You're the one who knew her best."

She broke out into a sarcastic laugh. "No one knew Kayla. Everyone wanted to get into her orbit. But the closer you got to her the more you realized how closed off she really was."

"So she told you nothing?" I asked skeptically.

"She told me what she wanted me to know. The good stuff. What extravagant gift her parents got her. What compliment some boy said. What award she was up for. But it was all positive."

"She never . . . I don't know, suffered setbacks?"

"I guess she did. She just didn't speak of them. Her failures, her weaknesses, those were her secrets. And they went with her to the grave."

"You must have thought about this, though," I pressed. "You have no theories about who might have wanted her dead?"

"No."

I tried a different approach. "Someone broke into my house recently looking for something. Do you know what that could be? Did Kayla have something anyone would want?"

"She had expensive stuff, but that all would have moved with her parents." She threw her hands into the air. "I don't know why you're doing this. You're not going to find any answers."

Here she was again, acting defensively. Just like when she'd first found out about my investigation. It made no sense. If they were such good friends, wouldn't she *want* to know who killed Kayla?

"Why are you so against me looking into Kayla's death?" I asked. "Why does it bother you so much?"

"Because it was my fault, all right?" She spoke the words fiercely. Then, again, softer this time, she repeated, "It was my fault."

I took a small step back and a branch reached out and scraped at me like a bony finger. "What do you mean?"

Faye let out a deep, rattling breath. "This isn't the first time I've inserted myself into this little love triangle."

"I . . . don't understand."

"Let me paint you a picture. Kayla cheated on Donovan. With Kane. I found out and did something I'll regret for the rest of my life. I told Donovan. Kayla was my best friend, and I should have been loyal to her. I didn't care about Donovan, and if she'd been cheating on him with anyone else, I wouldn't have told. I would have stayed out of it. But it was Kane. She could have had anyone in the world. Why did she have to take Kane? So . . . I wanted to hurt her. It was immature of me. But whatever. I told Donovan."

My stomach turned. "When?"

"The day she died."

My intuition was right. Donovan had been holding something back. "So that's why he broke up with her that day."

"Yes, and that's why I denied their breakup to you in the hall. And why I didn't want anything to do with your little investigation. Because this whole thing is my fault."

"I don't get how this makes her death your fault."

She threw her hands into the air. "If Donovan pushed her it was because of information I gave him. If Kayla was so upset after their fight that she fell down the stairs, it was because of something I set off." She put her face in her hands and let out a sob. "If I hadn't told, the day would have gone differently, and she wouldn't have died."

My heart went out to her. "Not necessarily. Not if there was something else going on. Someone who would have killed her whether or not you told Donovan."

She looked up, shaking her head sadly. Her guilt ran so

deep I doubted she was even listening to me. "It's my fault," she repeated. "And every Sunday, when I see her parents all dressed up in church, I smile and nod at them, but on the inside I feel sick. Because they don't know I was the cause of it all."

"Wait." I held up a hand. "Her parents still go to church here in town?"

"Yeah. They got a new fancy house in a neighboring town, but still like to return every Sunday to see their friends. I hear them chatting, you know, about work and decorating their new house and all that and sometimes I can't believe life is moving on without her. Just last week Mr. Sloane was saying that they're planning a big addition to the house to keep Mrs. Sloane occupied and get her mind off Kayla."

All dressed up? Chatting with friends about work and home decorating? These weren't the Sloanes I saw the other day. Something wasn't adding up. Maybe they didn't want people to know how badly they were grieving? That they couldn't even get to work anymore, much less keep up with some grand mansion?

"What mass do they go to?" I asked.

Faye frowned. "Nine o'clock. Why?"

From the Diary of Kayla Sloane

7 has always wanted me. I know this. And maybe the reason I never wanted him back in the same way was because he made it too easy. But I care about him. I always have. And I feel sick over what I'm about to take away from him.

But I know what I have to do. I feel terrible, but I have no other choice. It's 1 and 2's fault. I'll never forgive them. But I've figured out a way to make myself feel a little better . . .

I can give 7 a consolation prize. Make him happy and ease my guilt in one fell swoop. I may be taking away what he considers rightfully his, but I'm giving him the one thing he'd probably trade it for . . . me.

And what about 28? Well, he already looks at me sometimes like I'm this giant disappointment. So I might as well go ahead and do something to actually earn his disdain.

chapter 28

I stood awkwardly in the church parking lot, scanning the parishioners as they exited. Finally, my eyes fell upon the two people I'd come here to see. Mr. Sloane plucked a piece of lint off his suit jacket while Mrs. Sloane draped a black shawl over a beautiful deep purple dress. I moved toward them, overhearing the end of a conversation.

"It sounds like you've got a lot on your plate with this new company and now building an addition to your house," a man said to the couple.

Mr. Sloane placed his hand on his wife's shoulder and responded, "It helps to keep her occupied. The color choices and the decorating . . . it's work she loves."

"Excuse me?" I interrupted. "Mr. and Mrs. Sloane?"

They turned to face me with identically polite smiles on their faces. I could see them searching their minds for a name to match to my face, but coming up blank.

"Um, you don't know me," I said. "I live in your old house."

The polite smiles faded and the well-dressed man quickly excused himself.

"I'm very sorry about your daughter," I started.

"Thank you." Mrs. Sloane clutched her pearls. "That's nice of you to say." The words were spoken as a dismissal, and they began walking, clearly anxious to get away from me.

I boldly stepped in front of them. "I need to ask you something."

The force I spoke with surprised them *and* me. But my concern for their grief was gone. This little act they put on here in town, refusing to show weakness, maintaining this air of arrogance at all costs, materialism above all else. It bothered me. Enough to ease any misgivings I'd had about talking to them. Besides, I only had one simple little question.

"Someone broke into the house this week and searched the room that used to be Kayla's. Do you know why someone would do that?"

"Obviously to steal something of yours," Mr. Sloane replied coolly. "All of Kayla's belongings are gone."

"Are you sure?"

"Of course," he insisted. "We either kept them, donated them, or distributed them to her friends."

"Her friends," I muttered. "Did any of them ask for anything in particular?"

"No, we just gave a few of her closest friends some of her clothing," Mrs. Sloane said, but her husband's expression had changed. Like he was remembering something.

"Well, there was one thing," he said. "But it didn't exist."

"What?" I pressed.

He turned to his wife. "Remember, someone asked about a diary?"

"Oh yes." She waved her hand. "It was silly because Kayla never kept a diary. And if she had, we would have found it among her things."

Unless she hid it so well that it was still in the house, I thought. "Who asked for it?"

Mrs. Sloane tapped a manicured fingernail against her chin. "You know, I don't remember. It was the day of the funeral and there were literally hundreds of people coming up to me. And I was . . ." For a moment, the mask of togetherness she wore slipped a bit. "I was in a bad place."

"And I'm sure it has nothing to do with your break-in," Mr. Sloane said, leading his wife away. "Good luck."

Maybe it didn't or maybe it did. But the only person who knew for sure whether or not Kayla kept a diary . . . was Kayla herself.

Dad was coming home later that afternoon, and Marie was running around like a crazy person, cleaning the house and planning dinner. When I offered to play board games with Colby up in his room, I thought she was going to drop to her knees and kiss my feet.

"Thank you, Jade," she said, patting my shoulder. "You're such a help."

Guilt lay like a block of lead in my stomach. If only she knew what I was really planning.

Colby was on the floor in his room, paging through a Star Wars sticker book. I didn't want to involve him in this. But it was the only way. And I was doing it to save his life, after all. But that didn't make it any easier.

"Hey, buddy." I sat cross-legged beside him.

He looked up at me and smiled. One of his top front teeth was loose. It would fall out any day and that smile would be forever changed. Part of me didn't want it to happen, didn't want him to grow up, to lose his innocence. Even though, in a way, he already had.

"You know how I promised you that I'd make the ghost girl go away?"

The smile faltered, but he nodded slowly.

"I'm working on doing that . . . but I need your help, Colby."

He blinked his big brown eyes. "What can I do?"

"You're the only one who can communicate with her. And I need you to do it. Just one more time. I need to get some answers from her. And then I'll be able to send her away."

"For good?"

"For good," I repeated.

He pondered that for a moment. "Okay. I'll do it."

"Great." I clapped my hands together. "We'll just wait until the next time she comes around and then you can help me ask her some questions."

"We don't have to wait," he said, closing his book. "I can call her."

"You can . . . make her show up?"

"Yeah, I did it before by accident."

That could have been a coincidence, but I plastered on an encouraging smile. "Okay, then let's do it now."

He crossed to his bed and sank down, closing his eyes. Only a moment later, my whole body hummed as Kayla's now-familiar energy filled the room. I couldn't believe it. Colby could not only see her, he could summon her.

The temperature plummeted. Colby opened his eyes. His head snapped suddenly to the right and he fixed on an empty corner. There was nothing there, but I knew Colby saw otherwise.

A chill seeped into my veins.

His eyes never left the corner. "She's here."

As Colby sat on his bed, expressionless, I realized he was much braver than me. Sweat trickled down my spine despite the cold in the room. I slowly stood to my full height, though my bones felt like they were made of jelly. If I took one step forward, my legs would collapse underneath me.

I angled my body in the direction Colby was looking and cleared my throat. "I'm close to the answer you wanted, Kayla, but I just need to know a few things first."

My eyes slid to Colby.

"She's waving her hand," he said. "Like she's saying, 'Go on.'"

"Okay." I faced the girl I couldn't see. I pretty much knew the answer to my first question, but wanted to be sure. "Are you here all the time?"

Colby said, "She's shaking her head no."

"Did you see someone break into the house a few days ago and search the upstairs?"

"She's shaking her head no again, but this time she's frowning, too."

"Did you keep a diary?"

I looked over my shoulder at Colby and his confused expression as he tried to read her. "I think she's nodding," he said finally.

"I need to know where it's hidden," I said.

"She's shaking her head no."

"I need to read it, Kayla. Someone broke in here looking for it. There must be something in there."

"She's covering her face." Colby squinted as he watched her. "I think . . . she's embarrassed. She doesn't want anyone to ever read the diary. Yeah, she's nodding to that."

"I have to read it," I pleaded. "Don't you want me to figure out who did this?"

"She's pointing to herself," Colby said.

Meaning she wrote it and even *she* can't figure out who killed her.

"But maybe I'll see what you couldn't," I said. "I may have information you don't. And when it's put together . . . I could figure out who it is."

The room was eerily silent for a long moment. "What's she doing?" I asked.

Colby shrugged, puzzled. "Just standing there. Maybe she's thinking."

I wrung my hands as I waited. She needed to agree. *Had* to. My access to her friends was cut off. This was the only angle I had left. "Please . . ." I whispered.

Colby shot up and jumped off the bed. "Under there!"

"What?"

"She's pointing under the bed!"

That made no sense. People would have found it under the bed. This house was empty when we bought it. Still, I threw my weight against the frame and moved the bed a few feet over.

Colby pointed enthusiastically at a spot on the floor. "There! She's pointing there."

At . . . nothing? I got down on my knees and ran my hand over the hardwood. Maybe a loose board? I pounded my fist around haphazardly until the pressure on the end of one board caused the other end to lift up. I gasped.

Colby reached over me, his nimble little fingers pulling up the board in seconds. And there, underneath, was a black leather-bound journal. I picked it up slowly, then clutched it to my chest. I stood and spun around, ready to thank Kayla for trusting me. But the energy leaked out of the room, the temperature rose, and I knew she was gone.

Her secrets hadn't died with her. They'd been buried within the house the entire time.

chapter 29

I pulled an all-nighter. A feverish, determined, adrenaline-fueled night of reading. As everyone in town closed their eyes, mine raced across Kayla's looping script. While the house slept, I learned Kayla's deep, dark secrets. I knew why she hadn't wanted anyone to read the diary. Many of the entries were sociopathically devoid of empathy for other people. But I held back all judgments and read each one as evidence.

By morning, I had the quirks and curves of her handwriting memorized. She used a numeric code, giving everyone in her life a sequential number, starting with the first time they were mentioned in the diary. Her parents were 1 and 2 and so on. I'd figured out the identities of the main players, taken notes, worked on a chart, and finally discovered what Kayla hadn't.

I knew who'd killed her.

My phone chirped and I gave it a glance. Donovan calling again. This was call number . . . four? Five? Plus countless texts. I hadn't returned one of them. He hadn't lied to me, but he sure hadn't shared everything he knew, either. And I didn't know why.

Plus, since I'd found the diary, I'd been kind of busy.

But now . . . I had time to answer his call. Tell him everything I read. Ask him why he hadn't told me the big reason he'd dumped Kayla. My thumb hovered over the button, but the phone went silent.

Just as well. This was something better done alone.

I glimpsed my reflection in the mirror. Dark bags circled my eyes and my hair was a frizzy mess. But I didn't want to waste any time showering. I wanted to get this over with. The digital clock on my desk read 9:00 a.m. A little early for a Monday with no school. We had the day off due to some teacher conference. But I didn't want to wait. Not now that I was so close to finishing this. To giving Kayla the closure she sought — and to saving my family.

Going downstairs in the same clothes I wore yesterday, plus the haggard look on my face, was begging for parent trouble. So I stripped off my shirt and reached around the pile on the floor for whatever was closest. My hands brought up a tight green long-sleeved tee. Good enough. I pulled it over my head and was about to leave the room when I saw my jewelry box.

I carefully lifted the agate pendant out and held it up to the light. It was a beautiful brown stone with streaks of orange and yellow. It had always reminded me of a sunset, but I didn't choose it now for its looks. It was a truth charm. And that seemed fitting. I clasped it behind my neck.

It was time to confront a killer.

I checked to make sure the recording function worked on my phone's app, then slipped it into my pocket. I slung my empty backpack over my shoulder and headed downstairs. The TV was blaring SpongeBob, so I knew Colby was down there. I was disappointed to find my father sitting beside him on the couch. It was so much easier to lie to Marie.

"Where are you headed this early?" Dad asked. "No school today, remember?"

He wore a Celtics T-shirt and his flannel pajama pants. His arm was draped up over the back of the couch and Colby was tucked up against him, warm and safe. The sight tugged at my heart. I wanted so badly to join them. To sit mindlessly on the couch, giggling at SpongeBob and Patrick's escapades.

Hopefully I would do that, very soon.

"To Alexa's house," I answered, averting his eyes. "Study session. Plus a . . . um . . . group project."

"I hope you won't be gone all day," he said, disappointment lining his voice. "I was hoping for some family time."

"Me, too," I said. I put my hand on the knob of the front door and didn't allow myself the last glance over my shoulder that my heart wanted. "I'll be back."

Several minutes later, I parked my car and walked up to the door of Kayla's killer. I pounded my fist on the wood. And waited for footsteps.

A few moments later, a shuffling came from within the apartment, and the sounds of someone fumbling with the lock. I slipped a hand into my pocket and hit the button on my phone. Recording. Ready to provoke a confession.

Kane opened the door with a sleepy but open face that shut down as soon as he saw it was me. He wore blue athletic shorts and a thin white undershirt. Running a hand through his bed-head mop of hair, he squinted at me and frowned. "You look like a girl who's been up all night."

I straightened my shoulders and stared him right in the eye. Confidence bloomed inside me like an awakening flower. With a strong voice I said, "I have."

"Well, I'm sorry your guilt is interrupting your beauty sleep, but I'm not interested in whatever apology you came here to give." He started to close the door in my face.

I slammed my palm against it and pushed my foot in the opening. "And what about *your* guilt, Kane?"

He reopened the door a slice. "What are you talking about?"

"You tell me. What keeps you up at night?" The prospect of finally getting the truth emboldened me.

"Is this some kind of game?" He shook his head. "You're loonier than I thought."

"I know all about Kayla," I blurted. "How she cheated on Donovan with you."

Kane's eyes narrowed. "It wasn't cheating," he snapped, not even bothering to deny it. "It was the start of a new relationship. She finally realized that I was the guy for her."

"Then why was it a secret?"

He held my gaze for a moment. "Because she wasn't heartless. She had to find a way to break it off with Donovan."

"Here's a way." I heightened my voice an octave and said, "'Hey, Donovan, I'm seeing someone else. We're done.'" I returned to my own tone. "How hard was that?"

Kane's eye twitched. "Maybe she did it that day and that's why she's dead. Did you ever think of that? She dumped Donovan for me and he killed her."

"That would be a great theory, except Faye told Donovan about you guys. And Donovan broke up with Kayla that day. Not the other way around."

"I'm sure that's what *he* told you," Kane said defensively.

"Actually Faye told me. Last night. But that's not all I learned overnight. I found out the real reason Kayla finally gave in to you."

"Oh yeah? And what's that?"

I paused to add a moment of drama before I dropped the hammer. I arched one eyebrow and said, "Pity."

He flinched as if I'd slapped him. "Excuse me?"

"She was taking away your future, your dreams. And — like you said — she wasn't completely heartless. So she gave you something in return. Something else you've always wanted. Her."

"What are you talking about, my future?" His defensive tone turned confused.

"I know about the money."

He shrugged, then crossed his arms over his chest. "Clue me in, then."

I swallowed hard. This was the moment. I was ready to drop the bomb and see the guilt on his face. "The assumption was always that you'd get the Bodiford Scholarship. You were the one who fit the requirements: all-state athlete with the highest class rank. But Kayla would have gotten it if her parents' wealth didn't disqualify her."

"Yeah, and . . ."

I thought back to the entry in Kayla's diary when she found out her parents' secret. Her father had lost his job. But appearances mattered more than anything to the Sloanes so the spending continued, the lifestyle went on. Until they couldn't hide it from Kayla anymore. They were in debt. Their money was gone.

Suddenly, she had to worry about how she was going to pay for college — something that had never crossed her mind before. But then she realized, with her parents' wealth gone, she qualified for the Bodiford Scholarship. Kane's scholarship. She and Kane were both all-state, but her class rank was higher. It was hers now.

"She found out the money wasn't there," I said. "Her parents were broke."

"That's not true." Kane shook his head. "Her parents still have money."

"Have you been to their new address?"

"No, but —"

"It's an act. They pretend everything's the same, they cling to it because it's all they have left. But the money's gone. Kayla suddenly fit the requirements for the scholarship. And she was going to take it. That's why she finally showed you some affection, after all those years, even though she loved Donovan. Because she felt bad for what she was about to do to you. That was how she dealt with her guilt."

His eyes watered as he continued to shake his head. "It's not true. It can't be true. How would you even know this?"

He seemed genuinely surprised, but I wasn't going to fall for the act. "I found what you broke into my house looking for. Kayla's diary. Kayla's own words show your motive."

His face reddened. "You think I killed her?" he asked incredulously.

"That's why I'm here, yeah."

He was absolutely still for a moment and something in his stunned eyes made my stomach tighten.

"Jade, I was playing in a lacrosse game the afternoon Kayla was killed."

I opened my mouth to retort, but my nerve faltered.

He let out a long pained sigh. "I scored three goals. You can look it up."

I stumbled back a step. He had an alibi. A solid one, too. I'd been so sure after I read the diary. It had all clicked into place. It all made sense. But now . . .

A concerned female voice behind him called out, "Kane? Who is it? What's going on?"

I started walking backward, my throat dry and my face in flame. "I, um, have to go."

chapter 30

Defeated and hopeless, I came home and went up to my room. The school's website confirmed Kane's alibi. I scrolled down to last season's schedule and, yep, he'd been playing a game that day. His goals were listed right there in the public record. He hadn't killed Kayla. I was back to square one. I knew nothing.

My heart heaved, equal parts anguish and fear burning in my chest.

The diary lay open on the bed beside me, almost mocking me. I thought it would have the answers but it only gave me more questions.

Almost everyone in Kayla's life had a reason to kill her. She'd bullied Alexa. Used a giant lie to ruin Faye and Kane's chance at a relationship. Cheated on Donovan. Plus countless other pranks and random hazings. It was like a manual for mean girls. No wonder she didn't want anyone reading it.

I turned onto my side and curled up, closing my eyes. I'd been tired plenty of times in my life. But this was an exhaustion I'd never felt before. Full body depletion. Gauge on empty. I had nothing left. I didn't even dream.

Something woke me, hours later. I gazed around the room through half-lidded eyes. My shade was up but the sky was already turning gray. I'd slept through most of the day. I pushed myself up into a sitting position, wondering what had woken me from a hard sleep. As my senses came to life, I realized what it was.

A chill slowly crept into the room. I felt Kayla's now familiar energy sweeping around me. I didn't have to see her to know she was angry and impatient. I could feel it in the air. She wanted me to talk.

I closed my eyes and pressed the palms of my hands into them, hoping she'd just go away. That if I ignored her, she'd disappear. But a rush of energy blasted at my face and swirled all around me like concentrated wind. With it came an instantaneous deep freeze that I felt through my skin and into my bones.

My eyes snapped open at the sounds of shuffling paper. The diary was still on the bed next to me, but its pages were being flipped back and forth by an angry unseen hand.

I knew what she wanted to ask. *What did you find out? Where did you go? Who did this to me?*

"I don't know!" I shouted. "I thought it was Kane. He had the biggest motive, but I was wrong. It wasn't him. And I'm no closer to finding the truth than I was at the beginning."

The pages stopped flipping.

I inched back on the bed, away from the diary, the silence scaring me more than anything. My back hit the headboard and I pulled my knees up to my chest. My whole body trembled.

The diary rose up by itself and flew across the room, smashing into the mirror on my vanity.

My eyes watered and I squeezed them shut, not allowing the tears to spill down my cheeks. "You'll never know who did it and you have to accept that," I said, forcing a stern, confident tone. "Release the house. Leave my brother alone!" I opened my eyes. "It's time to move on, Kayla."

I sat in silence for several beats, waiting for whatever she'd try next, but nothing happened. My senses were so jacked up that I couldn't tell if her energy was still with me or not. Sweat beaded on my forehead. I tentatively stretched my legs out and slipped off the side of the bed. Stood in the center of the room. Waited.

Nothing.

Tears flowed freely from my eyes. Tears of fear and disappointment. I'd failed. I was desperate. There was only one thing left I could do, no matter the consequences.

My feet pounded down the hall. Colby called out from his room, "Jade?" But I kept going, down the stairs, into the living room where Dad and Marie were watching TV.

Dad sat up straighter in his spot on the sofa. "What's wrong?"

"What was that bang?" Marie asked.

"It was *her*," I spat, more angry than frightened now. "She's haunting this house. She's been threatening Colby. You didn't believe me before, and I tried to handle this myself. Tried to give her what she wanted to save Colby. But I failed, so now I need you to believe me. We have to get out of here!"

Marie crossed her arms and rolled her eyes, immediately on the defensive. She wasn't going to believe me. Again. Dad looked back and forth between us in confusion. Hot, angry tears burned my eyes.

"You have to believe me," I repeated. "We have to leave."

Small, slow footsteps sounded behind me. Colby was coming downstairs. I was about to open my mouth and continue the fight right in front of him, but something in Dad's eyes made me stop. His expression was uneasy and that frightened me more than anything else had.

Colby plodded forward with awkward jerky steps, his head tilted to the side. No one said a word. All eyes followed him as he came up beside me. His lips curled slowly into a disturbing and decidedly un-Colby-like smile.

"No one's leaving." Colby's sweet childlike voice was gone, replaced with an older, knowing voice that was familiar only to me.

Marie pressed her fist to her mouth, suppressing a scream.

Dad stood quickly, arms stretched out toward his son.

"Sit down," Not Colby barked.

Dad fell back to the couch, his eyes wide with panic. Marie's olive skin paled in horror.

This was it. My punishment for failing Kayla. The air tightened around me like strong arms across my chest, making it hard to breathe.

Not Colby turned and met my eyes. My heart seized as a wave of chills spread over my body.

"Finish what you started," he/she said, calmly, but with underlying menace. "Get me what I want."

I fought against the fear, reached out, and planted two strong hands on his shoulders. "You've made your point," I hissed. "Get out of him."

Not Colby gave me one last evil grin, then his eyes rolled up. I caught him as he collapsed and Kayla's spirit left. I wrapped him in my arms and pulled him close, putting my ear to his mouth. He was breathing, but his body was already heating up with the fever.

Dad sat motionless, hands on his knees. Marie's body trembled, but at the same time she seemed frozen, her unblinking eyes glued to Colby. Then they both looked at me, seemingly for answers, like I was the parent and they were my children, huddling on the couch.

"Dad," I said. "Take Colby, put him in the car." I stood, scooping Colby up into my arms and handed him off.

"Marie," I ordered. "Pack a bag. Quickly. Bring the Children's Tylenol."

Tears rolled down her face as she nodded.

I glanced at the walls one more time and said to the air, "We're getting out of here."

chapter 31

I grabbed Kayla's diary, my mother's jewelry box, and nothing else. I called Alexa on the way and asked if it was cool if we spent the night. Not wanting to go into details, I said the house had a gas leak that was being worked on.

I'd figured we could sleep in an extra bedroom but Alexa's family actually had a separate guest*house* in the back. It had two bedrooms, a bathroom, and a living room slash kitchenette. Alexa's parents offered to cook us a big dinner, but we explained that Colby wasn't feeling well so they left us to tend to him. Which was good. We needed privacy.

Night fell and Colby slept peacefully in one of the bedrooms, Tylenol in his system and cold cloths on his forehead. Dad, Marie, and I settled around a little table in the kitchenette. They each sipped from mugs as I told them everything. What Colby had been through. What I'd been through.

"Why didn't you tell us?" Dad asked.

"I told *her*." I pointed at Marie. "I tried talking to her about Colby seeing a ghost. Not only did she not believe me, she threatened me. And then I was supposed to tell her Colby had been possessed? She would've had me committed."

Dad looked to Marie, possibly for her to defend herself, but she didn't. She sat still and quiet, eyes on her clasped hands.

"Well then why didn't you tell *me*?" he asked, returning his eyes to mine.

"You would have taken her side and you know it," I said softly.

"That's not fair, Jade," he snapped.

"Leave her alone," Marie said, lifting her face. "Don't you see? It's our job to protect the children and we failed. Jade came to me and I pushed her away. None of this is her fault."

Dad pulled his hands through his hair and groaned. "You're right. I'm sorry. All that matters is that we're safe now. We'll figure something out. Sell the house. I don't know." The chair screeched against the floor as he stood. "I'm going to check on Colby."

He closed the bedroom door behind him, leaving Marie and me alone in the tiny kitchen. I didn't know what to say. I was surprised that she'd stood up for me. Seeing Colby change in front of her own eyes must have shocked her into believing.

Marie smeared a tear off her cheek. "I want to tell you how grateful I am for all you did to try to save my little boy."

"He's not just your son, you know," I muttered. "He's my brother. I'd do anything for him."

"I realize that and I'm sorry for the things I said." She gave me a long look. "I know I've made mistakes since we became a family, but you didn't exactly come with a manual."

"You didn't come with a stepmom instruction booklet, either." I waited a beat and admitted, "I suppose we both could've been easier on each other."

I glanced at the wall clock. It was getting late. I figured it was time for us to both head to bed, but Marie quietly said, "You don't call me Mom."

I was surprised at the pain in her voice. It had never been my intention to hurt her. I twisted my hands as I struggled to explain. "I already have a mother. I felt like it would be betraying her if I called you that. I don't call you by your first name out of disrespect. I just can't do Mom."

"I understand," she said, nodding lightly. "It just felt like you never accepted me."

"But it's not like you accepted me, either. You barely look at me."

Her eyes slid to mine. "Because you're the image of her."

My throat tightened so much it hurt to swallow. "What?"

"You are a carbon copy of your mother. When I look at you, I see her. And when you look at me with disdain in your eyes, I feel like it's her, looking through you, judging me for marrying her husband. And I know I can't compete. Not in your eyes, not in your father's. How can you compete with a dead woman?"

I rocked back in my chair, reeling. Those were the same thoughts I'd had about Kayla and Donovan. Meanwhile I never realized that Marie felt the same way. Like she was competing against the memory of my mother.

Marie and I had more in common than I'd thought.

I reached across the table and put my hand over hers. "My mother's gone," I said. "You're here. You, me, Dad, Colby . . . we're the family now." And in that instant I realized our problem. We'd been looking at each other as intruders. She was an intruder on Dad and me, and I was an intruder to her, Dad, and Colby. Two separate families instead of one whole.

But, as we smiled at each other from across the table, I knew that would change. It was too bad it took something like this to help us understand each other, but things would be different between us from this point on. Not lovey-dovey. Not mother-daughter. But better than they'd been.

Marie's eyes were rimmed with red. "I should have believed you," she said.

"I don't blame you." I shrugged. "Most people would think I was crazy for saying Colby saw a ghost."

"No." She licked her lips and glanced around nervously. "I didn't *want* to believe you."

"What's the difference?"

She looked down at the coffee mug as she spoke. "You never knew my father. He passed away before I came into your family's life. I loved him very much. He was a sweet and kind man, but . . ."

"But what?" I pressed.

She looked up at me. "He claimed he could see ghosts. Not every day. Only a few times in his life. But he swore up and down that it was true. Some sort of gift he had. I never believed him. I actually thought he was a little bit crazy because of it."

Everything clicked into place. Why she'd shut me down so quickly. Why she stuck her head in the sand and refused to see the truth. "So when I told you about Colby and the ghost . . ."

"I didn't want it to be true," she said. "Because that would mean this was some gift he got from my genes. My father had been telling the truth all those years and I hadn't believed him. And now my own son has inherited it? It was too much."

"We'll see this through together," I said. She let out a long, trembling sigh, but looked better. I was glad she'd shared the truth with me. This was something Colby had to know about, too. Kayla was the only ghost he'd ever seen but, then again, it was the only haunted house we'd ever lived in. Even after all this ended, he might see another one sometime and he had to be prepared. But that was a conversation for another day.

A yawn overtook Marie, and I quickly followed with one of my own.

"I'm going to head to bed," she said, standing. "Your father and I will sleep with Colby. You can have the second bedroom."

We exchanged a quick hug, and then I cleaned up the kitchen. Mostly because I was wide-awake and needed something to keep me busy. After I was done, I peeked in the bigger bedroom and all three were fast asleep. I felt grimy and chilled to the bone. A hot shower sounded like heaven so I steamed up the bathroom and stripped my clothes off. I stepped into the shower, the hot water rinsing the dried sweat and tears from my skin.

Things would be better now. Many truths were aired. My family was all on the same page. We would just never enter the house again and everything would be fine.

I heard the patter of little footsteps in the bathroom and saw the shadow of Colby through the shower curtain. He got up on a little step stool so he could reach the sink. After a moment he left, so I figured he'd gotten himself a drink from the tap like he did at home. The poor kid was so feverish he was probably half asleep.

After I was pretty sure I'd used up all the hot water for the entire property, I opened the shower curtain and reached around in the fog for a towel. It was one of those thick expensive towels and it felt so soft against my skin. I felt good. Like real good. For the first time in a while. I dried my face and wrapped the towel around my torso. Venturing out of the tub, one foot at a time, I squinted through the fog. Then froze. A prickle ran down my spine as I realized what I was seeing.

Words were written in the steam on the mirror.

I'M STILL HERE.

In a fit of panic, I rubbed down the mirror, wiping out the letters. But I couldn't erase them from my mind. I couldn't deny what they meant.

Kayla wasn't haunting the house anymore. She was haunting Colby. Her ability to possess him at will didn't end at our property border. It came with him, wherever he went.

We couldn't run. We couldn't hide. Colby would never be safe.

Gripping the towel tightly, I raced into the other bedroom. Colby was sleeping again. Dad and Marie snored lightly on either side of him. I backed out of the room, my heart pounding loudly in my ears. I retreated to the bathroom, put my dirty clothes back on, and tied my wet hair up in a ponytail. I padded into the kitchen and quietly grabbed the keys and the diary from the counter. I got halfway to the door and stopped.

Mom's jewelry box was on the table. My fingers reached in and, almost as if it was calling to me, I pulled out the stone I had in mind. Peridot. The one I never wore. The pendant swung lightly as I held it up to the light. It was a perfect circle, a beautiful piece, but my mother had worn it the day she died and — other than stuffing it into the bottom of the box — I'd never touched it since. Which is ironic, since the stone's main use was to help the wearer let go of the past.

But I felt the need to hold it now. Maybe for its secondary use — to guard against evil spirits.

For a moment, I watched the light reflect off the crystal in shades of green. Then, without thinking, I clasped it behind my neck and let the pendant fall under my shirt, against my skin. It lay in the hollow of neck, just as it had in my mother's. Rose and fell with my breaths, as it had with hers.

I took a moment to close my eyes and focus. I imagined the gemstone filling me with strength and determination. Then I opened the door.

This had to end now.

I didn't even remember driving to the house. I'd been on auto-pilot, fueled by adrenaline. One minute I was sneaking away from Alexa's home and the next pulling into the driveway of the house I'd promised myself I'd never step foot in again.

I closed the car door quietly, not wanting to wake the neighborhood. Our outside light was on a timer so I thank-fully didn't have to walk through complete darkness. I held the diary in my hand as I followed the stone path to the front of the house.

The tall outline of a person stood facing the door. At the sounds of my footsteps, the shadow turned around and morphed into a familiar face.

I gripped the keys tightly in the palm of my hand and steeled myself. "What are you doing here?"

chapter 32

"What are you doing here?" I repeated.

"I had to talk to you," Donovan said, holding his hands out palms up. "You wouldn't answer my calls or respond to my texts. I had to make sure you were all right." He aimed a thumb behind him. "No one's answering the door."

"That's because no one's home. We left. Kayla . . ." The words caught in my throat.

He moved closer and reached out for me, concern etched on his face.

I stepped backward. Holding the diary up, I said, "You lied to me. Kayla cheated on you with Kane."

"I didn't lie," he insisted. "Nothing I said was untrue. I'd wanted to change her, to make her into a better person. Then I found that I couldn't and broke up with her. All that was true."

"But what about the cheating?"

"I never told anyone about that. Why bother? To ruin her reputation? She was dead. I would've rather let people think she was better than she really was. Faye agreed to keep it secret, to protect Kayla's memory. I never spoke to Kane about it. He doesn't even know Faye told me."

He does now, I thought. I looked up into Donovan's kind eyes, the blue shining in the reflection of the light. He should have told me, I still felt that. But at the same time I understood why he hadn't spread the truth around. Despite the terrible things Kayla had done, Donovan was a gentleman to her — even in death. His integrity wouldn't allow him to badmouth her. He wanted to let her rest in peace.

Unfortunately, she hadn't.

Donovan reached out for my hand and I let him grasp it. "What happened?" he asked. "What is that? What did Kayla do?"

"It's her diary. I found it and read it, hoping to figure out who killed her. I thought it was Kane, but I was wrong. Then she . . . lost her patience with me." I shook my head at the awful memory. "She possessed Colby again. This time in front of my parents. They freaked and we all left. We're staying at Alexa's."

"Then why are you back here?"

"I found out she can possess Colby anywhere. I have to go in there. I have to — somehow — end this now."

Donovan glanced over his shoulder at the darkened house. "I'm coming with you."

My heart constricted at the idea of putting him in danger. "No, don't risk it. I'll do this myself."

He shook his head and gripped my hand tighter, protectively. "There is no way I'm letting you go in there alone."

I didn't argue any further, both because I knew he wouldn't change his mind and because I was less scared with him beside me. I found strength in being close to him as I used my key to unlock the door.

We stepped inside and I ran my hands along the wall until I found the light switch. It illuminated the staircase as Donovan closed the door behind us.

The air was unnaturally cold. Energy buzzed through the room with almost tangibly sharp shards. It nipped at my skin like thousands of microscopic teeth.

"Do you feel that?" Donovan asked, his eyes looking around wildly.

I nodded. My hair lifted up from my shoulders with static electricity. Kayla was all wound up. I'd never felt her energy this strongly before. I wished I could see her, communicate with her like Colby did. Just this once.

Why was she so mad? Because we left? Because I came back? Because Donovan was with me? I didn't know and without Colby I had no way to find out. But the unprecedented amount of energy both unnerved and motivated me. There was something different. Something added. And it made me feel like we were coming to the end. That Kayla was close to getting what she wanted.

"Come on," Donovan said, tugging at my arm. "Let's go upstairs."

I followed him up the stairs as the charged air swirled around us. It wasn't centered on me; it seemed to be everywhere. All through the house.

We stopped at the top and stood in the hallway. "What now?" Donovan said. "What's your plan?"

"I don't have one. I was just going to . . . try to talk to her, I guess. I don't know."

I felt stupid now. Unprepared. I gripped the diary tightly in my hand and yelled, "Kayla! I'm here to tell you this has to stop now!"

A rush of air swooped by me, headed down the hall. I stumbled back. As my hand touched the wall, a blue spark flew from my fingers, and I gasped.

"The air is charged with electricity," Donovan said, feeling the open space with an outstretched hand.

"This isn't going to work. I can't talk her down. She wants to know who killed her and she won't stop." Panic rose in my throat.

Donovan placed his hands on my shoulders. "Deep breath. Look at me. Jade, look at me."

I did and immediately my breathing slowed.

"Try to think," he said calmly. "Was there anyone else mentioned in the diary who would have a motive?"

"Well, yeah, but I'll never be able to figure it out. The whole diary is full of motives for murder."

"Wait." Donovan let me go and put his hands up to his temples. "But who knew it existed?"

I blinked. "What?"

Donovan spoke excitedly. "Whoever broke in here to steal the diary and erase their motive for murder . . . they obviously knew the diary existed."

I felt the blood rush to my face. I was almost dizzy. Why didn't I think of that before? Rather than searching for who'd had the biggest reason to kill Kayla, all I had to do was figure out who knew about the diary. Her parents didn't know. But someone else did. Someone had asked her parents about it. I held my breath as a tingling of memory buzzed in the back of my head.

"There was a passing mention," I said. "It meant nothing at the time. I was reading it for motives, nothing else. I read it all in one night."

"What is it?"

"Kayla did have an entry where she mentioned the diary to someone."

"Who? Who!"

I opened the diary, flipping through, searching for the entry. "Kayla used all these number codes for people. I figured out who was who, but it took a while . . ." I found the entry. My finger followed the rounded handwriting: *I already gave her some tips on handling boys and friends. Told her to trust no one. Keep her secrets to herself and her diary.*

I looked up sharply as I gasped. "I was right all along."

"Kane?" Donovan said, confused.

"No. The motive. I was right about the motive. But the killer wasn't Kane."

A creak of hinges made us turn around. Colby's bedroom door was opening. Slowly.

The peridot pendant felt strangely warm against my skin.

"I see you found what I was looking for," a solemn voice called out from the black of the room.

Donovan moved in front of me, arms spread wide, in an attempt to shield me. But I wasn't scared. Several feelings tussled for dominance inside me. Anger won out. This was why Kayla was so wound up. She'd been watching her killer search for her diary.

"Come out!" I called. "It's time for the truth."

One small foot stepped out first into the light, a black ballet flat. Then the rest of her came into view.

Ellie Woodward. Kane's sister.

"You were so close this morning," she said, in a small, almost-apologetic voice. "And I heard you tell Kane you'd found the diary. I had to come back one last time to try to steal it. It was the only evidence."

"You?" Donovan gasped. "You killed Kayla?"

"I didn't want her dead," Ellie said, her eyes wide and wet. "I never planned for it."

"But . . . why?"

I already knew, but I let her speak so Donovan could hear for the first time. Why Kayla had broken his heart and why she'd paid with her life.

"I started to wonder," Ellie said. "Why, after all this time, after all his years of trying, did Kayla finally give in to my brother? Why now? And why in this dirty, secretive way? I mean . . . cheating? Really? If she truly wanted to be with Kane, she'd have dumped you for him. But it wasn't like that."

I should have realized Kane's motive for murder was also Ellie's. They were so close. They told each other everything. Of course she'd know. "Did Kane question why she was seeing him?" I asked.

"Kane was in denial. He told me to keep my mouth shut and mind my own business. He said Kayla only needed time. He'd loved her for so long, I think he was happy to take whatever he could get from her. But I didn't trust it. Every move Kayla made was meticulously planned out. I knew there had to be a reason."

"What happened the day Kayla died, Ellie?" Donovan asked.

"I knew she kept a diary. I snuck into the house when no one was home."

"You used the trellis," I said.

Nodding, she said, "Kayla told me that's how she snuck out of the house sometimes. I just wanted to read the diary. To see what she'd written about Kane. To make sure she wasn't using him for something. I only wanted to protect my brother, that's all."

"But you never found the diary," Donovan pointed out. "Even when you snuck in again after Jade had moved in. So what happened?"

"While I was looking for the diary Kayla came home with you." She closed her eyes, remembering. "You were fighting. You'd found out she was cheating with Kane. You were furious. You broke up with her. She actually . . . begged for your forgiveness. Sniveling, crying. I'd never seen her like that — weak and vulnerable. She tried to explain herself, justify it."

"How?" I said, though I already knew.

"She cheated with Kane because she felt guilty," Donovan answered.

Ellie nodded. "She was stealing the Bodiford Scholarship. Just as you said at my house this morning."

I looked sharply at Donovan. "She told you about the scholarship that day? You knew and didn't say anything?"

Donovan said, "Yes, but it didn't matter. Kane had a lacrosse game that day. After I found out she'd died, that was the first thing I checked. I knew he didn't kill her and I never imagined . . ." His eyes went to Ellie. Her small stature, her innocent stare. No one would ever think her capable of murder. But, in protecting Kayla's memory and not telling anyone about her and Kane . . . Donovan had also protected a murderer.

"How could you?" he said to Ellie.

"That scholarship was rightfully Kane's," she spat. "It was his future. We have nothing. Our mother works minimum wage. And financial aid is such bull. He'd graduate six figures in debt. Meanwhile, Kayla grew up rich. Never had to work a part-time job on top of her studies like Kane did. She and her mother racked up charge after charge with designer clothes, five-hundred-dollar handbags. Sunglasses worth what my mother makes in a week. The whole family was always so concerned with appearances that they lived over their means and then when her dad got laid off, they had nothing. So now, out of nowhere, she's going to qualify for the need portion of the scholarship. And she was going to take it. She didn't deserve it."

Rage reddened Donovan's cheeks. "She didn't deserve to die!"

Ellie's chest rose up and down, but she ignored Donovan and continued in an eerily calm voice, "You left her alone, sobbing. You slammed the door. And I was standing in the hallway, taking it all in. My brother *worshipped* her and she was going to ruin his future. Just like that. The anger built up inside me. I was shaking with the power of it. And it just sort of . . . exploded out of me. I rushed down the hall and pushed her from behind. It wasn't until she landed at the bottom that I'd even realized what I'd done." She looked back and forth between us. "I didn't plan it, I swear."

"Was she still alive?" I asked.

"No. I walked down and . . . it was obvious. She wasn't breathing and her neck was . . ." She buried her face in her hands. "I wish I hadn't done it. I wish I had snuck out of the house while she was crying. Or, even if she saw me and ruined me at school . . . nothing Kayla could do to me could amount to what I've done to myself. I shouldn't have pushed her. I should have just gone home and told Kane. I should have left. If I had done that one thing, all our lives would be different."

"Does Kane know?" I asked.

"No. And when he and my mother find out . . ."

Ellie's mouth snapped shut as if she couldn't bear to finish. But I knew why the tears rolled down her cheeks. Not for Kayla. But because everything she, Kane, and her mother had worked so hard for — all the planning, all the work — it was all ruined now. Because of the one moment of Ellie's life that she lost control. One moment.

"If I could go back in time . . ." Ellie said, more to Donovan than me.

"I know," I said. I reached into my pocket for my phone. "We have to call the cops. Don't try to run."

She shrugged. "There's no point. You can't run from yourself. Part of me is glad it's finally going to be over. And I won't have to hold it inside anymore." She leaned up against the wall for support. "Secrets are like a disease. They infect you and destroy you from the inside out."

"I'm at six Silver Road and we need the police right away," I said into the phone and then hung up. The details could wait until they arrived.

The three of us stood at the top of the stairs, in the place where Ellie had pushed Kayla, and waited in silence.

Silence. I straightened. I'd been concentrating so much on Ellie's confession that I hadn't noticed Kayla's energy disappear. Had she found peace? Had she really left?

My mother's pendant had begun to irritate my neck. I reached for it and gasped as it burned my fingers. *What the?* I looked down. The green peridot seemed brighter than normal, glowing almost.

A sharp intake of breath came from Ellie. I looked up to see her head rock back. Her eyes shut. Her entire body shuddered as convulsions racked her small frame. I looked at Donovan, unsure of what to do. But before we could act, a strange, guttural sound came from her. She slowly opened her eyes, cocked her head to the side, then gave us a bitter smile. And I knew . . . it wasn't Ellie anymore.

Tendrils of fear unfurled in my chest. "Kayla," I whispered.

Donovan stared at her with growing horror as he realized what I already knew. Ellie/Kayla looked at him. Before, emptiness had filled Colby's eyes. But now Ellie's eyes were filled with love.

In a soft voice, she said to Donovan, "I'm sorry for what I did to you. You always did deserve better than me." And then, as if in suggestion, her eyes slid to mine.

"You got what you wanted," I said coldly. "Now go. Forever."

"I will," she said. "In just a moment. But, on my way out, there's one last thing to do . . ."

That familiar menacing smile spread across her lips. She took an awkward step toward the top stair.

"Wait," I said, suddenly nervous. "What are you doing?"

Ellie/Kayla looked over her shoulder at me. "Getting my revenge."

"No, don't!" Donovan yelled.

"We told the police," I said. "Ellie will be punished."

"A pretty little honor student with a wonderful sob story?" Ellie/Kayla snorted. "They'll call it an accident. She needs to pay."

My mother's pendant burned against my skin. I felt feverish — from the inside out. "Don't do this," I said.

"She did it to me," Ellie/Kayla replied.

"So be better than her!" Donovan said. "Be the girl I wanted you to be. Be the girl I thought you *could* be."

The hard look in her eyes faltered and softened for a moment. I thought he'd done it. Convinced her. But it was only a fleeting second and her determination returned. I realized it first and without thinking, reached out. I wrapped my arms around her from behind, hoping to have the strength to pull her back, away from the top step. But she was unnaturally strong. The writhing mass of our bodies tangled together and launched off the landing.

Donovan's eyes widened with fear. His hands reached out for me, but — too late — grasped only air. I screamed loudly in surprise as my feet no longer touched the ground. Ellie/Kayla had jumped, even with me attached to her. It wasn't a perfect swan dive, though. We fell forward and to the side, awkwardly, haphazardly. I let out a second, smaller scream of pain when my head smashed into the wall. And then, clinging to each other, we continued to fall.

Probably only two seconds had passed, but everything was in slow motion. It was like my mind knew — this is the last moment of my life. Slow it down, make it last. I was flying through the air.

Ellie lost her grasp. Like a cell splitting in two, we separated, identical expressions of horror on our faces as gravity pulled us down. Ellie's eyes were her own — terrified, confused. Kayla had gone, left us forever.

Left us to die.

But then, suddenly, my body was filled with electricity. My skin hummed with an energy like nothing I'd ever experienced. I felt connected . . . tethered . . . to something or someone else. And instead of falling, I was momentarily frozen in place. Instead of the pull of gravity, I felt the weightless sensation of floating. Of being held . . .

Cradled.

The scent of jasmine filled my senses. The sudden familiarity of it was overwhelming. An ache gripped my chest and my tightened lungs were unable to take in a breath.

But then my feet were planted on a stair. My hand reached out and grasped the railing. And the energy left me. Only a hint of jasmine remained in the air. And at the moment I realized I was safe, I heard the thud of Ellie's body hitting the bottom.

Head first.

chapter 33

Two weeks later, I walked out of the police station after giving my final statement. I sat on the steps to wait for him.

The carpet my parents had installed saved Ellie's life. The police arrived to find her unconscious body at the bottom of the stairs. Donovan and I were lucky that she lived, as it would've looked mighty suspicious if she hadn't. Despite a severe concussion, she was fine.

We left out the ghost stuff and kept it simple, telling the police that Ellie came to my house and confessed to Donovan and me that she was the one who had pushed Kayla. Then, in an ironic twist, she herself fell down the stairs.

A half-truth, but it was the most they were going to get.

The police told me there was going to be some sort of plea deal. So my work was done. No trial. That didn't mean Ellie would get off easy. But the specifics of her punishment didn't matter to me as much as finally knowing the truth about that day and bringing peace to my home.

Looking back, we'd all been haunted by the dead and buried. Not just the house. We'd carried ghosts inside of us, making our spirits weary. Dad, Marie, and I with my mother. Donovan,

Faye, Kane, and the others with Kayla. And perhaps heavier than the ghosts were the secrets we carried.

But we opened ourselves up and now, just as the house was free, so were we. At last.

At first, Dad and Marie still wanted to sell the house and move. It was like we'd flipped places. *I* was the one telling *them* the house was safe and we should stay. Colby helped me convince them. His mood had lifted and he was back to his sweet, cheerful old self.

Kane removed himself from qualifying for the scholarship — which might have been taken away anyhow. He was now hoping for a partial lacrosse scholarship to a state school. After everything that happened, I couldn't be his friend. But he needed someone now more than ever, with what his family was going through. So I told him something I'd learned from Kayla's diary. Something that made him give Faye another shot. They both deserved a chance at happiness.

Shuffling footsteps came from behind me and I looked up to see Donovan settling down next to me on the stairs. The tightness lifted from my shoulders. Just having him beside me made the sky seem brighter, the temperature warmer.

"Are you okay?" he asked, his blue eyes lit with concern.

Those were the same words he'd said that day, when my mother had saved my life on the staircase. I knew it had been her — the jasmine scent, the way she'd held me. I'd worn the pendant ever since, but never felt her presence again. Still, the gemstone that used to give me only anguish now filled me with a sense of tranquility. How my mother had managed to possess me — to save me — I don't know. Maybe her pendant had opened a door like the Ouija board had done for Kayla. Maybe Donovan was right when he'd said it doesn't hurt to believe in a little magic now and then.

I wove my fingers through his. "I'm great. How'd it go in there?" He'd had to give his final statement also.

"Fine. I'm just glad it's done." He brought my hand up to his mouth and kissed it. "And that you're all right." He took in a deep breath. "Talking about that day . . . remembering you falling . . . I was so scared that you were . . ." He shuddered and squeezed my hand.

"I'm here," I reassured him. "It's over."

He reached out to touch my face and let his thumb trail down my cheek and my jawline, sending a pleasurable shiver through me.

He spoke quietly, his eyes never leaving mine. "I spent months in this . . . limbo. I was alive, technically, but only going through the motions. Kayla had done these awful things and suffered a terrible end. I felt all this guilt. And everyone in school, aside from a couple friends, turned their backs on me. I think I just . . . lost faith in humankind." He took another deep breath. "But then you came along. You woke me up. Made me see the good in the world again. You saved me, Jade."

He reached into his pocket and pulled out a little box. "I wanted to give you a little something, a token or . . . whatever." His cheeks reddened as he stumbled over his words. "To tell you how much you mean to me."

I opened the black velvet box. A pair of drop earrings sat nestled inside, the gemstones a deep, dark green. Almost a match to my peridot pendant, but these weren't peridot. They were emeralds.

I didn't bother hiding the blotches on my neck. I was pretty sure he was used to them by now.

"For your collection," he said.

"Thank you." I ran my finger over the smooth stones. "They're beautiful."

"I chose them because, um, well I looked up the meanings online and I wanted, um . . ."

Seeing him so nervous was the most adorable thing I'd ever witnessed.

He took a moment to catch his breath and tried again. "Do you know what the gemstone means?"

I couldn't help the smile that overtook my face. "Emerald is called 'the stone of successful love.'"

"Yeah," he said, matching me smile for smile and blush for blush. "That."

ACKNOWLEDGMENTS

When I was in elementary school, I wrote my first book. It was only around ten pages long and involved a house that swallowed children who walked by. So I would like to thank my parents, for continuing to buy me horror books even after they read that. And thanks to my teachers for encouraging me. That little girl with the freaky story didn't grow up to become a serial killer. Just a writer.

As always thanks to my agent, Scott Miller; my editor, Aimee Friedman; and the fantastic team at Scholastic, including Lauren Felsenstein, Nikki Mutch, Becky Shapiro, Stacy Lellos, Bess Braswell, Elizabeth Parisi, Starr Mayo, Rachel Horowitz, Janelle DeLuise, Abby McAden, and David Levithan. You all rock!

Huge props to:
Susan Happel Edwards, for keeping me sane. Relatively.

Rebecca Micucci, for jewelry design info, letting me borrow all your gemstone catalogs, and being hilarious on a daily basis.

Much love to:
My parents, extended family, and the outlaws.

Mike and Ryan, who are always the highlights of my day.